I0823330

GRAY DAWN

ALSO BY WALTER MOSLEY

The Awkward Black Man

John Woman

THE KING OLIVER SERIES

Down the River unto the Sea

Every Man a King

Been Wrong So Long It Feels Like Right

THE EASY RAWLINS MYSTERIES

Farewell, Amethystine

Blood Grove

Charcoal Joe

Rose Gold

Little Green

Blonde Faith

Cinnamon Kiss

Little Scarlet

Six Easy Pieces

Bad Boy Brawly Brown

Gone Fishin'

A Little Yellow Dog

Black Betty

White Butterfly

A Red Death

Devil in a Blue Dress

THE LEONID McGILL SERIES

Trouble Is What I Do

And Sometimes I Wonder About You

All I Did Was Shoot My Man

When the Thrill Is Gone

Known to Evil

The Long Fall

The Further Tales of Tempest Landry

Inside a Silver Box

Debbie Doesn't Do It Anymore

Parishioner

The Last Days of Ptolemy Grey

The Gift of Fire / On the Head of a Pin

Merge / Disciple

OTHER FICTION

Stepping Stone / Love Machine

The Right Mistake

The Tempest Tales

Diablerie

The Wave

Killing Johnny Fry

Fear of the Dark

Fortunate Son

The Man in My Basement

47

Fear Itself

Futureland

Fearless Jones

Walkin' the Dog

Blue Light

Always Outnumbered, Always Outgunned

RL's Dream

The Fall of Heaven (play)

NONFICTION

Twelve Steps Toward Political Revelation

This Year You Write Your Novel

Life Out of Context

What Next: A Memoir Toward World Peace

Workin' on the Chain Gang

The Graphomaniac's Primer

GRAY DAWN

An Easy Rawlins Mystery

WALTER MOSLEY

MULHOLLAND BOOKS

LITTLE, BROWN AND COMPANY

NEW YORK BOSTON LONDON

Mulholland Books / Little, Brown and Company
Hachette Book Group
1290 Avenue of the Americas, New York, NY 10104
mulhollandbooks.com

First Edition: September 2025

Mulholland Books is an imprint of Little, Brown and Company, a division of Hachette Book Group, Inc. The Mulholland Books name and logo are trademarks of Hachette Book Group, Inc.

ISBN 9780316573238 (hardcover) / 9780316596954 (large print)
LCCN 2025933152

Printing 1, 2025

LSC-C

Printed in the United States of America

A NOTE FROM THE AUTHOR

I've been writing about Easy Rawlins and his coterie since somewhere around 1988. His first appearance was in a short story called, I think, "Rent Party." It was about an unnamed young man who had opened his Fifth Ward, Houston, apartment for a wild party. The story started with this young man standing at the front door, taking a ten-cent admission fee from friends, acquaintances, and those strangers who had heard about the event.

He greeted everyone, calling those he knew by name.

When a woman named EttaMae Harris walked up, looking fine and late-1930s hood-glamorous, he felt his heart throb. She was beautiful, strong, trustworthy, and willing, the young man knew, to stand up for her friends. He felt something akin to love for this woman. He would have spoken to her about this feeling except for one thing…That was the next person to show up at the door—Raymond "Mouse" Alexander.

Mouse was trouble. He cheated at cards, messed with the wrong women, disobeyed all the commandments and laws. Ray was everything that the young man was not, but still EttaMae loved him, loved him with all her heart and soul.

The young man greeted Mouse, who handed over his dime and then smiled, saying, "Hey, Easy, how you doin'?"

This was the birth of Easy Rawlins, a character I've never felt the urge to introduce because he had always been the teller of his own tales. But this time, with *Gray Dawn,* something has changed. Easy's experiences and his world have slipped far enough into the past that, it is possible, many will not understand the reason for his fictional existence.

Easy, and his friends, exist to testify about a volatile time in Black, and therefore American, history.

Ezekiel's combined tales are kind of like a twentieth-century memoir, a fast-paced unspooling of events that came from a people, an entire so-called race, that had been fighting for liberation and equality longer than any living soul could remember. Black people, during the Great Enslavement, weren't considered wholly human, and, even after emancipation, were promoted only to the status of second-class citizenship. They were denied access to toilets, libraries, equal rights, and the totality of the American dream, which had often been deemed a nightmare. These somewhat-citizens worked hard, suffered terribly, and, despite all that, made this country a shining example, a beacon of freedom in the face of freedom denied.

Easy is a passionate soul. He identifies with the underdog because he has been that man, because his children (by blood and by choice) are in danger of inheriting this unwanted mantle. He speaks for the voiceless and tries his best to come up with answers to problems that seem unanswerable.

His friends fall into categories that were, at the time, unimaginable for Black folk. In Jackson Blue and Paris Minton, you have IQ prodigies, both of whom can understand anything that has been written or postulated. There's Fearless Jones, the urban warrior who understands only what the heart demands. You also have Amethystine Stoller and Anger Lee (EttaMae too), women who survive, and even thrive, when the odds are steady against them.

There is, of course, Mouse. Raymond Alexander, a lifelong criminal, rebel, speaker of truths we'd rather not know, the only Black man you'll ever meet who is not afraid of anyone or anything at any time or place.

And then there's Easy, possibly the most dangerous character you'll ever meet. When you see Easy you think you understand him, but, in reality, he is always something else. He is the truth-seeker whom most people do not suspect of such grandiose purpose. They see a Black Man, a man who has been beaten so often that he could never pose a threat that is not immediate and physical. They have no idea that Easy has learned how to open any door, either physical or conceptual. He gleans your secrets, secrets you might not even know that you have.

These characters are not superhuman. It's just that their quite normal talents must be hyper-present in a world that is set against them for reasons that are clear and still make no sense. They face mouths and doors that utter the words "Whites only." They are stopped by authorities who see their guilt in the color of their skin. They are heroes whose purpose is to undermine enemies who often do not recognize their own culpability. Their history is almost from another dimension, a place, a series of events that have not happened for the keepers of the official history of this country, this world.

So, when a so-called white security guard stops Easy for being in an office building, a place where Easy has many powerful friends, and Easy's internal response is hatred, some readers in the modern world might not understand where that hatred comes from. They may no longer have access to the memories of poverty forced on a people, of lynchings based on a word or a glance, of doors to public institutions barred, of children who stolidly believe in their own inferiority.

I ask the reader of this novel to consider what I have said here in the many angry, anguished, and enthusiastic exhortations of life that inform the pages of *Gray Dawn*.

GRAY DAWN

1.

The phone was ringing. Ringing. Those evenly measured burps of jangled sound were a warning that my life was falling apart—that much I knew. I don't know how many times it rang, but my conscious count was up to six when I finally rolled across the king-size bed to the other side, where the night table stood. Before I lifted the receiver from the cradle, I looked out the window into the wafting mists and fog that inundated the mountainside all the way down to where the ocean was usually visible. It felt like a poisonous sky had come down to choke both land and sea.

"Hello?" I whined, as if begging for some kind of miracle or release.

"What's wrong, Daddy?"

"Feather? That you?"

"Uh-huh."

"What's wrong?" Fear for my daughter's safety pulled me from sleeping dread into wakeful worry.

"Nothing. I just thought I'd use the phone card to say hi."

I had just woken up, and I was already exhausted. It felt as if I had run full speed down a long city block, my heart thundering, breath coming in shallow gasps.

Feather was in Dijon, France, with a national high school group called the American Institute for Foreign Study. Gone for five weeks already, she was there to study French language and culture.

"What's wrong, Daddy?"

"Nothing. Why?"

"You sounded scared or somethin'."

"Maybe I was havin' a nightmare, sumpin' like that."

"Nightmare about what?"

"I don't know, honey, but I sure am happy to hear your voice. How's your classes goin'?"

"Good. I got top marks in everything."

"That's great." My fearful heart began to ease. "Have you heard from Bonnie?"

"She's in Ghana right now, but she's comin' when school's over. We're gonna go to Paris."

The joy in her voice was greater than the weight on my soul.

"That's great, baby. I know how much she loves you."

Bonnie and I had been lovers when Feather was an orphaned infant, lost in the world. We were the closest things to parents she'd ever have. And that was more of a blessing for us than it was for her.

"You sound sad," Feather said.

"A little bit. Jesus and Benita spend most'a their time on the water, and you're fifty-seven hundred miles away. All I got here is the dogs and June gloom."

"I don't have to go to Paris if you don't want."

"Yeah, you do. I'm okay. And I want one'a those little statues of the Eiffel Tower."

"Okay," she said softly. "But if you need me, I could come home."

"You havin' a good time?"

"Yeah," she replied with a little more gravitas than she meant to express. Probably thinking about a sip of wine, her first cigarette, or maybe a kiss. That's what I thought.

"I gotta go to a lecture, Papa," she told me.

"Bien. Allez," I said back.

The second after hanging up I was beset by a pack of dogs.

The two little ones felt like birds prancing wildly on my chest. But number three, Prince Valiant, weighed 180 pounds when the vet last hoisted him on a scale. PV was what Fearless Jones called *mostly bull mastiff*, stronger than your everyday wolf, friend to loved ones, and death to any threat.

I followed them down the stairs to the first floor and the exit to the backyard of our lighthouse-like dwelling. The smallest mongrel was Frenchie. He was the oldest and the titular leader of the pack. The next was a brown mutt who only wanted to play. These two each got a bowl full of dry food. The big dog, Prince Valiant, was fed three pounds of ground meat twice a day.

Back when I was a child in New Iberia, Louisiana, three pounds of prime ground beef would be enough to feed a family of three for two days. Back then I was, and everyone I knew was, so poor that the end of the Depression was no big deal because we didn't even know it had happened. In those days a nickel would buy a sandwich that lasted from morning till night. It was a hard life, but I felt loved and cared for. So, at the age of eight, I was terrified when my parents died and I had to hop a boxcar to make it to the Fifth Ward of Houston, Texas. I went there to find my grandfather. After a week of wandering around, asking people if they knew him, I met a madwoman who pointed the way. My granddad gave me a place to sleep but said I had to provide my own victuals. By the time I was used to supporting myself, Uncle Sam said I had to go to war in Africa and Europe. After World War II, I went to California, where, they said, a poor soul could sleep on the ground and eat off the trees.

I did well, became one of the few colored private detectives in Southern California, invested in real estate, and experienced a few fortunate windfalls. Now I lived in a gated community atop a mountain for the fee of a penny a year. I had money in the bank and in the ground. I adopted and raised two children and had quite a few friends, a couple that I even trusted.

Considering where I came from, I'd done very well indeed.

But two years ago I was involved in a missing person case, and by the time I'd found the victim—a forensic accountant—he was dead. That by itself wasn't so bad, but somehow I fell for the woman who hired me to find the man—her ex. She had committed a murder for which I would never have turned her in. She was justified but I had to let her go.

I went through the rest of the morning almost mechanically. After watering the rose garden on the roof, where I smoked my one cigarette of the day, I went down to the second-floor kitchen and made coffee and buttered toast. After that I donned a short-sleeved off-white dress shirt, brown trousers, blue-and-brown argyle socks, rubber-soled shoes made from black fabric, just in case I came across the unexpected necessity to run, and, finally, a dark, dark brown sports jacket.

Before taking the funicular down the mountain I went to the rough-cut Olympic-size, almost natural grotto of a swimming pool that was just perfect for my daughter to practice in for her swimming meets.

Looking down at the water, I could imagine Feather's laugh and the smooth, steady strokes of her hours of practice. For some reason this made me climb over to the edge of our mountaintop and scale down the side until reaching the tall, and sometimes electrified, twelve-foot-high razor-wire fence that circled the six homes comprising my community.

Sitting there at the edge of the barrier, I felt like this was some kind of symbol of my life, a prisoner in a paradise of my own making.

I wanted another cigarette but had none. I wanted the fog to dissipate, but that wasn't to be either.

"What are you doing out here, my friend?" a rough voice in a deep accent asked.

I didn't have to turn to know that this was Erculi Longo, sire of the four adult brothers who protected the rich woman's mountain. He was burly but not tall, old but looked less so, and deadly as a Tasmanian devil, at least that's what his sons had told me. His pants, shoes, and workman's jacket were neither gray nor brown, creating a kind of natural camouflage. His dark eyes and dark olive skin spoke of both sides of the Mediterranean, the Maghreb.

"Signor Erculi," I greeted. "What are you doing down the hill?"

"I saw you," he explained. "And I say to myself that you never have climbed down here before."

"I don't know," I confessed. "Just seemed like somethin' to do."

That called up what I'd come to know as the Sicilian Stare. It was a silent inquisition unafraid of what you might have thought or wished to hide. There was a powerful mind behind that weathered face, the kind of focus that few human beings could manage. His family had been through a decades-long feud with a rival clan. When a shift in power came about, and the body count was piling up, Erculi decided to move his sons to America, where they'd have a chance to breathe and breed. He somehow met Orchestra Solomon, the owner of our mountain, and she realized how he could protect her and those she had chosen to live in her little community.

"You miss Feather?" he asked at last.

"Yeah." I nodded toward the mist.

"But it is something else," he concluded.

It was my turn for silent reflection. This was probably the longest talk I'd ever had with the stoic warrior. I understood that his gaze was an offering that I had a debt to answer.

"I don't know, Signor. I feed my dogs, water the roses, go to work, and do whatever is asked of me. But it's all habit. I could lie on my bed all day long and that would be just the same. I eat food but don't really taste it. I drink liquor but it doesn't feel like anything."

Giving a shrug he said, "That is what we must do. Life is not pleasure for men like us. Life is only the future. It is our children...and their children. It is our young people. They see the world with new eyes when ours grow old and gray. We go blind and toothless...for them."

I hadn't been to church in many years. A minister's palaver about sin and eternal life, the sacrifices of the testaments old and new, the hope of forgiveness, none of that seemed, in any way, true. I'd lived with good and evil since before I could speak, and I had never been able to separate them. In the life I'd lived through, good men turned their backs on suffering and bad ones loved their brothers without reservation.

I hadn't been to church for a very long time, but it felt like I was in the pews on that mountainside with that patriarch who had also been a slayer.

"So, what should I do now?" I asked honestly.

"Go to work, my friend."

2.

Doing as the Sicilian elder suggested, I made it down the side of the mountain riding the vertical railway, descending into the mist as I went. Firing up the old brown Dodge, I made it to my office on Robertson Boulevard a few minutes before 6:30 a.m. I expected to have some hours alone to read and wait for the sun to burn away the fog. But after scaling the steep staircase to our third-floor offices, I found our receptionist and detective in training, Niska Redman, already at her desk and hard at work. Seated in her plush blue padded swivel chair, with one denim knee up to her chest, Niska was poring over one of six white-pages phone books open across her wide desk.

When I came in, she glanced up over a blue knee, smiled, and said, “Good morning, Mr. Rawlins.”

“Hey, Red,” I said, doing my best to keep the sadness out of my tone.

“I’m just wearing jeans until the office opens,” she apologized. “It feels more comfortable when I’m doin’ all this research.”

“What you workin’ on?”

“I put up a sign on the bulletin board at school offering to find missing persons or property.”

"You did?"

"Yeah, and this woman—a student—called me and said that she had this boyfriend that was missing."

"Oh? Missing how?"

"At first it just sounded like he'd left her, but after we had tea at the student caf it turned out that he emptied her bank account without her knowin'."

"How much?"

"Ninety-two hundred dollars."

"Whoa."

"Yeah. That was everything she had. It was money her grandparents had given her to pay for school. And this guy, he called himself Martin Durer, wasn't anywhere that she could think of."

"Why you say 'called himself'?" I asked.

"I called Captain McCourt's office and asked about him. You know, maybe he had a record or was wanted, or somethin'. It—it turned out that he'd done that kinda thing before, and if it was the same guy, he'd gone by Denton McDaniels, Mack Daniels, Dean Minton, Darryl Morley, Dax Mandel, and nine other names, all with the initials D.M. or M.D., except for one—Stanford Pride. His usual MO was to wheedle his way into a woman's life and run off with her money a few months later.

"He took Doreen's money like so many others'."

"Doreen who?"

"Anton, Doreen Anton. She's a grad student in economics. I went with her to the downtown police station and they, um, corroborated what Captain McCourt said."

"You talked to him? Not his assistant?"

"Yeah. I told Doreen that I'd look for Durer for two weeks and charge one hundred dollars."

"And that's what these phone books are about?"

"Yeah. I go through six books every morning looking for one or more of his aliases. Today it's Fontana, Ontario, Anaheim, Huntington Beach, Van Nuys, and Los Angeles County."

"Seems like you would have looked at LA first."

"I know," she said shyly. "I guess I was saving the best for last. I mimeographed fifty sheets with all the names printed on them and I'm checkin' off each one as either not there or making notes on the ones that are."

"You do this every morning?"

"I do."

"And what do you plan to do if you find this guy?"

"*When* I find him," she corrected.

"When you find him," I acceded, grateful for the grin her determination brought out in me.

"I'm going to go get a look to make sure it's him, then I'll get my client to come and see. After that I'll have her press charges."

Niska had been taking detective lessons from me for the past two years. She used the work she did for me and my partners to see what would work for her. She took her time, and I was proud to see how far she'd come.

"That sounds really good," I said. And then, changing the subject: "Saul and Whisper coming in later?"

"Uh-uh. Mr. Lynx is down in San Diego looking to see if he wants to take on this smuggling case he's been offered."

"Smuggling what?"

"I think he said something about guns, but I'm not sure. And Tinsford is on vacation in Hawaii with Shirley Brown."

"Just all of a sudden, he left for Hawaii? That's not like him."

"I think he's planning to ask her to marry him."

Niska had come to the office from working with Tinsford Natley, also called Whisper for his low voice.

"Well," I said. "Keep me updated on this case of yours. I don't want you doing anything reckless. And, um, don't tell Whisper about it until it's over."

"Don't worry, I won't."

Like most American men in the early seventies, Whisper felt that there was a deep divide between women's work and the labors of men. I felt that way too but, at the same time, the world was definitely changing. Taking a step back from my own prejudices, I could see that if Niska could prove her ability as an investigator, then what she became was not up to me.

"Okay," I said. "Keep up the good work. I'm gonna go back to my office."

"Do you want me to tell you about calls or visitors?"

"Sure, why not?"

Sitting behind my overlarge desk I experienced the desire to have a simple and straightforward case like Niska did. Just thinking that there was somebody out there that I could find, a manhunt that needed doing, seemed to offer solace. It would be a joy to lose myself in a job.

I hadn't taken on any cases in the last six months, and very few in the year and a half before that. Jobs came in, of course, but I passed them on to Saul and Whisper. But maybe it was time to shake off the stagnation and melancholy of a lost love that had been consecrated by the deaths of two men who might have been saved.

I had a copy of Katherine Anne Porter's *Ship of Fools* in my bottom left drawer. I bought it secondhand, drawn to the title. A fool adrift, that was me.

* * *

I'd been reading for a few hours when I realized that, though I really enjoyed the prose, I didn't retain very much of the story at all. I had just let the words wash over me like sometimes when I'd stand in the shower for a very long time.

There came a tapping on the doorframe. I looked up from the book that I was no longer reading to see Niska's head peering in.

"There's somebody here who wants to talk to you," she said.

"To me specifically?"

She nodded. "He said that he wants to see Easy Rawlins."

"Not Ezekiel?"

She shook her head.

"Okay then, show him in."

Her head withdrew, leaving me to wonder if I had somehow conjured up this visitation.

A few seconds later Niska came through. She was wearing a coral-colored dress and yellow pumps. Her face was made up and her straightened hair was piled at the back of her head. The man who came in behind her was dressed in dirty overalls with tears here and there and a gray T-shirt that had once been white, and shod in shit-brown clodhopper boots.

"Mr. Santangelo Burris," Niska said, "this is Mr. Ezekiel Rawlins."

The detective in training then left me with my visitation.

If I didn't exactly smell him, I imagined that I could. It was as if he'd just fallen off the back of a farm truck and tumbled upon my doorstep. He had the build and hunched posture of a wild boar—not tall but brutish. His face contained many emotions, none of these pleasant. By turns he seemed angry, suspicious, and as determined as a soldier before a battle.

The only thing about him that wasn't piglike, threatening, or foul was a thick gold ring he wore on the pinkie of his left hand. This singular piece of jewelry was festooned with a large hunk of topaz, inlaid with a silver torch or some other kind of scepter.

"Saint Angel," I said idly.

His expression of mere anger elevated into rage.

"What you say?" he cried, half raising his right fist.

"That's what your name means," I said by way of apology.

"That's what—what they called me at school. Called me little angel and homo and stupid." He was on the verge of shouting.

"Sorry about that, man. I was just thinking about the Italian."

"What Italian?"

"The word, Santangelo, it's Italian."

The beast-man's eyes bulged and looked around for something, anything to hate.

"I don't know about all that," he said. "I'm here about my auntie, Lutisha James."

"Okay," I said in my most placating tone. "Why don't you have a seat, Mr. Burris?"

The man's breath came in angry huffs. He looked at the three wide-bottomed walnut chairs arranged before my grand desk. I could imagine him asking which chair I wanted him to take. Instead, he pulled an outer chair away from the other two and hurled his backside into it.

Thinking that I'd have to get the chair cleaned, I paused for a second or two and then leaned back in my swivel seat.

It occurred to me that I had rarely been with someone whose breath was loud enough for me to hear it.

"Where did you get my name, Mr. Burris?"

"What?" he challenged.

"I was christened Ezekiel. Only those who know me call me Easy."

"I'ont know about that," he replied defensively. "All I know is that I aksed a man if he knew how I could find somebody missin' and he said go to Easy Rawlins."

"Who was this man?"

"What?"

Very slowly I said, "Who is the man that told you to call me?"

"I don't know." Almost every word he uttered was loud. "It was this dude down in Compton across the street from the hotel where she stayed at."

"What hotel was that?"

"Ummmm, Orchid. The Orchid."

Finally, something I knew.

"I went there," Saint Angel continued, "to find Auntie Lutie, but she was gone. Nobody knew where she went so I aksed the man who owned the sto' across the street if he'd maybe seen her go. He's the one said about you."

His hard breathing did not abate. Anger seemed to vibrate with every word, every gesture.

"So, you went to the Orchid to find Lutisha James. She wasn't there and a man you didn't know told you about me."

He stared at me wondering, I believe, if I had more to add. When I didn't, he said, "Yeah, yeah, that's right." Then he moved the gaze from me to the ceiling and continued from memory. "My grandmama called me up from down home and told me to get Auntie Lutie to call her. She said that they said at the hotel that she had moved out. So I went down there to find out where she gone."

"Where's down home?"

"What?"

"Where does your grandmother live?"

"She live in Pistol."

"She lives in a gun?"

"No, fool, Pistol, Pistol, Texas."

"Never heard of it."

"I cain't hep that."

I wanted to say *Touché*, but instead I asked, "Is this some kind of emergency?"

"Sure is. I told you, my grandmama want me to find her."

There wasn't a doubt in my mind that this man was lying about something. But that didn't matter, not right then. It was my job to reveal lies. That's what detectives do.

"Do you have a picture of your auntie?"

"No. Don't have no camera. My grandmama got a portrait'a her on her dresser back home."

"But that's in Pistol."

"Yeah. That's where she live at."

"What kind of work does your auntie do?"

"She takes care'a old people an' chirren. Old people an' chirren. She pretty good at that."

"Does she have any hobbies or other interests?"

He couldn't even ask *What?* about that query. He just stared vacantly, with only a hint of rage.

"For instance, does she, uh, collect china plates or play any board games?" I suggested.

That got me my first smile from the feral man.

"She play hearts," he said through a wide grin. "Hearts. She really good at that. Sometimes she play for money. Good money."

"She play any other kind of card games? Bridge? Poker?"

His shoulders told me that he didn't know.

"What about some other job, other than a domestic, I mean?"

"She not married."

It took me a moment to realize that the word *domestic* dredged up marriage from the cauldron of Santangelo's experience.

"Does she do any other kind of work?" I asked.

He thought so hard on that question that his eyes nearly closed.

"Um," he began. "Uh. Back down in Texas she used to, um, take numbers over the phone in her house. That's the only way she could afford to have a phone."

I could think of more questions, but I doubted that the answers, if they came at all, would be of any use. While I stared at him, his nostrils opened wide, unconsciously testing for danger.

"Why does your grandmother need to talk to your auntie?"

"That's her private business."

"Okay," I said. "All right. But you have to understand that I can't be lookin' for people if the one who pays me is out to settle a grudge."

"It's my grandmama wanna talk to her daughter. What kinda grudge could there be in that?"

"You'd be surprised at the number of times people want to use me to get at somebody."

"Why my gram wanna hurt her own blood?"

It was at that point I wondered why I was even entertaining the conversation. This shitkicker out of deep Texas obviously did not have the $125 a day to pay for my services. He couldn't afford to hire me, so why tease him?

It was this last thought that upset my neatly stacked applecart. I went into this business because poor Black people rarely got a break or official assistance. It once was that I did the work and they paid what they could. Often, we'd trade in favors, not having to deal with money at all. I wanted to get back to that way. Back then I was a happier man.

"Look here, Santangelo, you need to see this from my side'a the table. I don't know you or your grandmother. I don't know the man works across the street from the Orchid SRO. How am I to be sure that you don't have some score to settle with this Lutisha James?"

"She my auntie, man. She my blood. I just need to get her the message that her mama want her to call."

He had calmed down, was looking at me with the closest he would probably ever get to sincerity. It was something, but not enough.

"I'll tell you what," I said. "I'll look for your auntie. And if I find her I will tell her what you said. If she wants to see you, I'll make that happen. Or I can just pass on the message about making the call."

Santangelo Burris's murky eyes concentrated on me for at least two minutes. This gaze was so intense I thought that if he had had a gun I might have died right then and there.

Then he nodded and said, "Okay. How much it cost?"

I knew he wouldn't be able to afford my going rate, and I didn't want to say I'd do it for free. I also didn't want to offer to trade favors with someone who was that angry.

"How much to find your auntie?"

"Yeah."

"I charge by the day. Seventy-five dollars."

"How, um, how many days would it take?"

"If I can't locate her in a week, I'll probably never find her."

"And so that's seventy-fi'e dollars a day for seven days?"

"That's right," I agreed, thinking that this man wasn't as stupid as I'd assumed.

He gave me another two-minute stare, nodding almost imperceptibly, and then pulled out a thick roll of ten-dollar bills. He peeled off fifty-two notes, counting them out one by one as he laid them on the desk before me. It was dirty money, greasy and worn. After returning what was left of his wad of cash to a jacket pocket, he reached into another pocket, came out with a crumpled wad of green and slowly unfolded it into a five-dollar bill. This he laid upon the stack of tens.

It surprised me that a man looking like he did knew how to do numbers in his head.

"That enough?" he asked.

"Um. Yeah."

"Okay then," he said and then rose without using his hands for extra leverage.

"Do you have any idea of where your auntie could be?"

"Naw. If I did I would go there myself."

"But she stayed at the Orchid?"

"Yeah. I aksed them where she went but they didn't know."

"You think she might work numbers here in LA?"

"I don't know nuttin' 'bout that. I just need you to go out and find 'er."

Giving up on getting any more out of the boar-man, I asked, "How do I get in touch with you?"

"What for?"

"To tell you what I've found."

"Oh. How long you think it'a take?"

"Maybe one day," I said. "Maybe never."

"But you gonna get into it right away, right? My grandmama need to talk to her."

"It's the only job I got right now. I'll be on it this very morning."

"Okay."

"So, what's your number?"

"Don't worry about that. I'ma—I'ma—I'll call you."

"It'd be better if I could call you."

"I'ont have a number right now. I'll call you at the end'a the week."

I shrugged and nodded.

"Okay," he said. "I'll call Friday. You be here, now."

He turned and walked down the short hall from my office to the front door.

I followed him to make sure that he didn't take a bite out of or stamp on Niska.

3.

“Wow,” Niska commented a few seconds after Saint Angel left out the front door of the WRENS-L Detective Agency. “What was that?”

“That’s the kind of clients you get sometimes.”

“He scared me.”

“Me too,” I admitted.

“Really?”

“Look, Niska, if that man didn’t raise your hackles, you got no excuse to be in this business.”

She was seated behind her desk but still reached out as if she was going to touch my arm. It was a friendly gesture.

“I’m gonna go out for a while,” I said. “I want you to lock the doors downstairs and upstairs too.”

“Okay. Where you goin’?”

“To check out Mr. Burris’s case.”

“You’re gonna work for that awful man?”

“Oh yeah. Not everybody comes to you gonna be a sweet co-ed.”

Down around 103rd and Central there was a block-wide four-story building that had a barnlike fourth floor. This air-conditioned space was called, had always been called in all its addresses and reincarnations, John's Bar. John didn't have a liquor license nor any other kind of certification. It was just a place that Black people could go to feel down-home, no matter where that home was.

The hours for the establishment were 8:00 a.m. to closing, seven days a week. I got there at about 9:00, so there weren't many patrons. There were only a couple of day laborers who needed a snort before a long day in the Southern California sun and a few others who came for the morning paper and coffee.

John was standing behind the long mahogany bar wiping it down with an ocher chamois cloth.

The lifelong bartender was an inch taller, two inches wider, and maybe twenty percent stronger than the mythical steel-driving John Henry. He could bust up any fight or crack any jaw without breaking a sweat. One time the strongest man I knew, Fearless Jones, told me, "I wouldn't wanna have ta tangle with your friend John. He look like he got a serious bite."

"Easy Rawlins," John hailed.

"Hey, brother." I extended a hand, and he gripped it. "I thought Millicent ran the early shift while you worked out back."

"Oh yeah. She do. But today is special."

"Special how?"

"She and me gonna get married and she makin' her own weddin' dress."

"That's great! Congratulations, man. You and her were made for each other."

Millicent Roram had come to work for John as a bar girl. She served the tables, cleaned up after hours, and, after a few months, started keeping records on materials and money. A year later, when he came to the current address, she moved with him into the apartment that made up the back rooms.

"Yeah," he agreed. The grin on the bartender's face told of a deep joy.

"When's the big day?"

"Monday after next," he said, as satisfied as a shark that had just swallowed a baby seal.

"Next Monday? When did you propose?"

"Day before yesterday. When she said yes, I told her we could drive out to Reno after closin' up, but she say she don't wanna get hitched on the Lord's day. That's bad luck. So, that's why we have to wait so long."

"Can I come?"

"Oh yeah, Easy. You could even be my best man if the deputy mayor don't want that job. Drink?"

"It's a little early for me."

"You on a job?"

"Maybe. I gotta check out a few things first."

"Like what?" John stopped rubbing the bar. He could smell that I was there for information.

"What are the best numbers schemes around here?"

"Only one that really matters."

"Who runs that?"

"Brother Forest."

"Ah, shit. That man's like a cancer in your balls."

John laughed loud and hard.

"He still out behind that elementary school on Denker?" I asked.

"Naw. He moved the policy shop up to Hollywood. He Mr. Big Businessman nowadays."

"Hollywood? A tar-ass Negro like that?"

"You bettah believe it," John declared. "Cops down around Watts nowadays like wild beasts. They don't mess with street brothahs ’cause they might fight back, and there ain’t no profit in that. But if you got a business, legitimate or not, then they lean hard.”

“They on you?”

“Uh-uh. I found the right pocket to line and they lea’ me alone.”

“It ain’t like the old days when the ofays stayed away from where we lived,” I said, feeling the wisdom of the words.

“Come on now, Easy,” John argued. “If we was twenty years old again, it would be the old days right now.”

I was all the way to the car before deciding on the next destination. The choice was between heading down to Compton or out to Hollywood. Without even flipping a coin I nosed my Dodge in a southerly direction, down Central till getting a little ways past the two hundred block.

LA has always been a transient city, as was, and is, the United States, on the whole. Urban folks are always moving in and out, or just away. Compton used to be a primarily white area. Back then there was a rivalry between Black Wattsonians and Caucasian Comptonites. One of the reasons gangs started to develop in Watts was because of raids from Compton. But by 1972 Blacks started to colonize their southern neighbor. Working-class folks bought homes, rented apartments, and looked for jobs close at hand.

I don’t know what the Orchid SRO was before, but now it was a four-story down-at-heel residence for women only.

I parked my pretty much nondescript car right out front and strode in like I belonged there.

But I didn’t belong there.

The first floor was a large living room–like space where there were couches, chairs, and tables for women to sit alone or with others to converse. It felt as if every eye in the place was on me as I made my way toward the reception desk at the back of the room.

"Ladies," I greeted now and again as I went.

Some smiled and nodded, others frowned and turned away. Almost all the residents were women of color, from high yellow to midnight blue-black. It was a bastion of colored femininity and therefore felt different in a way that maybe you could learn from.

But the intelligence I'd come to gather had nothing to do with gender except for the fact that the person I was looking for might have at one time been a resident of the Orchid.

They didn't have a proper reception desk, only a library podium with a young brown woman standing behind it. There was a nameplate that read GINA LIMA. The young woman, who might have borne the name on the plaque, gazed at me with what my distant cousin-by-law Riley used to call a belligerent eye.

"Is it Leema or Lyema?" I asked in my most pleasant voice.

"What the hell you say?" was her answer.

"The last name," I said, gesturing at the nameplate that hung from two nails driven into the front side of that plinth.

"You don't need to know my name or ask me questions. This is a place for women only and you are not a girl."

"I know that, and I will be gone just as soon as I can ask a question."

"You already asked a question," she barked, just before slapping a vicious-looking hunting knife down on the podium.

I was a little shocked that walking into a building and making a simple request could turn into a life-and-death situation just that quickly.

"Aw, come on now, lady," I pleaded. "I'm not lookin' for any trouble."

"You gonna get some, you don't walk yo' old Black ass outta here."

I was very aware that my two years off the streets, up on my mountain, had slowed me down. Boxers call it ring rust. Whatever you call it, I needed a good oiling.

Her hand was laid across the hilt of that Bowie blade. Any smart man would have backed away ten steps and then run. But I had a question, and it made no sense that I couldn't get an answer.

"Ezekiel Porterhouse Rawlins," somebody said in a contralto tone that was juicy and deep.

Without turning away from Ms. Lima, I said, "Stella Voorhes."

"Baby, what you doin' flirtin' with li'l girls like Gina?"

"He ain't flirtin' wit' me," Gina complained. "Bettah not if he don't wanna lose whatever little he got."

Gina lifted her blade as Stella sashayed into view. Peroxide-haired, black-skinned, of a mature age, and with a generous figure, Miss Voorhes was a pinup of the mind.

"Gina," she said in as stern a timbre as her diva voice could muster.

"What?" the younger woman complained.

"What I tell you about that knife?"

"I told him to leave, and he didn't," the younger woman said by way of explanation.

"Do you like your job?"

"Yeah," Gina replied in a much softer tone.

"Because if I see that mothahfuckin' blade again I'ma fire your butt and take away your room. You know I don't need the city comin' in here threatenin' my license because you hate every man you see."

"But—"

"But what?"

"Nuthin'. I'm sorry."

"Okay. Now, go on upstairs and bury that knife away in that trunk'a yours."

Gina Lima walked past me carrying the knife in her left hand. I made sure not to make eye contact with her, just in case.

When the young woman started walking up the stairs, Stella turned to me and said, "Easy Rawlins. You know sometimes I wake up at night with your name on my lips. You evah think about me like that?"

"Every chance I get."

"You got your chance right here, right now."

"Honey, I'm on the job right now."

After giving me a contemplative stare, she said, "I heard tell you live in a castle on a glass mountain like that princess in the fairy tale."

"Not a castle, just a big house. And it's a mountain all right, but one made outta soil and stone, not glass," I confessed, "but... yeah."

"Could I come up there and see you one day, maybe?"

"Just as soon as this job is over," I lied.

"Yeah. I bet."

"C'mon, Stella, gimme a break."

"You got good shoulders, Easy Rawlins. Strong but not sharp like some'a these fools out here today. I could ride them bones all day long."

Her smile was a thing out of mythology. I was resisting temptation, but if a conversation like the one we were having went on too long... there was only one place it could go. So I decided to cut it short.

"Lutisha James," I said with a ring of finality to the words.

Amazingly, seemingly without a muscle moving on her face, Stella's broad grin turned into a grimace.

"What about her?"

"I've been hired to find her."

"She lost?"

"Her mama wants to hear from her."

"I'm surprised a bitch on wheels like her even got a mama."

"Why you say that?" I wondered mildly.

"Lutisha is old-school. She got a knife longer than Gina's in her handbag and dynamite in both feet and hands. I once seen her knock a full-grown man to his knees. She is serious business."

"She gave you a hard time?"

"Naw, uh-uh. She was quiet enough, and civil too. The only problem I evah had wit' Lutie was that she liked to play poker in her room, and she wanted to have men in the game. I couldn't allow that. You know, once you let men in, they hang around like dogs, beggin' for whatever scraps you got."

I liked talking with Stella. She brought the best of the old days to mind.

"The guy hired me said that he was her nephew," I said.

"Fireplug of a man look like one'a those men clean out chimneys?"

"That's him to a T."

"An' he the one payin' your fee?"

"He is."

"And he said he was her blood?"

"He did."

"I hope you ain't takin' to believin' just anything that some fool tells ya," Stella challenged. "When that man came here all I tole 'im was that Lutie was gone, and I didn't have no idea where she went to."

"I can understand that, but in my business, I try and give everybody the benefit of the doubt."

"That's what they call castin' pearls before swine."

"Yeah, yeah," I said. "I know. What I'm doin' is lookin' for her to ask if she wants to be found."

"And you had to climb down from your glass mountain 'cause you couldn't see her from up there?"

"Can you help me, girl?" I asked in faux exasperation.

She gave me a leery look and then reached out to take me by the hand.

"You know I really do like you," she said.

"And I like you too, Stella."

"My mama, God rest her soul, used to tell me that it was better to hook up with a man you liked instead'a one that you loved. She said that like lasts a lot longer'n love."

There was nothing to say to that.

"If I help you," she said, "will you return the favor someday, if I should happen to need it?"

"Absolutely."

We both smiled on my oath. That was better than shaking hands.

"A white man come by one day in one'a them fancy limos. I think he was a professional driver 'cause he wore a suit and that kinda military hat with the brim only in the front. He took her and her suitcase outta here."

"Where'd he take her?"

"Up to some rich people house, on a fancy street in LA somewhere."

"Did she know 'em? Was she gonna work for 'em?"

"Work, yeah. To take care of some old lady. Andit, Ortit, sumpin'."

It was good to go down to the Orchid. Being there reminded me of things that most of my people would rather forget. We'd rather forget, all the time knowing that the only way to survive is to remember.

4.

Dave Kleiger, the Russian grocer across the street from the Orchid, could not remember meeting a man matching the description of Santangelo Burris, and he had never heard of an Easy Rawlins. So I left the wide swath of Black LA for an address John had given me. That was on Cherokee Avenue in Hollywood. I didn't want to go there, where Brother Forest was supposed to have set up shop, but seeing him would be like a crash course for ring-rusted instincts.

Brother Forest was from the streets of the Fifth Ward in Houston, Texas, streets I'd once known well. He could squeeze money out of bone and there was no act he would not undertake if it meant that he got what he wanted. Men like him could be found in maggot-infested back alleys and whorehouses where the women were nothing but drug-addicted slaves. Men like Forest came up on you out of nowhere, when you least expected it.

But no matter what it was that I expected, it was not a well-appointed eight-story building, constructed from rich, dark brick and broad, green-tinted windows. At first I was sure that it was a mistake, that John had somehow gotten the wrong numbers, or maybe there was a Cherokee Street somewhere nearby.

Then two men and a woman walked out the entrance of the posh building. The men wore business suits, gray and dark blue, and the woman a purple, red, and yellow minidress of paisley. But what they wore was less important than the fact that they were all white.

I was stuck. There was no other building on that block or the ones north and south of there that had more than six floors. The address John had given was suite 702. Finally, I decided that all I could do was walk in and get redirected to the right alley.

There was an actual uniformed guard behind a desk there at the back of the entrance hall. That clinched it. Brother F had to be someplace else. Had to be.

"Can I help you, sir?" the guard called out. Not young, he had blond hair and pale skin. Rising from his chair, he stood to a full six foot one, tall enough to look me in the eye.

I hesitated then. This was different. I'd been used to being in close quarters with white people for thirty years, all the way back to when I was slaughtering them from North Africa through Italy and France, and finally in the fatherland itself. I could face blood and bombs and insane hatred, but what could I do in this sedate office building talking to a very respectful man?

"Sir?" the guard urged.

"You got a…a man name of, um, Pinklon Frost here?" I managed to pull the name out from the depths of memory. That was Brother Forest's real name. No one ever used it, and it was only the desperation of my history that culled it from so many years ago.

The guard paused to consider my question. He didn't have a

badge, just a navy-blue uniform and a name tag that read C. JORDAN.

Then he smiled and said, "Seventh floor, suite seven-oh-two, Sales and Support. Are you applying for the job?"

There was no spite or disrespect in his query. He was infinitely pleasant and patient, honestly wanting to know why I was there.

"Yes," I said. "Yes, I am. Thank you."

I boarded an elevator that was big enough for four. A white woman in a green/gray plaid skirt and a tan button-up blouse stepped in on the second floor.

"Good afternoon," she said, smiling sweetly as she had been taught to do in good company.

"Hey," I replied. "How are you today?"

"Fine," she answered, looking up at the level register. "But I missed my floor. You know whenever I get into one of these things I think it's gonna take me where I want to go without pressing the button."

"I do it all the time."

By then we'd reached the seventh floor and so I stepped out into the hallway.

"Have a good day," the young woman blessed as the doors closed.

The first door I came across down the seventh-floor hallway had an oversize silver-and-black sign attached to it. The sign read SALES AND SUPPORT. The door was unlocked, so I walked in.

It was a long and somewhat slender room with ten little tables down each side. There were men and women of all ages and races sitting at nineteen of the twenty little desks. The empty seat, I thought, must have been the job C. Jordan told me about.

Each station was big enough for two burly black phones, a pad of paper, and one well-dressed operator.

The phones were ringing mercilessly, accompanied by an off-beat and continuous chorus of many voices answering calls, saying the same three words, "Sales and support," in many different keys and pitches.

The experience was disorienting, for a moment throwing me back in my bed with the clouds closing in.

At the far end of the hall of telephoners sat a Black woman with no table before her. The chair was set up about six inches from the floor, on a dais. She was studying a newspaper with rapt attention when she looked up and noticed me. Then, letting the newspaper fall to the floor, she rose effortlessly from her overseer's chair, descended the stage, walked up to me, and said, without even a shred of sincerity, "Can I help you?"

There were two questions balled up into that one—the first was, *Is there anything I could possibly do for you?* And the second, *What the hell are you doing here?*

Up close she was a knockout, from figure to face, from dun-orange heels to conservative brown-and-green two-piece dress suit.

I probably smiled.

The expression on her face assured me that I could not be helped.

And then I said, "I'd like to speak to Brother Forest, please."

Her countenance froze for a moment. The request I'd made was not meant to be spoken aloud in that space… ever. Her eyes worried over my fate, and maybe hers. When I didn't turn away, running from a faux pas, she said, "Um, come with me."

To the left of her administerial throne was a door. This she opened, gesturing for me to follow her through.

"Close it behind you," she said, leading me to understand that no one was supposed to even suspect our destination.

Seven steps later we came upon another door.

She knocked.

I waited.

"What?" a gruff voice said.

"Somebody here askin' for you," the Knockout replied.

"Who is it?" the voice threatened.

Realizing she had not asked for my name, she turned.

"Ezekiel Rawlins," I provided.

"Ezekiel Rawlins," she repeated.

Then came the wait. I wasn't worried, but the lady was. I got the feeling that this little interaction was pretty far above her pay scale.

Maybe a minute passed, and then the door slowly opened.

The lady stepped backward, bumping into me. I moved aside, leaving her room to flee. Then I walked through the doorway feeling as if I were entering a neolithic cave.

It was a largish space illuminated by blue lightbulbs set in the ceiling. There was a broad table that would have probably been white under normal lighting. Behind the table stood Brother Forest / Pinklon Frost.

He wore a suit that was what would have been dark blue in regular light and a maybe-yellow shirt with no tie. Almost anybody else would have been deemed presentable dressed as he was. But Brother Forest was a thug that no suit of clothes, address, or governor's pardon could clean up or legitimate. The strain in his face would look like last-leg fatigue on a good man, but instead the deep creases, the old scars, and the darkness of Pinklon's eyes told of hatred and determination, an entire history of whips and chains, illiteracy and cunning on a genius level. He was black like the black mold that gathers between old, cracked tiling. His teeth were deeply stained from the dozens of cigarettes he sucked down each day. His sour breath filled the room with its diseased scent. His hands were large, and his smile, when he smiled, was hungry for whatever you had.

"Sit'own," he ordered.

There was a chair on my side of the table. I made use of it. He paused for a moment, eyeing me warily, and then sat down on his side of things.

"What you want?" he asked. This was high-level hospitality from a man like Forest.

"I'm lookin' for a woman named Lutisha James." I put emphasis on the last two words to test a hypothesis.

The big man leaned back in his chair. This brought a whine from the straining wood joints. What emotion, I wondered, was hiding behind Pinklon's intense gaze? The blue light made me doubt. He might have just been angry that I was there wasting his time.

"I'ont know who you talkin' 'bout," he complained.

The tone of that denial exposed the full range of his fear.

"Come on, man," I said on a sneer. "Stop lyin'."

"What you mean—lyin'?"

I learned many things from this reaction. One was that whatever it was Santangelo Burris wanted, it was more than just a call to his grandmother. I also understood that even a man as heartless and reckless as Pinklon was afraid of the woman I was looking for, or, at least, he was afraid of what she represented. Brother Forest had changed. He was older and he had something he didn't want to lose. Maybe it was a wife and family. Maybe, as time encroached, he'd become aware of death. Whatever it was, Brother Forest had moved to Hollywood out of fear.

All that was a big deal, and I had to concentrate not to laugh in his face.

"What you want wit' 'er?" the bad man asked.

"What do you care?"

"What you say to me?"

"You heard me. I come here lookin' for Lutisha James and you tell me you don't know 'er. If you don't know, then my business is still mine."

"Fuck you, Easy Rawlins."

"Okay." I made to stand.

"Wait a minute."

"Okay." I slumped back down into the chair.

"I might'a heard about a woman of that name."

"What you hear?"

"Why you lookin' for her?"

"C'mon, man. Do you know her or don't you?"

"Who you in dis wit'?"

"Look here," I said with supreme authority in my voice. "I'm lookin' for Lutisha James, me, I'm lookin' for her. If you know where she's at I might let you in on what I'm doin'. If you don't, then you don't."

The dialect coming off my tongue meant that I had shed most of the ring rust. I was ready to throw down with that man, then and there.

But Pinklon was not so brash. He sneered and gave me some hard looks, but that didn't mean a thing.

"I didn't do nuthin' to that woman," he testified. "Not a damn thing. She worked a desk just like everybody else and I paid what I promised to."

That was about as much of an answer as Pinklon was liable to give. Realizing this, I stayed silent.

"So, is she?" he asked.

"Is she what?"

"Don't you fuck with me, Easy Rawlins. Don't you fuck with me. I ain't afraid'a you or your friends."

"That's where you and me's different, Pinky."

Calling him Pinky was the most dangerous thing I did that year.

"Different how?"

"I'm afraid of banana peels and little girls in pigtails. I'm afraid of a car behind me with no headlights." I was just talking by that time. He was free to make what he would out of what I said.

"So—so—so she want in?"

"I have no idea what she wants, man. I'm lookin' for her, not workin' for her."

Pinklon was a smart man. Smarter than I am. But he was so scared that his brain was no longer available for logical conclusions. He stared at me in that blue haze like a wildebeest that had his haunches clamped onto by a crocodile.

"Then we ain't got no business," he finally realized.

I nodded and stood.

"Why you even come here?" the thug cried out.

"Because I knew that she worked the numbers and I been told that you the only game in town."

If he wasn't so relieved by whatever it meant that Lutie James wasn't after him, I do believe that he would have tried to hurt me. I wasn't worried, though. No. I wasn't worried, I was a fool, believing I could make brash challenges against bad men without paying for it.

Luckily Brother Forest could see that impudence in the set of my shoulders, misinterpreting it as true confidence.

"Get the fuck outta here, niggah," he said.

5.

Back in the long aisle of operators, the Knockout was waiting for me. She seemed impressed that I made it out unscathed. Her skin was almost as dark as her boss's hide, but this blackness was more satin at midnight than diseased misery.

"You get what you wanted?" she asked.

"Some."

She seemed to like my tone—certainty edged with ambiguity.

"I'll walk you to the door," she offered.

Nineteen pair of eyes followed us to the door, which she opened.

The surprise came when she accompanied me into the hall.

"You need anything else?" she asked, closing the door behind.

"Yeah. Do you remember an operator workin' here name of Lutisha James?"

"Yes, I do."

"What was she like?"

The policy shop manager took a moment to consider the question and then said, "Lutisha was different."

"Different how?"

"To begin with, she was extremely intelligent, could speak

Spanish and French. She never made a mistake with her paperwork, and you only had to explain an operation to her once. After that she knew whatever it was well enough to teach it to anybody else."

"Spanish and French you say?"

"She would talk to some of our Latin employees in Spanish and once she said something to me in French."

"Why she do that?"

"I don't know," she said, rather wistfully. "I guess—I guess it felt like she was testing me."

"Testin' you for what?"

"Same reason that any house cat swivels its head. They're always on the hunt, it's in the blood."

"You said 'to begin with,'" I prompted.

"Huh?"

"'To begin with, she was extremely intelligent,'" I said, repeating her words to me.

"Oh, right. Mr. Frost gives me all the names of the people he wants me to hire, but Miss James came in looking for a job. She was the only one who was ever invited back to his cave. She would go there, have lunch, and come out smelling like scotch."

"A drinker, huh?"

"She always did her job impeccably."

"Yeah, but I guess you wouldn't want the other nineteen operators to start havin' liquid lunches."

"There's no personnel department here, Mr. Rawlins. Here, if the boss wants his friend to have a drink with him, that doesn't mean I have to let anybody else do so."

I did like the way she talked.

"What's your name?" I asked.

"Ida Lorris." She held out a hand and I shook it, smiling into her dark auburn eyes.

"So," she said, still holding my hand. "Who is Ezekiel Rawlins?"

"You mean what do I do for a living?"

"I mean who are you to barge in on Brother Forest and then walk out again without a bruise on your face?"

"I'm a man with many friends."

"Mr. Frost doesn't have any friends."

"I'm not talkin' about his people."

"Who then?"

That was when I relaxed from the ordeal of interrogating Brother Forest. I'd been ready for a fight to the death with the numbers man, but now Ida's talk had switched the dial.

I held my hands palms up to indicate helplessness and said, "I don't know what to tell ya... People."

"Anybody could get you in our back room is not just people."

"Yeah, well, I guess some folks might think that a few of my friends are pretty scary."

"Like whom?" She pursed her generous lips into a gesture that dared you to kiss them.

I was very impressed to hear her using the object form of *who* in a two-word sentence.

"Um," I said. "There's a man named Redbird, whose extinct tribe was native to this continent, a war hero named Fearless Jones, and, um, uh, then there's Charcoal Joe the Black gangster and Raymond Alexander."

"Oh," she sang in a higher register than before, indicating that she was impressed, though not revealing by whom.

"Now you can tell *me* somethin'."

"What is it you want to know?"

"How does this place work? I mean, I know you're takin' bets, I just didn't hear anybody callin' out numbers."

She liked something about the question, looking at me attentively and asking, "You want to go downstairs and grab a cup of coffee?"

Crenshaw's Coffee Klatch was up on Hollywood Boulevard. We walked the four blocks, talking as we went.

"To begin with," she said, "we really do phone sales at S and S."

"You do? Sellin' what?"

"Mr. Frost has a woman named Tina Aren working for him. She puts ads in business sales papers and makes cold calls to people who might want our services."

"And who are those people?"

"Anybody with a legitimate need."

"And what do you sell to these unknown bodies?"

She smiled at the wordplay and then, when we stopped at a red light, said, "Whatever anybody wants to buy. Goods and services, penny stocks, cleaning products, frozen meat and fish, even vacation packages for airlines. We cold-call clients from lists that Tina supplies and we take calls from people who have read our ads. We also reach out to businesses for other businesses. And we charge twenty percent below the nearest competitor, so if anybody investigates us, they can see that we provide a thriving service."

"So, you're completely legal?"

"Oh no. Not in the least. We are a straightforward policy shop. The daily number is chosen from the last dollar digit for the win, place, and show of the fourth race of whatever track is active right then. It's clean."

The light changed and we made it all the way to a table at the Coffee Klatch before continuing the discussion.

"But what if you're making calls to sell magazine subscriptions and all the phones are busy when a client is calling in to make a bet?"

"Only ten phones at a time can be making legitimate business calls and the other ten are open for bettors. Each station has a number, and we switch back and forth between even and odd every half hour or so."

"But what would you do if the cops came in to bust your operation?"

"When a call comes in for the number of Acme Plumbing Equipment, APE, the person taking the call fills out the standard form for any sale, using the same format we would for any other solicitation. The only difference is that the details identify the person calling, the amount of the bet, and the number they want."

"And if the cops come in, everybody starts makin' calls so the phones don't ring," I imagined aloud.

"You'd be good at this."

"So, it all looks copacetic?"

Ida had a beautiful smile.

"And how do your phone operators get paid?" I asked, before taking a bite out of my glazed buttermilk doughnut. "I mean, twenty-one employees make for a big number on the right side of the ledger."

"You know accounting?"

"I own a little property, and I like to keep track of my own debits and credits."

"Huh." It was as if I had just come into focus for her. "The sales force gets a percentage of whatever profit there is from what they sell. Mr. Frost gives them one seventy-five an hour over that."

"Damn. That's a really slick system you got there."

"It is pretty neat."

"The only thing I don't understand," I said, "is you."

"My pronunciation is off?" she asked on a smile.

"No. Your pronunciation is perfect. More'n that. You sound educated and you don't seem to be truly bent. So why would you be workin' for a dog like Pinky?"

Miss Lorris's soul was alive in her eyes. She'd been playful enough on the walk and when we were talking about the procedures of their particular policy scheme. But when it got personal, those fun-loving orbs transformed into those of a full-grown and wronged woman.

"Educated," she said, regarding the word as an offense and me as something somewhat less than human. "You think my schooling means anything?"

"Doesn't it?"

This question caught her off guard. I was hoping that this meant she sensed my sincerity.

"No," she said, not quite angrily. "I am Black, and I am also a woman here in America hardly fifty years after women received the right to vote. Most people, men and women, think I should be having babies, cooking my no-good man's dinner in case he decides to come home that night, and cleaning up any shit I find or fall into.

"We get paid less than men for the jobs they let us have. Our husbands leave us and then forget to pay for their kids. Is that the education you were referring to?"

I didn't respond immediately. I'd heard this kind of complaint too often to deny it, not only its truth, but also its complexity.

Western women were coming out of a centuries-old coma-like state in the 1970s. They didn't want what they'd been *given,* and, to some degree, they didn't want to lose what they were told they had. I knew these things, but also, I understood that I could not speak to them.

It was like Niska wanting to be a PI. Of course she should be enabled to practice that trade. I shouldn't have any say in that. But, on the other hand, she needed me, or someone like me, to open that door and even to hold it open for a little while.

"What?" was Ida's challenge to my silence.

"No," I said softly.

"No what?"

"No to all of it. I mean, you're right. I got no reason to be questioning you. You doin' the best you can with the cards you been dealt."

"And the deck is stacked."

"Yeah. It is."

There wasn't anything to add. So I sipped my coffee and ate some doughnut while she looked like she was staring at me, but I suspected that that gaze was inward. The silence expanded into a basketful of minutes.

Finally, she said, "At least at S and S all the women on the line get paid the same amount as the men. And as long as I'm running the room, I make sure that they have what they need for their kids and their own well-being. At least that."

"I see what you mean," I said.

She then fell into another tub of contemplative minutes.

I had a job to do, but I didn't mind waiting. The pastry was fresh, and Hollywood Boulevard always had something new to reveal.

I saw a man walk by in a full clown suit, makeup and

everything. Then there was a woman wearing what might have been a bear coat walking an animal that looked an awful lot like a brown bear cub. A young woman wearing very little stopped an older white-haired man, probably in his sixties. She asked him something with a smile on her lips and he answered her question with a pleasant look, echoing her own. She nodded happily, he crooked his elbow, making space for her left arm to snake through. Then they both walked on, happy with their choices.

"What are you doing for dinner?" Ida asked.

"What?" I replied, shocked back to our little table.

"My pronunciation again?"

"No. I just thought I'd made you mad or somethin'."

"You didn't. Men like you can't help that they feel superior because they might be stronger than I am. At least you know it."

"Can I have your number?"

Our talk seemed to be about different things, but it wasn't.

She wrote down her number on a napkin and I folded it away.

"What kinda food you like?" I asked her.

"Good food."

"That shouldn't be a problem."

6.

Most often, when it comes to the detecting profession, I prefer to work alone. I don't want or expect assistance, but on the other hand, I try to give help where and whenever it might truly be needed. So, when I have to ask for aid, I do so with the feeling that I've earned it. This intricate excuse in mind, I went to a phone booth on Cherokee, after walking Ida back to the front door of her office building.

I called a number from memory.

"Hello?"

"Vu?"

"Easy?"

"I need to talk to him."

"What's your number?" the lapsed Vietcong asked.

I read it off the dial.

"Okay," she said, and then she hung up.

I held down the receiver lever with a finger and two minutes later the pay phone rang.

After releasing the lever I said, "Ray?"

"Easy." You could hear the smile on the killer's lips. "How you doin', brothah?"

"Okay here, not so much there."

"I hear ya."

"What's goin' on wit' you?"

"Vu's pregnant."

The ground seemed to shift under my rubber soles. For a second, I wondered if this was another earthquake, like the half-billion-dollar one that happened in the San Fernando Valley the previous year. But then I realized this feeling was a response to Raymond's news.

Raymond Alexander, called Mouse by many, was a man of violent moods. He could be your best friend or your executioner, a lover of epic proportions or a madman swinging from the rafters. And so any strong emotion coming from him was a sign of potential danger to anyone who knew him well.

"Congratulations," I cheered.

"Yeah, man, this is a good thing. Very good."

"How soon?"

"She won't tell me."

"Why not?"

"She say, because she don't want me gettin' all ovah-protective like Americans do, that her pregnant sistahs would do night work rebuildin' the Ho Chi Minh Trail till the baby was about to drop."

"That there's a tough woman."

"You bettah fuckin' believe it, man."

"So, what you gonna do?" I asked, knowing that there was something there.

"She and me lookin' for a house."

"Where?"

"Up in Laurel Canyon."

"Really? Why there?"

"She says that that's where the stars line up. It's pretty safe and

Vu like the sky ovah her head to be close up and clear. What about you? You still all heartbroken?"

"No," I lied, knowing that he knew I was lying. "I'm okay now. I just met this woman might be right for a minute. How 'bout you, you readin' anything good?"

This question had three purposes. One was to get him off the subject of my love life. Two was, since Mouse became a reader, he was always surprising me with the books he landed on. And three, you needed to give him time before getting down to business. If you didn't, he'd feel used, even abused, and that was never good.

"Yeah, man," he said. "I been readin' this book about India and stuff. A guy name of Rag Heaven wrote it. Hol' up, I got it right here." I heard some shuffling around and then: "Here it is: *1971: A Global History of the Creation of Bangladesh.* That's it."

"Why you readin' that?"

"It's all about war and revolution and shit and it's international, you know? Vu's always tellin' me that Americans only worry about what we do and the world's a helluva lot bigger'n that."

Mouse was a madman and a killer, but he was also a lot more. If he'd been abused a little less, he might have been a professor at Harvard or, more likely, Howard.

"What about you, Easy?"

"What am I readin'?"

"No. Why the fuck you call me?"

"Yeah. It's not too much," I said. "I got hired by this guy lookin' for a woman and I wondered if maybe you might know her."

"What's her name?"

"He says Lutisha James."

The few seconds of silence over the line told me that I had crossed over into dangerous territory.

"In a hour, meet me at the place before last," he said, and then he hung up.

Mouse lived a criminal's life, at least in part. He was a heist man who did work with a continental syndicate that had the capability of striking anywhere in North America. Some branch of the federal government got on his scent a few years before, and so he had to limit the number of people who knew where he was at any particular moment. This meant that I had to keep a mental list of the last five places we'd met.

The place before last was the outside food court at the Farmers Market at Third and Fairfax. He was already there when I arrived, leaning back in a red rubber-coated metal wire chair and wearing a bright yellow suit with a royal blue shirt. His shoes were sharkskin dyed a uniform medium gray. His upper left incisor, which was on display from inside an affable grin, was embedded with a high-quality emerald that was at least half a carat.

"Ray," I greeted.

"What you wanna eat?" he replied.

Mouse got a kind of gentrified Mexican food plate with hard-shell corn tortilla tacos, refried beans, so-called Spanish rice, and a few slices of avocado. I bought a hamburger and fries from one of the many food concessions.

When we were seated again, the emerald went away and Mouse asked, "How the hell you lose your way an' end up at Lutie's front door?"

"A man named Santangelo Burris, look like he come from the back end of a sharecropper's outhouse, hired me to look for her."

"He paid you?"

"He did."

"How much?"

"Five hundred twenty-five dollars."

"An' he look like shit?"

I nodded.

"And that didn't make you wonder?" he asked, nearly closing his left eye.

"I don't know, Raymond. I guess it made me feel like the old days back down in Fifth Ward. You know, back when all we had was each other. I remember when the preacher, undertaker, blacksmith, and even any police we got were Black people. And you made a deal with anybody wanted your services, whether he had money or not."

"But this dude didn't ask for no deal. He pulled the bills out his pocket..." My friend looked up then, a question in mind. "Was they new, clean bills?"

"Dirty, and greasy too. I didn't like handlin' them."

"Huh," Raymond grunted.

"What?"

"If it was dirty money, then it coulda been his. So, you been out lookin'?"

"Some."

"Where at?"

"I went down to the Orchid Hotel in Compton. She had stayed there but then she moved."

Mouse glanced at his left wrist, where he wore an expensive-looking watch. Then he asked, "Where she move to?"

"I don't know. Some old white woman hired her for live-in or somethin'."

"Yeah," he said nodding. "Where else?"

"Santangelo told me that she would be a phone runner for the numbers sometimes, down Texas. So, I went to John and he suggested I go see Brother Forest."

Just the mention of the numbers man got Mouse to smile again.

"You went to see Pinky?"

"I did."

"I hear he got this fine-ass woman workin' there."

"There was one. I don't know if it's the same girl, but she was fine."

"What Pinky say?"

"He was scared that Lutisha was gonna try and take over his business. That's when I knew I had to call you."

"Had he seen her?"

"Not only that, she worked there for a while."

"Oh, so this ain't no jive. She out there, an' people lookin' for her."

"Her nephew is, maybe."

"More'n that, Easy. More'n that."

"Why you say that?"

Looking at his watch again, he said, "Because I know from a long time ago that Lutie goes to be a live-in domestic when she needs to lay low."

"So, you know how I can get to her?"

Mouse leaned way back in his chair and studied me, like I was a mark, an enemy, or a fool. And then without any warning he started to recite a poem of sorts.

Lutisha James don't throw no shadow
Lutisha James don't play no games
If Lutie sets her eyes upon you

You had better sign your papers over
In your loved ones' names
Lutisha James is death no foolin'
Lutisha James had Satan's son
If you see her comin' duck down quick
Before you hear that thunderin' gun

I was a little stunned by the use of verse. Even though it had the earmarks of a song, it was also a poem. A poem that Raymond Alexander had committed to memory.

"Where'd you get that from?" I asked.

"They say Brownie McGhee penned that ditty but it coulda been Sonny Terry. I mean, it coulda been Lightnin' Hopkins. All three'a them know her."

"She a singer?"

"C'mon now, Easy. You heard the words. They wasn't talkin' 'bout no singer."

"Okay. Then what do they mean?"

Holding up his pinkie he said, "Typhoid Mary," the ring finger, "Lucretia Borgia," the middle finger, "Boxcar Bertha." I thought that that was it. But then he held up the forefinger and said, "And the Bitch of Buchenwald too."

It was true that Mouse had changed since the days he started to read, but much of the knowledge he cherished carried the stench of the profane.

"So, what you sayin'?" I asked.

"Not me, the song. 'If Lutie sets her eyes upon you...'" Raymond's swaying head expressed the pity he felt for a lost fool like me. Then he looked at his watch again.

"What kinda timepiece is that?" I asked, taking a little break from our two-way interrogation.

"This here is the Rolex Oyster Perpetual Explorer II." There was that emerald again.

I held up my right hand, showing a leather-banded wristwatch and saying, "This here is what they call a Q Timex. Cost me one hundred twenty-five."

"Mines costed ten thousand."

I leaned back and grinned.

"Okay," I capitulated. "You win."

Mouse accepted his victory with a brief head bow and then went right back into the subject at hand.

"She a shadow outta darkness. You will never see it comin'. And you should know that, Easy. The minute you seen Brother Forest hang back, you shoulda known what you was inta."

I started laughing. It was a deep belly laugh that was so strong it scared me a little. I couldn't stop. For a few moments I couldn't breathe. And there wasn't a shred of humor in it either.

"What you laughin' at, fool?" Mouse asked. He was smiling.

"You know I know what I'm into. You been here, where I am right now, many, many times."

"Yeah," he opined. "Jackson Blue talked to me about it one day. He said that this dude like a psychologist said that it was the, um, come—com—compulsion to repeat."

The laughter died in my chest.

"You mean you and Jackson were discussing Sigmund Freud?"

"That's his name. Yeah. I aksed Jackson how come some niggahs be makin' the same mistake ovah and ovah and he told me about that Sigmund man."

Mouse had bought an encyclopedia and swore that he read in it every night. He'd been my friend for thirty-seven years and he still surprised me.

"So," I said. "This Lutisha James, she's like a crime boss or somethin'?"

"Somethin'."

"What's that supposed to mean?"

Mouse looked up at me, his smile at the ready. He was about to say something when…

"Hi there, Raymond, Easy."

We both looked over to see Vu Von Lihn in all her war-torn splendor. She was clad in olive-green long-sleeved coveralls that somehow accented her figure. Vu had been in a bomb blast in the service of the Vietcong against South Vietnam and the U.S. military. The lightning-bolt scar down the right side of her face traveled directly through that side's eye, killing it, and leaving in its wake a slightly nacreous white scar in the form of an after-eye-like orb.

Raymond bounced up to his feet, fast as a hare who just heard a dog bark. He pulled out a chair and seated her like the finest trained waiter.

"I seen a booth make that salad you like," he said at her ear. "Just gimme a minute."

He hurried away.

"He's so sweet," the onetime communist insurgent said, looking at him moving away down the long outside aisle of shops and restaurants.

"Especially when his woman is with child," I appended.

"He told you?" Vu asked.

"Proud as any man can be."

When talking to Vu I tended to look into her dead eye. There was something beautiful about that wound. It made you feel that you were in the presence of a living secret.

"He's a good man," she answered.

"As long as you not on the other side."

Vu laughed and tapped my knee.

"You are always on his side, Easy. He loves you."

"I once knew a man raised a lion from a two-week-old cub in the property out behind the back of his house. He'd go back there to feed and play with her almost every night. She loved him like he was her natural mother. But when that three-hundred-fifty-pound cat run up on him and raise her front paws to rest on his shoulders, you better believe that that love was hard to bear."

Vu leaned forward, looking me in the face. "You are like the old wise men in the village where I lived," she said. "You teach with stories and make me want to smile."

"Here it is," Mouse announced. He was carrying a largish cardboard bowl, filled with Caesar salad. "I aksed him for extra anchovies."

It was a pleasant visit after that.

Vu said that she was going to sell the garage, which had a chop shop on its lower level.

"You gonna do somethin' else?" I asked.

"I'm thinking of going to school to study Asian history."

"As a corrective for Western stupidity?"

"I love Black men," she replied, blowing me a kiss.

We talked for maybe an hour or so. Mouse was happy and Vu was too. I told them the news from my rose garden and Raymond told us that he planned to spend more time at home.

After a while I decided to leave.

I'd made it all the way to the parking lot in front of Du-par's restaurant when he came up behind me.

"Easy."

"Yeah, Ray?"

"Look, man," he said. "If you want my advice, you should give up lookin' for Lutie."

"Yeah, I got that."

"But you gonna keep on?"

"For a little while."

7.

From the Farmers Market I took Wilshire eastward driving toward the heart of downtown. I kept on going until the addresses dwindled down to almost zero and the late-day traffic attained its densest, most sluggish flow. Those six or seven square blocks are LA's sweet spot, where the banks and other financial institutions, and the corporate headquarters of many a mogul, thrive on the lifeblood of the people, having dug in like ticks, making themselves at home.

Just a few blocks from the end of the fancy boulevard, on the north side of the street, stood one of the city's tallest glass-and-steel skyscrapers. This edifice represented the crux of business in America: the mining of the sweat and blood, hopes and dreams, of people who have never and will never see the upper reaches of possibility that their squandered labors have wrought.

I could see my destination from four blocks away. In other parts of the city, and the countryside that surrounded us, I felt most like just another man living his life by steady steps, slips, and slowdowns. But traveling on that tarmac thoroughfare I always realized that I was no more than a simpleton cell occupied with the business of a behemoth so large that it made less sense to one such as I than the stars do on a cloudless night in the middle of the ocean.

I had witnessed that star-strangled sky on my way to World War II.

The parking lot was on Sixth Street, a block north of my destination. The rate was an initial three dollars and then seventy-five cents an hour after the first two. Five years earlier I could have left my car all day for one dollar.

The building I was going to was completely occupied by P9, an international insurance company of French origin. The lobby was full of men and women in business attire, all of them moving with intention, like they were going somewhere important. There was the hubbub of conversation and bursts of laughter now and again. Almost every person in that great space was white, that's just the way it was.

A small man, more gray than white, dressed in a muted olive-hued uniform, moved to stand in front of me.

"Can I help you?" he asked, and just that fast a half-forgotten rage welled up in my chest and made its way down to my fists.

After all I had accomplished. After all that I had learned, this little man with a halfway-Hitler mustache, graying at the edges, placed his body in my way and asked a question he knew for a fact I could not answer. He knew that he could pull out a pistol and shoot me in front of all the dozens of people surging in and out of that international hub of finance. He could shoot me down and say that I threatened him, that I reached for my jacket pocket, and he feared that I had a knife. All I'd seen and experienced, everything I had built, meant nothing up against the lying word of this high school dropout rent-a-cop. At that moment the most important thing in my mind was to grab that man by his throat using a thumb twist I'd learned while serving in the American army in the European theater. The torque would break his windpipe and nothing short of a tracheotomy could save him.

The security guard had a rectangular name tag over his left breast pocket. WARREN, it read. Warren couldn't even imagine who I was or what, but still he posed confidently, believing that he was keeping the world in its proper order. I honestly hated him after less than three seconds of our encounter.

Nothing of this feeling showed on my face.

"You mind if I take out my wallet, Warren?" I asked in a pleasant tone.

I'm sure he did not like me calling him by his Christian name, but that was the only identity his tag offered.

Uncertainty worked its way into his forehead and brow.

"Okay," he mouthed slowly, the question mark in his mien.

Taking a dusky green eel-skin wallet from my back pocket, I produced an identity card. This I held out to Warren.

At first, he just looked at the hand, wondering how this gesture fit into his worldview. A few seconds later, when this offer was not withdrawn, he plucked the item from between my forefinger and thumb. Glancing downward he saw the laminated card with my name, photograph, and security clearance as an employee of the vast insurance company that also employed him.

I was not a regular employee of P9, but French-born Jean-Paul Villard, the president and majority stock owner of the international corporation, was partial to the Black soldiers he'd encountered when we liberated France. So, he gave me a consultant's ID because whenever he needed a hand that he could depend on, he called on me or one of my friends.

"H-h-how'm I s'posed to know this is you?" Warren asked from his stance there upon the thinnest ice.

"Does it look like me?"

"I can't tell." He might as well have added that *all you people look alike to me.*

"Then do what it says on the bottom'a the card."

"What?"

"Call the security chief, you know him, your boss, Christmas Black."

Christmas was the coal-colored eternal soldier who was the head of all security at that corporation. It was then Warren understood that he'd gone from master of his limited domain to the possibility of food stamps and unemployment checks until they both ran dry.

"Um, um, uh, yeah," he said. "Excuse the mistake, Mr., um"—he looked down to read my name off the ID—"Mr. Rawlins. Go right on ahead, sir. Um, right on ahead."

Walking toward the elevators I considered what had just passed between me and Warren. I had made sure that that little gray man would hate me even more. He would resent it that I could rise to a level so high that he could never even imagine reaching it. Never. I almost regretted what I had thought and done, but the truth was, I had to stand up to him in order for that hint of uncertainty to lodge itself in his mind. His hate-trained brain was a prototype of the white world. An infection of the sort I provided, here and there, meant that he and his ilk would have to think before they ignored or acted against me and mine.

On the thirty-first floor I was met by a very handsome, tall, and even strapping young Black man clad in a black suit made from a fine fabric I couldn't identify.

"Mr. Rawlins?" he asked in an even tone that sounded like education.

"Yeah. What's it made of?"

"What, the suit?"

"You got it."

"Vicuna wool."

"You take Jackson's job?"

"No, sir. Why would—why would you say something like that?"

"Even Jackson would have to dig deep to afford enough vicuna cloth to make a suit."

"I got a girlfriend from Peru." The man's boyish smile revealed his playful side. "Her uncle has a farm where he raises the things. She wove it into fabric, and I hired a tailor. Follow me, sir."

Jackson Blue's office was expansive, with floor-to-ceiling windows that looked far enough west that you could see the blue of the Pacific. The walls of the thirty-by-thirty-foot room were lined with floor-to-ceiling bookshelves. There were hardback collections and one-off publications, paperbacks, dictionaries, novels, reports, biographies and histories, exposés, and a small corner dedicated to pornography in twelve different languages.

"Easy Rawlins," scrawny Jackson announced, leaping to his feet. He wore a maroon-colored suit, loose cut to hide how skinny he was.

"Jackson."

"C'mon, man, c'mon and sit ovah here."

"Here" was a ten-by-ten-foot area defined by a dense red-velvet rug. There he had three sofa chairs that faced a vacant central point and, therefore, one another. The chairs were upholstered in sheepskin, the fur of which had been dyed lemon yellow.

After we were seated, he asked, "So what can I do you for, Easy?"

"Lutisha James."

"Oh," he uttered in a tone that expressed how impressed he was. "What's your problem with her?"

"Nuthin' that I know. A man callin' himself her nephew wants to find her."

"Who's the nephew?"

"Santangelo Burris."

"Oh."

"You know him?" I asked.

"Nope. Never heard the name."

"I don't know him either, but he came to my office and said that his grandmother, Lutisha's mama, needs to talk with her."

"Her own mother don't know where she's at?"

"That's what he said."

"And why come to me?" Jackson asked.

"Come on, Jackson, I been comin' to you for twenty-five years askin' 'bout people in the streets."

"If you hadn't noticed, I don't frequent the streets no mo'."

I had known Jackson since I was a teenager in the Fifth Ward, Houston. Along with Raymond and John, he was one of my oldest acquaintances from that hardscrabble life. It just so happened that Blue was a genius. He met Jean-Paul somewhere and convinced the insurance tycoon to hire him to develop a computer system. From there he went on to strategies and foreign investments. He had risen to become the highest-ranked VP in the entire company.

"Do you know who Lutisha James is?" I asked.

"Yeah. She's a gambler mainly."

"What else she do?"

"I don't know exactly, but whatever it is, it's not on the Wilshire Boulevard side of the law."

"You mean she's honest?" I joked.

"I haven't heard her name in a very long time," Jackson offered after sharing a smile at my witticism.

"If you had to find her, how would you go about it?"

At that my old acquaintance-cum-friend squinted, indicating thought. He swiveled his head this way and that and finally turned to regard me again.

"Not enough data, man."

"Stella Voorhes from down at the Orchid told me that she left the hotel in a fancy car headed for a place on the rich side of LA."

"Damn, man. I haven't thought about Stella in years. She was one fine woman."

"Still is."

"You got a name Lutisha went to stay wit'?"

"She said Andit or Ortit, somethin' like that."

"Huh," he grunted. And then for a while he committed to silent thought.

After a bit he said, "You know, one time I seen Lutisha at a jazz club called Paradise. She was playin' five-card stud... winnin' too."

I just nodded. I didn't want to engage him in conversation because when Jackson set his massive intelligence to working out a problem he had to approach it stealthily.

He grunted again and then said, "You hear about them bank robbers up around Fresno, in Riverdale, went after this UCB branch?"

This question meant that Jackson wanted to conversate while trying to solve the problem of Lutisha James at the back of his mind.

"No," I said. "What about 'em?"

"They had been plannin' a straightforward robbery, but when

they looked at the layout of the buildin', they saw that one of the foot-thick walls to the vault was probably made from plaster. So, they went back to the drawin' board, found the wall in a dentist's office next door, and went through that on a weekend and then took down the plaster wall to the safe. They got away with seven hundred seventy-eight thousand two hunnert forty-six dollars. That's how much the bank admitted to."

"That's a haul," I said in reply to his talk-thinking.

"Woulda been except one'a them motherfuckers couldn't help but brag. Add that to the fact that the bank put a ten percent reward on the robbers' capture, and he signed the warrant for the whole crew..." He was about to say something else when a thought came to mind.

He snapped his fingers and cried out, "Mister! Mister!"

The young Black man in the vicuna suit hurried in.

"Yes, Mr. Blue?"

"Bring me the *Southern California Social Register.*"

"For how long back?"

"Last twenty years."

Without another word the young man named Mister departed.

"I bet you the name they gave Stella was Corbet Orbit," the top VP said to me.

"What's that?" I asked.

"It's a company that does radar designs for NASA. It was started by a dude name of Corbet, Lawn T. Corbet. He had a wife named Millicent. Yeah. The Corbet Orbit Corporation."

Mister brought in the many tomes that comprised the upper crust of LA's social register for the previous twenty years. Jackson rummaged around the pages until he found what he wanted.

"That's it," he said. "Lawn T. Corbet. He's dead but his wife, Millicent, still around. She old, though. If Lutisha doin' domestic work, I'm sure Millie could use it. She up in Bel-Air, the rich side'a town, just like Stella said. We could get the company Rolls to drive you over there. That way they'd kinda have to let you in."

"Thanks, Blue, but I have a date to get ready for."

"Hot date?"

"Simmering."

"She got a friend?" Jackson asked, sporting a hopeful grin.

Here he was, one of the most powerful men in international finance and technology, married to one of the top real estate moguls of Southern California, and still, when someone mentioned a woman who might let him kiss her neck, he was willing to lose it all.

"Why would you wanna go after some tail in the street, man? I thought you said you didn't get out in the hood no more."

"Just 'cause I don't, don't mean I don't wanna."

8.

"Hello?" she answered after the fourth ring. I was calling from a phone booth next to the outside garage where my car was parked.

"Miss Lorris?" I asked.

She tittered and said, "You could call me Ida, Mr. Rawlins."

"And you can call me Easy."

"That's an odd name for a man."

"Not if it's an antonym."

"Oh. Smart, are we? Where'd you go to college?"

"Up at the university."

"Which one?"

"The University of Life."

Her laugh was just what I needed at the end of a concentrated day of detecting.

"Are we still on for tonight, Mr. Hard Knocks?"

"I can pick you up anytime."

"I'm on the eleven hundred block of South Genesee." She gave me the address and added, "You can't miss it. It's the only blue house on the block. You could get me at seven."

"I'll be there."

There wasn't enough time to go all the way home, so I made my way to the WRENS-L offices because I kept a few changes of clothes there.

Niska was still at her receptionist's post, deep in thought. The telephone books were gone and instead she had on her desk a single sheet of paper with a yellow No. 2 pencil in hand. This configuration—a solitary wooden pencil and a clean sheet of paper on a bare desk—reminded me of her first boss, now my partner at WRENS-L, Tinsford Natley. Tinsford was one of the best detectives on the West Coast and it was no wonder Niska picked up habits from him. She had changed out of her coral dress into a dark blue ensemble that I knew from previous appearances came down to her calf.

"Hi, Mr. Rawlins," she said.

I knew, when she didn't look up, that she'd identified my footsteps on the outer stairs.

"How's the detective work going?"

That was when she raised her head to regard me. The big smile on her face told the whole story, a silent tale she backed up with the words "I think I found the guy."

"What's his name?"

"The one he's using is Delroy, Delroy Magi. That's one of the aliases Captain McCourt's assistant told me about. It's such a strange name, it's like he got it out of a book. I called the number and it's at a rooming house. The guy that answered was very friendly and he liked how my voice sounded, I could tell. So, when he told me that Delroy wasn't in, I pretended like I needed to talk with him soon. I said that I found something of his and I wanted to return it."

"Did he want to know what it was you found?" I asked, proud of my only student's first maybe-success.

"I said that it was a letter addressed to him. I looked up the name on the envelope and got his number. The guy said that Delroy was on a date with some girl, that he probably wouldn't be back until tomorrow. I asked if I could bring it to him somewhere else, like where he worked, and he said that he had the afternoon-evening shift at Chieftain's Cigar Mart on Cahuenga Boulevard. I looked it up. It's a fancy place out in the Valley."

Niska talked all in a rush. She was so excited that I got a little worried. That's why I pulled up a chair and asked, "What's the plan from here?"

"I need to make sure," she said. "Doreen gave me five photographs of him. It wouldn't take more than a glance, I don't think. Just get a quick look."

"So, you go to the cigar store..." I posed.

"Yeah."

"What then?"

"I go in and look at him, see if he's the one."

"What's your plan for that?"

Niska peered intently at me, the question in her eyes.

"I look at him and leave," she said.

"No."

"No?"

"You get dressed up and made up like you were going on a first date with a really fine guy. You wanna get him a cigar 'cause he likes to smoke 'em and you heard him say that he likes Cohibas."

"What's that?"

"It's a Cuban cigar."

"But aren't Cuban cigars illegal?"

"Now you're starting to understand. You can't just walk in and stare at the guy behind the counter and walk out. You got to be dressed up, to know what you're lookin' for. You walk in there checkin' out the merchandise. You don't even notice him at first. It's only when he tells you that that brand is banned, or when he offers to sell you some contraband stock, that you look him in the face. You're not there for him. You're there to get your new man something he wants."

Niska's excitement was gone. Now she was concentrating on the intricacies of the job.

"So, so," she wondered aloud, "I got to plan out how I go about it before going in there."

"Exactly. When you walk into that shop, the only thing on your mind is cigars. Cuban cigars. Seeing the salesman's face is no more than a necessary evil."

"And should I buy a cigar if he offers one?"

"If you, and your client, can afford it."

Nodding thoughtfully, she said, "So first, you think, I should do some research."

"No question. Because if this guy's a serious con man, he will see you looking at him for identification purposes. I promise you he will."

"That means if he hears about my call to his rooming house, he might run. I might've messed up."

"Water under the bridge, honey. Get the job set in your head, and then, tomorrow, go to the cigar store."

Nodding solemnly, she said, "I have to know everything before I go in there."

"No."

"No?"

"Look, Niska, there's a thousand situations you can't plan for. He might not be there. If he is, there might be another salesman that gets to you first. The sto' could be closed. And you can't rely on the information you got from a stranger over the phone. Your man might never have worked there.

"You can't know everything. All you can rely on is a solid base to work from. Whether it works or it don't, you follow the plan. You're there to buy an original Cuban Cohiba for a potential boyfriend."

"And why am I dressed up?"

"Because you're a good-looking woman and this guy makes his livin' off'a girls like you."

"So, I'm kinda like bait?"

"You got a problem with that?"

"I don't want to kiss him or anything."

"Your client don't want that either. But you don't have to worry. You're gonna be on the other side of the counter and you need his attention on anything but your intentions."

"Oh my God."

"What?"

"This—this is for real."

"Yes, it is."

Our assistant of many years sat back in her comfortable chair. Her face was as serious as a policeman's battering ram about to knock down a suspect's door. After a moment the determination she felt became tinged with a touch of fear.

It was then that I knew she'd make a good detective.

I went back to my office, took a shower in the master bathroom of the old-time mansion, and dressed in dark gray slacks, a nacreous white shirt with nearly transparent buttons, and a baby-blue sports jacket. The shoes were fabricated from dark blue leather.

The full-length mirror on the bathroom door told me that I was ready for my first date in fourteen months.

* * *

I parked in front of the only blue house on the eleven hundred block of South Genesee Avenue. It was a stone cottage with a faux thatched roof that rose high above the attic floor and curved downward to the tops of the high windows at the front of the house. The large stones that made the walls were painted a creamy blue and the lawn was perfectly manicured.

I'd made it about halfway up the cobblestone path leading to the front door when Ida Lorris came out wearing a loose yet alluring red dress that looked like a distant cousin of the kimono. Not a long gown, the hem came down only to the top of the overseer's knees. One shoulder was bare and the other held up a thick strap of red cloth. The fabric wavered over her extraordinary figure without giving away anything.

"Hi," she said, hurrying down the path in medium-blue high heels with no trepidation or wobble.

"Hey."

We met there, at the halfway point.

"You look nice," she complimented.

"And you look great."

She smiled slightly and then asked, "Where we going?"

"A place called Minor's."

"Like coal miners?"

"No. It's a family name using the possessive."

"Okay," she said.

I led her to a 1967 blue-black four-door Lincoln Continental that we kept in the building garage in case we were out on a job where we had to look good.

I drove west and north until getting to Mulholland Drive. About a mile up into the mountains we turned onto a dirt road and followed that, finally reaching a driveway that led to a large and rambling ranch house. The property was well lit and there was some activity. I drove up to the front of the house and my door was opened by an employee of Minor's Restaurant. Ida's door was also opened, and we were shown to the entrance.

To the left of the double-wide mahogany front door a big man sat on a huge chair that might have been made especially for his girth.

"May I help you?" the big man in the outside throne inquired. The tone of his voice carried a note of doubt.

"Rawlins," I said with some emphasis. "Reservation for two."

"You sure it was for Minor's?"

This wasn't like the little gray man at P9. Minor's Restaurant was a truly exclusive establishment. They gave trouble to everybody but the most famous.

"You think I just got lost goin' to Jack in the Box?" I replied.

"Do you have a word or two to substantiate the reservation?"

"Blue moon."

Reluctantly the sitting man rose from the portable throne. He pushed the door open, and we were greeted by the horns, strings, and drums of big-orchestra, pre-bebop jazz. The room was large, the size of a small auditorium, and there were tables of many designs where at least a hundred people sat and talked. On a dais at the other side of the room, the jazz orchestra played.

"What is this place?" Ida whispered in my ear.

"It is what you see," I answered. "How the other half lives."

"Mr. Rawlins," a throaty voice welcomed me.

"Hannah."

"It's so nice to see you. It's been ages."

"As a rule, this place is too rich for my blood," I said to the hostess, who looked to be clad in a close-fitting frock of liquid silver. Her hair was golden and her eyes the blue of an ocean. The emerald at her throat could have bought a middle-class home and the diamond on her left forefinger might have purchased an entrée to mortal heaven.

"There are no rules like that here, Easy." When Hannah looked into my eyes, I thought it better to let her have the last word.

"Hannah," I said, starting a new conversation. "This is Ida Lorris. A good friend."

"Very beautiful," Hannah complimented. "Both of you are. I will have to seat you where others can appreciate your charm."

We were led to an elevated table that was to the right of the jazz band. After seating us side by side, Hannah smiled, then went away to pamper her other guests.

The band played on.

"I don't, um, well, it's not that I don't understand," Ida said. "It's just that I've never been anywhere like this."

"Most people have never been anywhere like the back rooms of S and S."

This observation earned a smile.

"Are you trying to impress me?" she wondered aloud.

"Yes and no."

"Meaning?"

"Like my old mentor's wife used to say, I been in a mood for a while and then I met you."

She grinned and said, "What kinda mood?"

"Like everything was the same and nuthin' new on the horizon."

"But I'm the one who asked you out," she said, exploring any possible chinks in my explanation.

"And here we are."

Ida touched my forearm and smiled. It was a genuine smile, telling me that there would be no more social and political tussling that night.

"Are they going to bring us menus?" she asked.

"Not exactly."

There was confusion on my date's face and a question on her lips that didn't have time to become words.

"Good evening, Mr. Rawlins," a man said. "Miss Lorris."

He was standing by my side of the table. A tall man in an impeccably tailored black suit. His skin was copper brown and his eyes black.

"Horvat," I greeted.

"How did you..." Ida began. But then she went silent, remembering, I think, that I'd introduced her to Hannah by her full name.

"Do you eat meat?" Horvat asked Ida.

"Yes, I do."

"And do you have any allergies?"

"Not that I know of."

Horvat's face was long and severe, expressing little. But I saw a hint of a smile on his lips.

"Any foods you abhor?" the waiter out of Plato's cave inquired.

"Not really."

Then Horvat went into his spiel. "We will start with vichyssoise, followed by a lime sorbet for the palate, then lamb shank in a red wine sauce along with roasted baby potatoes, green beans amandine, and tempura-fried squash blossoms. For dessert we will serve a simple French apple pie.

"Does that sound acceptable?"

"Yes," my date said. "Very acceptable."

Horvat nodded and backed away.

* * *

Our meal came in the order the elegant waiter promised. The jazz was so good that, in my mind, it almost conflicted with the exquisite feast. At times I felt guilty eating while the clarinetist and trombonist were helping each other climb to the heights of their potential.

"Where you from?" I asked Ida just after the main course was served.

"Washington."

"The state?"

"DC."

"Your people in politics?"

"In a way."

"What way?"

"They were domestics for an eastern senator who came from wealth and expected to be served."

I had no quip for this confession.

"They made good money and took good care of me and my younger brother, Ira," Ida said, maybe with a little defensiveness in her tone.

"And you went to Howard?"

She leaned toward me, smiling broadly.

"Good guess," she said. "But no. I went to Spelman College."

"Atlanta."

"You're a continual surprise, Mr. Easy."

"As are you," I replied, holding a champagne flute for her to tap with the rim of her glass.

When we got back to her place I parked in front of the house.

"Can I walk you to your door?" I asked.

Her response was a full-mouthed kiss that had no intention of quitting. Her hand was on my neck and, after five minutes or so, the middle and ring fingers of my left hand had found their way to the center of her left inner thigh. The digits moved, ever so lightly, in circles until she moaned aloud, "Easy."

"Yes?"

"I have to go."

9.

The ride home was wonderful. I felt excitement in my heart, mind, and nether regions too. It was a feeling akin to how I felt about my first true love, Anger Lee, the stolen-goods-monger of the Fifth Ward. Back then, when I was fourteen and Anger seventeen, I was at peace with the world. For the longest time, many months, Anger treated me like a little brother. It wasn't until I got stabbed trying to save her life that she promoted me to temporary boyfriend status. The time I had to wait for Anger's love seemed to echo inside the space I'd have to occupy until I could be with Ida again.

Cosmo Longo came out of the little sentry hut that stood before the gate to the entrance of the mountaintop I called home. The Sicilian had a powerful build, with hair everywhere. He was probably the gentlest of the brothers. The kind of man you wanted as a babysitter for your child.

"Mr. Easy," he greeted.

"Hey, Cos, how are ya?"

"You have a visitor," he said instead of answering.

I looked toward the lighted door of the shedlike guard post. At that moment she emerged, as if waiting for me to turn that way.

"Amethystine," I think I said. Maybe the name only reverberated in my mind. I had been wanting to see her every day since the day I told her that I'd never see her again.

"Hello, Ezekiel, can I come up?"

I knew what I should have said and what I wanted to say. But instead, I said, "Okay."

The Sicilian caretaker unlocked the gate to the inner property, revealing a short pathway that led to the bottom of the mountain. He opened the sliding door of the fancy funicular car and then bunged us in.

When the machinery engaged and began to drag us up the mountainside, we kissed. It wasn't me kissing her or her kissing me. We came together naturally, after two years of being apart. It was alchemy and gravity. What was to be without a doubt.

Walking along the pathway, which was blue in sunlight and gray at night, to my tower of a home, we stopped here and there to resume the kisses and touching, unbuttoning and caressing. When we got to the front door, disheveled and hot, I fumbled around, finally working the key in the lock. I pressed the door open and ushered her in before I remembered Prince Valiant, the 180-pound killer guard dog.

"Watch out!" I shouted, but it was too late.

Valiant leaped out of the darkness, knocking Amethystine to the floor. He'd jumped on top of her before I could react. But when I got to him, he was already licking her face as she was tousling the thick fur below his ears.

She was laughing and he was crying—he was that happy to see her, a woman he had last seen as a few-weeks-old puppy.

"Oh my God," Amethystine exclaimed. "He's wonderful."

"I don't understand it," I said, pulling at his collar. "Every other time he's ever met a stranger, he growls and bares his teeth."

"He must smell you on my hand," she said. "He knows what this is."

She was the kind of woman who knew and didn't mind the fantasies of men. We'd almost made it to my top-floor bedroom when she mounted me on the stairs.

"Feather's not here, is she?" she whispered, rising from and descending onto my lap.

"She's in—in France."

It was as if I was caked with the filth and detritus of a lifetime, and now this woman came with a rough-bristled scrubber and hand rake to scour me clean and raw.

That night was spent throbbing with pleasure and pain too. I couldn't remember the last time I'd had a sleepless night that didn't involve a case, or one of my kids getting sick.

"I want to devour you, Easy Rawlins," she said maybe five minutes after sunrise. We were in my bed by then, taking a breather. "I been thinkin' about this here every day, every day."

She rose above me on her left elbow and looked down.

"I been dreamin' about it, but whatever I imagined, I never thought it would be like this."

"Like what?"

"Like dogs at their meat after they'd been starvin' a week."

I had to kiss her, didn't I?

* * *

Later that morning, we had breakfast in bed. I made lemon waffles with maple-cured bacon and a simple salad of butter lettuce dressed with vinaigrette. Somewhere in the middle of the meal I remembered Ida Lorris. I'd had a wonderful evening with that woman. She was friendly and intelligent, just bent enough that she wouldn't run away screaming from the life I inhabited. I remembered her the way I thought of parts of my life that had happened long ago, far away.

"So, what's your day like, Ezekiel?"

"I'm on a job."

"What kinda job?

"Lookin' for people probably don't wanna be found, runnin' into those don't want me lookin'."

"Wouldn't you rather stay up here with me?"

"What I want and what I have to do are two different things."

"Can't you hire some young man to run the streets with a target on his back instead of yours?"

"That's next year on the life plan. What about you?"

"What about me?" When she turned over on her stomach, the sheet rolled under her, showing off her fine flanks and two marks that told of healed violence. One scar was small and round, not unlike Vu Von Lihn's eye. The other was long and centipede-like due to the many stitches that had to be used to hold it together.

The long gash I remembered from the few weeks we knew each other. The bullet wound, though, that was new.

"What you been doin' since I seen you last?" I asked her. "Still workin' for Jewelle?"

"No. It didn't feel right working for your friend's wife. I left there and started working for a man named Charles Clinic."

"Now, that's a name. What's Mr. Clinic have you doin'?"

"Dr. Clinic," she corrected. "He's a physics professor at USC, pretty arrogant, really. I hired on to keep his house clean because his wife left him. He told me that he was doing very important work and that when he was in his study he didn't want to be disturbed, even with cleaning noise. So, one day when he wasn't behind a closed door, I asked him what he does in that study of his. He got all snide and said, 'Particle physics.' To which I said, 'Oh, you mean quantum mechanics.' His lips got all twisted. He said I coulda learnt that from some note he threw in the trash or sumpin'. I told him, no, I could read real books just as well as anybody else."

I knew what she was saying was true. Amethystine could debate someone on the level of Jackson Blue about the meanings and values of mathematical theory.

"So, what did the good professor have to say to that?" I asked.

"He thought for a minute and then asked me what the maximum number of electrons in a quantum shell was. When I said two-N-squared, he almost shit himself." Her grin was hard and self-assured. "He asked me more and more questions over the next few days. Sometimes we talked for hours. By the end of that week, he hired me to transcribe notes for a major paper he was slated to deliver at the end of last year."

"So, your job is to clean out his toilets and write his physics papers?"

She smiled and said, "Not anymore. When I made up my mind to come see you, I quit."

"Why?"

"I realized that I was just marking time, waiting for this."

I was listening to what she said but I was thinking too, and when her story was over, my mind kept on going.

"What?" she called into my silence.

"You killed that man," I said with deep conviction, referring to Harrison Fields, aka Sturdyman, who had murdered her ex-husband. She'd shot the old guy in his eye, leaving no clue but a whiff of perfume. I was the only one who knew the identity of the murderer, and so, because I didn't turn her in, I felt complicit.

"You woulda done the same to somebody murdered one'a your loved ones," she countered.

She'd said the same thing two years before, but for some reason, back then, I didn't hear it as truth. But time had changed me. I remembered talking to my adopted son, Jesus, pronounced in the Spanish articulation, *Hey Zeus*. He told me that I needed a woman in my life.

Somewhere between assigning Ida a place in memory and accepting Amethystine's hard truth, I stalled. In hindsight, I suppose it was good for me to be conflicted about love instead of the deadly danger that Mouse said awaited me with Lutisha James.

"Ezekiel?"

"Yeah."

"What you thinkin'?"

"How's Garnett and Pearl doin'?" I asked, coming up with a topic that had no weight. Garnett and Pearl were fraternal twins, her much younger siblings. She'd taken care of them since they were infants.

"They're fine. I sent them up north to a co-ed academy. He's gotten into painting, and she says that she wants to go into law."

"That sounds expensive."

"They're both very smart. Most of the cost they get in financial aid."

"They don't mind being away from you?"

"I go up to see them on the weekend every two or three weeks.

And they come home for the holidays and part of summer vacation."

"That's good. Those private schools can be hell on a sensitive child." I knew this from my daughter's prep school experience.

"You told me about Feather. What's goin' on with Jesus?"

"Him and Benita raisin' my beautiful granddaughter and they're makin' pretty good money at deep-sea fishin'."

"Really? I read somewhere that the mackerel were running less around Southern California."

"Yeah, it's been kinda dry. Jesus is a real fisherman, though. He goes down into open sea outside of Mexican waters."

"I wanna see you," she said out of nowhere.

"Me too."

The smile those two words earned brought me all the way out of the funk I'd been in for the last two years. You could say that she saved my life right then and there.

I left Amethystine in my mountain home with her scars and my killer dog. I hadn't broken it off with her due to any lack of trust. I did it because being with her was like being back in the Fifth Ward ghetto, back when the only laws were heaven and hell, black and white, good or evil.

The gates to the curved driveway of the Bel-Air address were open wide. I traveled up the long and curving cobblestone coachway and then parked at the curb before the heavy oaken double doors of the three-story manor. I disembarked the work Lincoln, walked up to the entrance, and was about to press the doorbell button when I noticed the right-side door was just a bit ajar.

I stood there for a full sixty seconds wondering what to do next. It was probably nothing. People up in that fancy neighborhood weren't worried about a neighbor coming to see if their door was unlocked and what kind of money they kept in the underwear drawer. Nobody wanted to steal your cracked china or some pair of three-year-old size-eleven shoes.

It was probably okay to ring the bell but, then again, I was unarmed and by myself. I had kissed one woman and made love to another. My life was going well, quite well. Why should I put that good life on the line for a man who looked like a demon that had been misnamed Saint?

Because he paid you, that's why, my secret voice advised. *Because you're in the business to do right by your people.*

My people. Blacks and Mexicans, those who were too old or too young. I identified with immigrants and wage slaves, those who were confused and the ones who were too smart for their own good.

I pressed the button.

The deep reverberation of three gongs sounded through the heavy oak, emanating from the interior of the ridiculously large house. I rang four more times, just in case the people therein were late sleepers. Three minutes had passed. My left hand pushed the right-side door inward. That's what it felt like, like my hand and not my mind decided, however unwisely, to enter the place.

The foyer was rendered in the shape of the long half of a twenty-foot oval, mimicking the lengthwise dissection of some ancient Roman gladiatorial arena. This hall was furnished with four padded chairs of blue and a stark, dark red love seat. Opposite the front door was a wide entranceway. This led to a room that went up all the three floors of that house, where a skylight, aided by well-placed mirrors, brought down a great deal of sunlight.

This meant that the atrium was also a solarium, where dense plant life flourished. There were at least a hundred different varieties of flora. It was like a fancified jungle in there—rosebushes, dwarf palms, cherry and walnut miniatures, just to name a few. Two very colorful birds, not native to this continent, squawked and fluttered at the height of the room, flitting back and forth in the passion fruit vines. I remember thinking that they must've had a gardener working at least three days a week to keep everything watered, fertilized, pruned, and harvested.

From the sunroom I entered a sitting room that was just big enough to hold two reclining chairs and a single bookshelf. This room was heavily infused with pipe smoke. The next room was a very large kitchen that looked as if it had never been used—it was that clean.

"Anybody here?" I called. "Lutisha, Lutisha James?"

I passed through a few more rooms that didn't have names in my architectural vocabulary. Then I finally got to a chamber that was occupied. The residents were corpses, three adults of differing ages. There was a barefoot young woman in her early thirties, clad in a T-shirt and jeans, an older man who looked to be in his eighties, and a younger man, maybe forty, who wore a burgundy housecoat that hung open. They were all white, dead, and had bled, copiously. There were marks of violence on their faces, and they had gunshot wounds to their chests. The old man had had two fingernails ripped out, telling me that this had been a straightforward torture scene.

There was no elderly white woman among them, nor some Black lady old enough to be the mother of Santangelo Burris. There was dried blood, the faint smell of gun smoke, and then there were a dozen or so flies. The ravenous little creatures' buzzing sounded like applause. They were feasting and no doubt planting eggs.

This last revelation coincided with my decision to leave.

I strode down a long hallway, coming to a hexagonal room that would have most certainly been called the library. There were floor-to-ceiling shelves against all six walls, filled with books, mostly hardback and jacketed. All other things being equal, I would have taken a moment to investigate the literary tastes of the house.

But things were not equal, and I was more interested in an exit than in the printed word.

That's when the ghost appeared.

A hideous scream broke the silence of the home. I turned to see a banshee running at me. It was all white, like a Klansman from hell, shrieking in a tone so high it would have been impossible for any living mortal to make. It was a vengeful spirit, intent upon rending my soul and dragging me to hell.

A second later, the spirit slammed into my side.

I felt the blow. There was no immediate pain, but I knew from the war that injuries didn't start out with pain. That would come later. I screwed up my courage to face the demon. But then it was just a child wearing a very light blue nightgown that went down past her feet. She'd wrapped her arms around my waist, holding tight and hollering words that I couldn't understand.

I put my hands down under her armpits and lifted her even though she struggled against me. When I hugged her close, her arms clamped down around my neck and she screamed and screamed.

10.

There I was, a Black man with three dead white people two rooms away and a white girl-child, maybe nine years old, shrieking and holding me around the neck with such strength that the only way to disengage her would have been to cause injury. After what felt like a long time she stopped yelling at the top of her lungs for maybe one minute, holding tight, panting like a small animal surrounded by fire.

Then she started yelling again.

As the time dragged by, she took little breaks now and then before starting up again. If we weren't so removed from the neighborhood, I might have worried about someone hearing her loud complaints, but the size of the mansion and the huge property itself, I felt, would swallow any sound a human could make.

After a while the sporadic spans of silence got longer.

During one of these pauses I began talking to her.

"Does anything hurt you?" I asked.

Her response was to double the volume of her complaint.

"Do you need some water?"

That time she nodded before crying bloody murder again. Carrying her in my arms, I went to a cabinet, threw it open, and found that it contained only cooking spices, then the next cabinet was filled with plates of varying sizes; the third cupboard specialized in large, probably handmade ceramic mugs. The girl was still hollering, but I paid no attention. I lugged her over to the double-basined aluminum sinks, ran water, and then held the fat vessel to her lips. She had to stop crying in order to drink, and after the third swallow she had to take a deep breath to get the right volume.

I became inured to sounds of terror, this because I was terrified myself, frightened of being discovered and lynched just for being there.

When I was a child they hanged Black people without a trial, without any excuse whatsoever. That reality lived inside me, a colony of long-toothed tapeworms writhing in my gut.

When the girl took another break from screaming, I asked, "What happened to you?"

To my surprise, she said, "My—my—my Uncle Rolfo put me in the secret room in the hall closet and said not to make a sound."

"He did?"

She nodded.

"Why did he do that?"

"Because they broke the front window."

"Who did?"

The child couldn't find words and started screaming again. She wouldn't let me put her down, so during this bout I sat on a tall stool that stood before a kitchen counter that loomed like an island in the middle of the immaculate kitchen.

When next she paused, I asked, "Are you okay?"

"Where's Uncle Rolfo?" she whimpered.

"I don't know," I lied. "Maybe we should call the police."

More shouts and screams. More holding on tight.

Then, "We got to look for him," she commanded.

"I'm too scared," I said. "I want the police."

More crying. This time it felt as if she might have been crying for me.

"What's your name?" I shouted over her screams.

"I'm scared," she answered.

"Me too," I replied honestly. "We need the police to protect us."

"Are the police like—like—like you?" While asking this she rubbed her small hand over my forearm, making me wonder if she was referring to my dark color.

Not knowing what answer would soothe her, I said, "They're my friends."

"Your real friends?"

"Yes."

"O-o-o-okay."

There was a phone next to one of the kitchen doors. Lifting the receiver from its cradle, I dialed a number I knew well.

"Melvin Suggs's line," Myra Lawless said in my ear.

"Hi, Myra, Easy Rawlins here. Please tell me he's in."

"Is it important? He's trying to finish a presentation he's doing for the chief."

"I'd say it was life and death, but really it's only just death."

Three clicks and: "Melvin Suggs."

"Hey, man, Bel-Air's in your jurisdiction, right?"

"Yeah." We were such good friends that there was no need to stand on ceremony.

"Well, I'm here at..." I gave him the address. "There's three homicides and one frightened little girl. It's bad."

"Anatole's in West LA right now. I'll send him and a few uniforms out there."

"Tell 'em there's a Black man here. There's a Black man here and they shouldn't shoot him. Make sure they know that."

"Talk to you later, Easy."

He hung up and it was just me and the girl, with death in the other room, and retribution on the way.

"Are they coming?" she asked.

"Yeah. They're gettin' into their cars and drivin' all the way out here."

She smiled at what I said but I didn't think that it had to do with the information imparted.

"They came in through the broken window, I think," she said with prodding. "I could hear Mamie screaming like she was hurt."

"Did anybody hurt you?"

Shaking her head, she said, "Only Uncle Rolfo when he pushed me into the secret room at the back of the closet where they keep the towels. Where is he?"

The ghost child had to be always touching me. She was seated on my lap, sipping her water with one hand holding the mug and the other on the side of my face. I took the mug, holding it for her to drink from while she used the free hand to grasp my sports jacket lapel.

Time was passing by sluggishly, bringing to mind thick molasses dripping from a crack in a crockery jar at the back of an unheated winter pantry that belonged to my grandfather. Sometimes I'd go out there to sniff at the sweet, burnt-smelling leak.

"What's your name?" I asked to fill in the moments.

"Geraldine, but they call me Gigi."

"Gigi?"

"Yeah."

"Did a woman named Lutisha used to stay here?"

"Lutie!" she cried, grinning broadly and nodding.

"She had black skin like me?"

"Yeah. She's my best friend."

In the distance sirens whined.

"Was Lutie here last night?"

Gigi shook her head no.

The sirens were getting louder.

"Did you see anything that happened after you went in the secret room in the closet?"

She went stock-still and stared at me.

"It's okay. You won't get in trouble."

Hesitating, she said, "I had to go to the bathroom, so I got out really quiet and I—and I saw Uncle Rolfo screaming at this man that had on a suit jacket that was like a checkerboard. The man hit him real hard and I ranned back to the closet."

"The checkerboard suit jacket was red and black?"

"Uh-uh, yellow and black. I'm sorry I ranned out."

"Don't worry, honey, everything you did was perfect."

She nestled her head against my chest and then a cop burst into the room. He had his pistol out and was pointing it at me and Gigi.

"Don't move!" he shouted, and Gigi started her banshee's cry.

Another cop, also with a pistol in hand, ran in from another room. That direction, I knew, was from where the dead bodies were.

"Let the girl go!" the second cop commanded.

I put my hands up next to my ears.

"Come to me," the second cop said to Gigi.

"Go away!" she screamed at him. It felt as if she was trying to climb into my sports jacket.

"I'm the one who called you guys," I said.

A third uniformed officer came in then. His gun was out too. I was hoping beyond hope that Gigi would stay holding me because I believed that it was only her physical proximity that could protect me from a dozen bullet wounds.

"Put those guns down!" someone yelled. Just hearing his voice sent cold prickles down the back of my neck, replacing the fever of absolute fear.

The voice walked into the room. It was Captain Anatole McCourt.

"You okay, Rawlins?"

"Ask me that after my heart slides back down into my chest."

"You two go back to the crime scene," he said to the first two cops. "And you, Rath," he said to the third man.

"Yes, Captain."

"You call down to the precinct and get a full team up here."

"Yes, sir."

"And don't give 'em any details. Just say that we need a full team to examine a suspected crime."

"Yes, sir."

When the gunmen were gone, Anatole walked over to us and sat down on a stool like ours.

Gigi's eyes opened wide at the sight of McCourt's great height and breadth. The red-haired, green-eyed cop was at least six six, blessed with a Neanderthal's chest.

Gigi held tight on to me while appreciating the gray-suited captain.

"Okay," Anatole said in a world-weary tone of voice. "Let's hear it."

I told him almost everything. Why not? I was looking for Lutisha James, it didn't matter who knew it. Santangelo said it was to call her mother. Nothing wrong with that. But when it came to talking about the dead bodies in the other room, I softballed it for Gigi's sake.

Anatole was the kind of student who never took notes, but he listened very closely. When I finished, he requested that we stay in the kitchen. Gigi and I were happy to comply.

Some time went by while various police officials came to inspect the crime scene. Gigi left my lap only once, when I had to carry her to the bathroom, wait, and then bring her back to our stool in the kitchen.

The child was too frightened to maintain any kind of conversation. Whenever we spoke about anything beyond creature needs, she tended toward tears. My only job, right then, was to hold her.

Maybe two hours later Anatole came in with a woman clad in a dull orange dress and boatlike dark brown low-heeled shoes. She was white, somewhere around forty, with a smile that seemed forced under the vise of her squashed-down face.

"Mrs. Alice Fabricant, meet Ezekiel Rawlins," the giant announced.

"Pleased to meet you," she said dismissively. Then, bearing that forced grin, she said to Gigi, "And who is this?"

My temporary papoose turned her face away, burying it in the fabric of my jacket.

"This is Gigi," I said.

Alice Fabricant gave me a sour look.

"She will have to come with me," she said. "I represent Child Services. Um, and who are you?"

"Mr. Rawlins," I replied formally. "I just met the young lady. She seems to think of me as a kind of protector."

Mrs. Fabricant reached out a hand to take Gigi's arm.

"No!" my charge screamed. "You leave me alone!"

"But, honey," Alice said softly, "you have to come with me."

"No! I want to be with my friend, Easy!"

That battle went on for some time. I tried to help, but Gigi was absolutely sure of what was best for her. No one could gainsay that.

After a long while Fabricant went away and then came back with a pint bottle of lemonade.

The social worker pretended to take a sip from the bottle and said, "This is really good lemonade. It's sweet and tart and helps you to relax."

She held the bottle toward Gigi, but I put up a hand. I looked Anatole in the eye, the question unspoken. He nodded at me, and I allowed Fabricant to commit her misdemeanor.

A few minutes later the little victim child laid her head against my chest again and yawned.

"Hand her to me, Mr. Rawlins," Fabricant requested.

"She's not asleep yet, lady."

"I have a time schedule to keep."

"Keep whatever you want, but Gigi's not asleep yet."

"I—" she started to say.

"You will wait," Anatole interrupted, using that cop's commanding voice that would stop anyone short of Mouse.

"Your superiors will hear about this," she warned Anatole.

"Oh yeah? You got your MD on you, sis?"

"What?"

"I don't think you have the license to prescribe lemonade. Do you?"

Fabricant's brows furrowed while she worked out the quality of the cop's threat.

Finally, she said, "I'll be outside."

* * *

A few minutes later Gigi was in a light sleep. I carried her out to the social worker's car and strapped her into the child's seat in back.

Gigi woke up then and looked at me sleepily.

"Easy," she said.

"Yes, baby?"

"Are you gonna come see me?"

I kissed her cheek and whispered, "Wherever you are, just say you want to see me, and I'll come to you."

Watching the Child Services car roll down the path toward the street, I felt a little pang for the girl. I was about her age when I lost my one surviving parent, my father. Gigi was like me in that she was going to have to make it in a world that didn't know to care. I hoped that she had someone, somewhere.

There was an ambulance-like van parked in front of the house.

"That the coroner's truck?" I asked Anatole.

"No. It's for the old lady."

"What old lady?"

As if my words were a magical incantation, the front doors of the mansion flew open and out came a man in white. He was pushing a wheelchair that held an ancient woman, swathed in a blanket and strapped to the chair. She was moving her head from side to side, trying to get a look at the man, while yelling hoarse curses at him. She weighed no more than seventy pounds.

"Millicent Corbet?" I asked.

"She was in a room upstairs," Anatole said on a nod. "Sitting in her own waste. I guess the killers didn't think she was worth the effort."

Another male nurse climbed out of the dark van and helped his friend wrestle the old woman and wheelchair into the back of that specialized ambulance.

I watched as they drove off.

"So, Easy," Anatole said to my back.

"Yeah."

"You have anything else to add?"

I turned to face him. "You got your car here?"

"I got driven out by Officer Rath. Why?"

"Will you ride with me back downtown?"

"That Lincoln yours?"

"It belongs to the company."

"I don't know if I want to ride to headquarters in a pimpmobile."

"You take your whores in secret?" I retorted, thinking, What the fuck he mean calling my car that?

"You don't have to be so sensitive, Rawlins. I'll take a ride."

11.

I took surface streets on the drive downtown. I find it less distracting than the sixty-mile-an-hour route. After we made it to Sixth Street it was a more or less straight shot to our destination.

"How's it been goin', Anatole?"

Ignoring me, he turned toward his passenger's window, looking at something there in the streets. If he was a witch, his familiar would have been some kind of feline that spent night after night hunting down prey.

After a few minutes he surprised me by answering, "I never liked you, Rawlins. You know that, don't you?"

This aggressor's question reminded me of a time over twenty-five years earlier. It was nighttime and I was out on my own, not far from our barracks in the city of Hamburg in Germany. That devastated town had been *pacified* and was deemed safe. I saw the shadow of a man skulking down an alleyway. I shouted, "Halt!" and he began to run. I ran after, service pistol in hand. That was an automatic reflex after three years of combat. I ran the guy down. He was a little older than I, some kind of officer with no weapons and no hope. He was undernourished, you could see the bones in his face. His skin was very pale, and he sported a dark, untrimmed mustache.

"I surrender," he said, before falling to his knees. "I surrender. A prisoner of war. You must arrest me and give me my rights under the Geneva convention."

I thought that he'd probably learned those words just so he could plead for his life in a situation like that. He knew, as I did, that German officers were being beaten and sometimes killed by our soldiers. Especially Black soldiers who weren't allowed the same privileges as captive German officers were. That's why my prisoner was begging for his life.

Luckily for him I'd lost my taste for blood.

I let him go.

"Why?" I asked the LAPD captain.

"Why don't I like you?"

I nodded.

"Because... you're a—a—a, you know."

"A Negro?"

"I'm not prejudiced, Rawlins."

"No? Then you just about the only one who ain't."

"I've never called you a derogatory name. The only times I ever came after you was when I was trying to solve criminal activity. You might be useful sometimes, but you cross that line way too often."

"That derogatory name, you ever say it out loud? You know, in a parley with your cop friends?"

Silence.

"I just asked you how's it been goin'," I said to break the muzzle clamped down on the conversation. "That's all."

"There's been a lot goin' on," he said, ceding to my request. "People are down on cops nowadays. They don't trust us. That makes doing our job harder. What about you?"

"What's been goin' on with me? Is that what you're askin'?"

"Yeah."

"Never been better," I said. "But that don't quite make things good."

Anatole actually smiled.

"You could have been Irish," he said, giving me the best compliment he could think of.

"Yeah, the Englishman's nigger."

He looked like a man who had just been slapped.

"I just, um, wanted to thank you, Captain," I said. "I know you don't like me, but you still do the right thing, mostly."

"That's my job."

"Yeah. I know Niska's been callin' your office and askin' questions that your people don't have to answer. I just wanted to thank you for helpin' her."

"I like Miss Redman. She's not all angry like so many'a your people are."

We were at a red light, and so I swiveled my head to look into his eyes. In the back of my mind, I had a whole document of the unwritten history of the people he was referring to; the death by violence, self-immolation, and spiritual suicide that we saw among our own on a weekly basis; the money we squandered looking for some kind of recompense; the children we tried, and failed, to protect from these truths.

But I knew that there was no way for him to understand.

My truth was not his.

The light turned green, and I drove on.

* * *

The captain and I went our separate ways when reaching LAPD headquarters. I went to the admissions desk, where I told them I was expected by Melvin Suggs, the third or, depending on how you gauged it, the fourth most powerful cop in the LAPD. They made me sit on a wooden bench, called Mel's office, and then went about shuffling papers. After ten minutes or so a stocky, olive-skinned woman came out from some back room and called, "Ezekiel Rawlins?"

I was the only person on the bench.

"Here."

"You can go on up. Do you know the way?"

Melvin's office was on an upper floor, lost in a maze of hallways and doors. But I made it there and knocked, as protocol required.

"Come in," a woman said, her voice raised for the task.

By the time I'd made it past the door, the professional police receptionist was on her feet. Maybe five five, 160 pounds, past sixty, gray-haired and with somehow intense brown eyes, Myra Lawless was the pit-bull grandmother who protected Melvin against all comers.

"Mr. Rawlins," she said behind a synthetic smile. "Did Captain Suggs summon you?"

"He did."

I knew that Myra didn't dislike me. It was just her instinct to put any visitor at a disadvantage.

"Fearless says hi," I said, eliciting a genuine smile.

"Oh. How is Mr. Jones?"

"He's all right."

I hadn't talked to Fearless in months, but if I had seen him and told him that I was going to see Mel, he would have definitely passed along good wishes to Myra.

"Easy," Melvin Suggs said from his office door.

He looked good, five eight, in good shape for fifty, with healthy skin and fawn-brown eyes.

"Hey, man," I said.

"Come on in."

I bowed my head to Myra and headed for the seat of power.

Mel maintained a man's office. Papers everywhere, bookshelves that had files, statuettes, one or two tiny dying plants that probably had not enough water or sunlight. The smell was somehow of leather. And I could feel the grit of the floor under my rubber soles.

"Sit, sit," my host offered.

The maple-wood visitor's chair had a broad bottom and a curved back. It was a comfortable place to sit, something that humans have sought after since the days before we were actually human.

"Look, Easy, the old man was Lawrence LaCraig, also known as Rolf, a very rich cattleman."

"Like a cowboy?"

"A real one, from down around South America. They say he owns a dozen ranches down there. The other man, Joseph Toledo, was Larry's nephew, and the woman was Barbara, called Babs, Sentril—mother of the child and wife of Mr. Toledo."

"Why didn't Babs take Toledo's name?"

"Don't know," Mel said. "The old man was an important part of a certain community, so there's gonna be some pressure brought to bear."

"I didn't know anything about the man till right now."

"Then how did you get there?"

"I'm lookin' for a woman name of Lutisha James."

"What for?"

I told the story of Santangelo Burris and the job he'd hired me for.

"Do you think she might have killed the people in that house?"

"The girl that survived said that it was a whole gang of people. They tortured the family before killin' 'em. As far as I can tell, James was a live-in domestic."

"Were the killers hippies?" Mel asked.

"I don't know for a fact, but I don't think so."

"Why not?"

"Gigi, the child, said they were wearing sports clothes, and the victims were tortured like you do when tryin' to get information. That makes me think that the attack was pretty well planned out. That's not a hippie thing. But—but why would you care about that anyway?"

"Because we can't have another Charles Manson kinda thing."

"Oh. Yeah. There wasn't anything in blood on the walls. Did they steal anything?"

"A wall safe the size of a small vault. Good one too. Made by Underwriters Laboratories."

"What difference that make?"

"Means whoever took it is gonna have a bitch of a time gettin' it open."

He asked a few dozen more questions and was, I think, satisfied with my answers.

"Is that all?" I said at the end.

"Pretty much," he said. "Except for this thing about Jesus."

"What about my son?" Anybody hearing my tone might have heard a threat therein.

"A guy name of Oglethorpe with the BNDD says that two of his agents have targeted him."

BNDD was the abbreviation for the Bureau of Narcotics and Dangerous Drugs, predecessor of the DEA. According to the *LA Times*, Richard Nixon and the CIA were working both with and against them at that time.

"Targeted him for what?" I wanted to know.

"Dope."

"Heroin?"

"Marijuana."

"You mean like he gets high now and then?"

"For smuggling tons of marijuana."

"Smugglin'. Jesus?"

"They say he's bringin' in regular shipments of grass in that fishin' boat'a his."

"That's impossible," my lips said, but my mind was racing far out ahead. For the past two years Jesus and his wife, Benita, had been doing deep-sea fishing. They had been going farther out because of overfishing and pollution along the coast. Jesus had told me that he was drifting farther and farther into Mexican waters. It made some sense that he would at least be suspected of smuggling.

"Who are these agents?"

"I asked to meet 'em, but Oglethorpe said that informing the LAPD was more manners than meat."

"So, they're after him?"

"They came to one of my captains who works narcotics. Told him that a kid named Jesus Rawlins was under suspicion. He knows that the BNDD is being investigated by the CIA for corruption, so he came right to me. He said that they almost caught up to your boy, but he scuttled the boat and got away."

"In Mexican waters?"

"That's what they said."

I was unmoored. My head felt like a buoy floating on a sea rocked by a far-off storm. Suggs was doing his best to help me. He didn't have to say a thing about the trouble gathering over my son's head. As a matter of fact, it would have been better for him to keep me in the dark, or even to try to wheedle information out of me.

"Thanks, Mel," I said at last. "Thanks, man."

"You need anything else?"

A new name and a different country to call my home, I thought. But, instead, I asked, "Could you ask somebody to give you any records you got about a Lutisha James and Santangelo Burris?"

"Okay. I will. But that Burris guy, he's your client, right?"

"He is."

"I don't understand. If you don't trust the client, why would you even take the case?"

"That's a very good question," I said. "And I have an equally good answer, but in a language that you have never learned."

12.

It was rare for me to get blindsided while on any case or in life in general. I was usually in the driver's seat, sitting comfortably in my old Dodge, following at a safe distance or parking down the street from my target, lying in wait, secreted under the deep shade of some huge oak or carob tree.

This time, however, I'd been struck, unexpectedly, by multiple blows. A house full of rich, dead white people and a child who somehow locked me in place like manacles to a wall. The police, who would have kept me in jail for months and might have never let me go if it wasn't for McCourt and Suggs. There was Amethystine Stoller coming up out of nowhere, leaving me stunned in the water like a fish reeling from a depth charge.

And then there was Jesus. My son. The most intuitive human being I had ever known. The federal government was after him. The federal government.

I went down to the Redondo Beach marina, but their boat, *The Proud Lion*, was gone from its berth. If the boat wasn't there, it meant that they were out fishing and Essie was with either me or Benita's mother, Jaunice. If the boat was there, then they would probably be there too because they lived on *The Proud Lion*.

Jaunice Flagg lived in a third-floor apartment on Grosvenor Street in Inglewood. She was Benita's mother. Her husband, a man named Clifford Brown, had left her for the pleasures of the street when Benita was just four. Jaunice and I didn't have much in common, except for the fact that Jesus's seven-year-old daughter was our granddaughter.

I climbed the external stairs to the third-floor landing, finding her front door open, revealing a latched screen.

"Anybody home?" I called into the shadowy living room.

Toward the far end of the room, in a backlit doorway, I could see the small and round shadow of a woman.

"It's me, Jaunice, Easy Rawlins."

"It is?"

"In the flesh. I'm lookin' for Jesus."

"Oh Lord."

Coming to a decision, Jaunice moved quickly across the room, barely lifting her feet. The fabric of her silken house moccasins slid across the pine floor, sounding most like a copperhead moving in rectilinear locomotive gyration through dry grass. She unlatched the screen door, ushered me in, and then closed both screen and front door behind me.

"Have a seat, Mr. Rawlins," she said, while turning on two lampshade lights on either side of a long green couch. I sat on the right side of the sofa while she alighted on a padded wooden chair that looked like it belonged to a nonexistent dining room set.

Jaunice was sitting but she wasn't still. One of her slippered feet was toe-tapping and she was wringing her hands.

"That son of yours is in deep trouble," she said.

"What kinda trouble?"

"I don't know *what* it is, I just know *that* it is."

"Okay. All right. Who told you that he was, um, in this trouble?"

"Police."

"What kinda police?"

"The kinda cops that wears suits instead'a uniforms."

"Did they show you their badges?"

"Yes, sir, they sure did."

"What did the badges say?"

"I didn't read 'em," she said angrily. "They was badges and they was real. That's all I had to know."

"They came here lookin' for Jesus?"

"They was after Benita too. Here she just a girl, a young mother, and they after her for what your boy done done. They come here three times. Three times. An'—an'—an' ev'ry time they come they got more threats."

"What kind of threats?"

"They said I could go to prison along with them. They aksed how I couldn't know what my own daughter was doin'. They aksed was I stupid or what. I told 'em. I told 'em that they was hardly evah here. I told 'em that I never see them anyplace except when they come to visit or leave little Essie with me."

"What were these policemen's names?" I asked.

"They must'a said but I don't remember. All I remember is those badges and threats."

"What was it they said Jesus was doin'?"

"They didn't." Jaunice had light gray eyes with whites that had the scars of a long life of seeing too much. "I don't know what they want 'em for."

"When was the last time you saw your daughter and Jesus?"

"Two days ago."

"Their boat's not down at the dock. Did they tell you where they were going?"

"Yeah," Jaunice said, almost sick with fear.

"Where?"

"They didn't give a address or nuthin'. They just said that they was goin' to stay wit' somebody name of Mama Jo."

I decided not to go looking for my son and his little family until after the sun went down. The day hadn't turned out the way I wanted, so I went to a little coffee shop near La Brea and Olympic and ordered a chili size and fries.

While my meal was being prepared, I went to the pay phone up near the cashier's desk. I called Niska to find out if Santangelo had checked in. He had not. I called Melvin Suggs to see if he had any more information about my son, but he was out or busy. Accepting these failures, I went back to my vinyl booth, devoured the meal, then ordered a cup of black coffee.

Sitting there, I let my mind roam over all the various aspects of the past couple of days. Niska was going out on her first case, while Jackson Blue lived like a spoiled prince in the uppermost reaches of P9's castle. There was Amethystine Stoller, who might very well be the death of me, but still, that would have been an improvement on the stagnation and gloom that had become my daily meat.

Something about my dejected mood for the past two years made me think of the funky and unkempt Santangelo Burris. The memory of his destitute state brought back the opposite—that ring he wore. That ring. It meant something, something that I just couldn't get a hold on.

Back at the diner's pay phone I called my house.

She answered after the eighth ring: "Hello, Easy?"

"Hey. I thought you'd gone."

"I was outside with Prince Valiant. He's very strong."

"That's his job."

"How are ya, honey?"

"I wanted to talk to you about something."

"What's that?" she asked in a tone that said she was going to be serious.

I told her about Santangelo's topaz ring.

"Huh," she pondered. "You think it was a college ring?"

"I'd be surprised if he made it through high school. And rings like that usually have some kinda writing on them. This just had that torch or whatever. Like the symbol was all that was needed."

"So then," Amethystine said, "probably not a sports thing either. How about a club or brotherhood?"

"That's it!" I exclaimed. "The BFNE. It's their symbol. *The eternal torch that lights up the longest night.*"

"What's that?" Amethystine asked.

"Excuse me, sir," a different woman said.

It was the waitress who had served me.

"Yes, ma'am," I replied to the redheaded server.

"What?" Amethystine asked.

"Not you, honey. The waitress needs something," I said to my fate. Then, to the waitress: "What can I do for you?"

"Do you plan to pay for your meal?"

I handed her a ten-dollar bill and said, "Keep the change."

"But the bill's only six dollars."

"Your lucky day," I said, shrugging nonchalantly.

"Your loss," she said, and then walked away.

"I'm back," I said into the receiver.

"The BF what?"

"The Brotherhood of Free Negroes Everywhere. It's an old private organization, ancient by American standards. It's said that the brotherhood predates the Civil War."

"I never heard of 'em," Amethystine admitted.

"But without you I might not have remembered. Thank you so much, honey," I said to the woman I really didn't want to love. "I think this might be the first clue that don't threaten to hit me upside the head."

"What time you comin' back?" Amethystine asked.

"I'm not sure."

"Because if it's early enough maybe I could go shopping and you could make us dinner."

"I'm not sure, but it's probably gonna be pretty late."

"Well, if you're not coming, I might go home."

"That's okay. I probably wouldn't be very good company anyway."

"All right then," she said in a soft tone. "Be careful."

"I will," I said, probably not knowing it was a lie.

The phone directory told me that there was a Los Angeles chapter of the BFNE on San Pedro down in South Central. When I saw the address, I remembered that it was lodged in the deconsecrated Church of the Savior.

A few years earlier, the loss of that church's holy spirit was gossiped about all over the Black community of South Central LA. The minister, a man named Kearn, Samuel Arthur Bethune Kearn, and his wife, Lillian Kearn, née Renquist, had overseen the church and its congregation for six years. The head deacon was Fallon Potts, from Mississippi somewhere. Fallon's wife was named Beatrice. Beatrice was a beauty and very sensual, the kind of woman that men would brag they could not resist.

Reverend Kearn, it was said, had a powerful voice and a deep understanding of the Bible and other religious texts. He worked closely with Deacon Potts and therefore spent some time with his wife.

The years passed and everything seemed to be fine. That is, until the minister invited Reverend Gregory Simms to take his place while he and his wife took a well-deserved two-week holiday to Jordan, where they planned to float on the Red Sea.

During that time Reverend Simms gave a powerful sermon about fealty, monogamy, and fidelity in marriage. It must have been a potent sermon indeed, because Beatrice Potts felt the Spirit enter her, and it would not rest until she had confessed to the open congregation about her many years of sin with Reverend Kearn.

Fallon and Beatrice Potts met every day for ten days with the visiting minister. They prayed together and read the Bible together. Gregory Simms talked to them about forgiveness being the closest any mortal could come to godliness. Toward the end of these ministerial meetings, Fallon and Beatrice had renewed their marital vows and could be seen going everywhere, hand in hand.

The sin, the confession, and then the revelation of the words of the Lord seemed to prove that faith could overcome any human problem.

Everything had worked out so well that Deacon Potts volunteered to meet the Kearns' flight back from the Middle East. He shot the minister right there at the gate and then turned the gun on himself.

The night before, Fallon Potts was at peace with going to meet Reverend Kearn. He planned to forgive the minister at the gate.

But that night an evil thought crept its way into the deacon's mind. Finally, he confronted Beatrice, asking her if their children were his or Kearn's. Beatrice was absolutely sure about two out of three of the progeny.

SO MUCH SIN—that was the headline of the *Los Angeles Sentinel,* LA's largest Black newspaper. The cheating wife and minister, the murder and suicide, marked the Church of the Savior with the sign of Cain.

The congregation drifted away, seeking places of worship that were free of sin. No other church wanted to take over the building. So the BFNE bought it for a song.

I called up the number of the new West Coast headquarters of the runaway slave social club.

"Hello?" a man with a boy's voice answered.

"Yeah," I said. "My name's Ezekiel Rawlins and I'd like to come by and talk to a man named Santangelo Burris."

"I've never heard that name before, sir," the man-boy said. "But maybe our membership office would know who that is."

"May I speak to someone in membership?"

"You can when they're here," he said. "But we're closed right now. Daily hours are from eight a.m. till six p.m. And Mr. Lorn won't be in his office till day after tomorrow. He only works three days a week."

13.

The sun had gone down, and a deep shadow settled across Los Angeles—a kind of darkness that only the desert sky or the heavens above the ocean many miles away from shore could approximate. Almost total blackness blanketed each moonless night of the city I called home.

It was time to drive southeast again, all the way to Compton once more. The drive was shorter, but that heavy curtain of night made the journey feel longer.

Mama Jo lived in one of the last bastions of wilderness out there. It was a large tract of land that was buggy and overrun by an acres-deep thicket of lively and durable bamboo. It was a dense cane forest that was nearly impassable unless you knew the secret paths that Jo had carved into it. The slender shoots of rattan were over eight feet tall, and they resisted all attempts at exploration with fibrous tenacity.

Mama Jo had set up a false wall of bamboo at an isolated border of this unrelenting grove. If you knew where to go, and Jo was willing to remove the camouflage screen, you might could slide your car into a secret cove she maintained back there, hidden from the world.

At that time Jo kept a trio of pet wolves that dissuaded those more intrepid explorers who wanted to investigate her wastelands. The whole area looked abandoned and wild, but one of Jo's patients, a man she'd saved from a death the doctors promised was coming soon, had bought the collection of lots and signed them over to her.

I stopped at a gas station a few miles away from the hidden entrance and made me a call.

He answered after maybe a dozen rings, "Who is this?"

"It's Easy. I'm ten minutes away from her."

The man who answered hung up and I went back to my car. I'd never met the sentinel whose number I called. I didn't know his name. All I knew was, if I dialed his number, he would somehow get a message to Jo, one of my oldest friends and mentors.

By the time I got to the bamboo scrim, it had been pulled away, revealing the car-wide path that went maybe thirty feet before coming to a clearing. I drove the route, parked, and by the time I got out of the car, she was there.

Mama Jo was tall, her skin the matte hue of finished wire-brushed onyx. She was dressed in a simple frock that was designed for hard work without denying femininity. Jo looked ageless but I knew that she was at least seventy years old. She was my height, had been even taller in her youth, and she was strong of mind and of sinew. Her face was handsome or beautiful, the ideal of any race, human or not.

"Easy," she greeted, and she kissed me on the lips like a mother or a lover or an innocent child.

"You lookin' good, Jo."

She smiled and said, "You lookin' for Jesus and them?"

"You got 'em out here?" I asked.

Nodding, she said, "In a little cabin out behind my place. I'll show you."

Leading down a footpath through the thick brush, she marched maybe twenty paces before the wolves joined us. They were gray wolves, about a hundred pounds apiece. When they neared me, my heartbeat increased. I don't know if this was from excitement or fear. These were wild animals loyal to one another and to Mama Jo. If she had wanted to, she could have had them kill me right then.

We skirted Jo's grass-covered hut and went in a direction that was unfamiliar to me. The center of Jo's property was inhabited by huge oaks that hid the buildings she maintained.

The wolves left us and at last we came to an aluminum hut that I'd not seen before.

"They're there," Jo told me. "You know the way back to your car."

"The wolves won't mind me walking alone out here?"

"Not unless you mess wit' 'em."

I walked up to the door of the metal shelter and knocked.

"I'll get it," I heard a child shout. A child I knew well.

"No!" a woman cried.

But it was too late. The door swung open and little Essie looked up at me and smiled, saying, "Hi, Granddad."

Hefting little Essie up in my arms, I walked into the odd-shaped room to see Jesus and Benita, the former with a pistol in his hand and his wife holding a silvery knife that had a five-inch double-edged blade.

"Hey," I greeted. "How you all doin'?"

"Hi, Dad," Jesus said on a relieved sigh.

Benita put down the knife, kissed my cheek, and hugged me while Juice put away his gun. Benita had a slight frame and was medium brown in color. She'd once had a dalliance with Mouse, but when I brought her home after an attempted suicide, my son fell for her and, luckily, Raymond didn't mind.

The room was larger than I'd expected, with beds against opposite walls, a woodstove, and a twelve-foot-high ceiling. There were chairs and a table in the middle of the floor, between the beds.

"This looks homey," I said.

"Sit down, Mr. Rawlins," Benita offered.

Jesus, Essie, and I sat while Benita brought out beers for the men and a lemonade for the child.

"What you think of it out here in the bamboo?" I asked my granddaughter.

"They got three big dogs that like to play. And—and—and there's a pomegranted tree and a lemon tree too."

"That sounds delicious," I replied, running my tongue over my upper lip.

Essie laughed because she loved me.

Thinking about love, I turned to my son and said, "I hear the BNDD wanna talk to you."

"Yeah."

"You did what they say?"

It took a few seconds before he admitted, "Yeah."

"Essie," Benita said.

"Huh, mom?"

"You wanna go up to Mama Jo's house and play with her house lynx?"

Essie was excited to go, but then she looked at me.

"Are you gonna come, Granddad?"

"Right after I have a little talk with your father."

"Is he in trouble?"

"Not with me."

She laughed and leaped from her chair. Two minutes later my son and I were alone in Jo's visitor's cabin.

He avoided my gaze but that wasn't a problem.

"What you wanna do about it?" I asked him.

He turned to me and said, "Whatever you say, Dad."

"If that's so, then why you didn't come to me about this shit in the first place?"

"Embarrassed, I guess."

When he was a toddler and I took him in, Jesus never talked, not a word. It wasn't until Feather came to live with us that he began to make conversation with her, secretly. He never needed corrections, punishments, or lectures. He was as sure of himself as any athlete training for a competition. So, for him to defer to me meant that he was aware that he was way out at the shark-infested end of the pool.

"Why they after you, son?"

"'Cause I wanted to stop dealing dope for them."

"What? They had you dealin' for them? Like some kind of informant?"

"Naw. They straightforward pushers."

"And they got their hooks into you?"

"Yeah. Those federal agents are all-the-way bent."

"I don't understand, boy. Why would they choose you to be their mule?"

When he turned away, I knew that he'd opened the door to his own troubles. There wasn't any rush. For that matter, there wasn't any one person or persons that bore the guilt. I should have talked more to him about his fishing success. Amethystine was right: There *was* a depression in the Southern California fishing business.

"At first we was just havin' fun," he said. "We went down to Ensenada before every fishin' trip. We met these people who were great. Mexican Mexicans that liked to party. We'd get high sometimes but there wasn't anything wrong with that."

"How long ago did all this start?" I asked.

"Around when we came back down home from Alaska. Just about two years. And then one time, about a year ago, this one dude, Diego, gave me a pound of weed and asked did I know people I could sell it to. I didn't know anybody but he said that he had some friends." Jesus shrugged, a nonverbal admission of his mistake. "By the time a year had gone by, we were dealin' in tons."

"Tons," I repeated.

"It was so easy, Dad. I mean, when you're way out there on the water, there doesn't seem to be any laws, you know what I mean?"

"How long were you dealing the heavy weight?"

"About nine months."

"How much?"

"Me and Nita made around two hundred fifty thousand."

"Dollars?"

He nodded.

"What you do with it?"

"Buried it out in Baldwin Hills. Near one'a the oil derricks. Number—"

"I don't need to know the exact location. I mean, you trust me and all, but money like that can cause anybody to go crazy."

"Yeah," Jesus said. "Yeah."

"So how did the BNDD get involved?"

"I don't know how they found out, but they did. We brought in a shipment to the usual port dock, and they were waiting. These two agents confiscated the load and then locked us up for three days."

I remembered then a time when Jaunice called me because Jesus and Benita were supposed to get Essie after a fishing run, but they hadn't shown up. By the time I had got it in mind to go out and find them, they were back.

"What happened after you were arrested?"

"They told us that if we did two more runs for 'em they'd lose the arrest records. We did the runs, they took all of both loads, and after the last time I told 'em we was finished."

"And what they say?" I asked, my anger rising.

"They said that we'd be finished when we were dead."

That pronouncement was accompanied by a necessary spate of silence.

Then: "You know anything about these guys?" I asked.

"Not too much. But one time I did the drop alone. I told them that Essie was sick and Benita was takin' care'a her. But really Benita went to where I dropped off the load and she followed 'em to a warehouse out in Bellflower. It was called Warehouse Eighty-Six."

My son was calming down now that he had someone to talk to, someone who at least offered a glimmer of hope.

"What's this about you sinkin' your boat?"

The question caused the young fisherman to gaze at me quizzically. That was when he first began to wonder how much I knew.

"I just stopped workin' for 'em," he said on a shrug. "I figured that they couldn't do anything after all we had done together. I went back to fishin' while Bennie stayed out in Watts with one'a her sisters."

"Then what happened?"

"I was out past Catalina checkin' these nets I set for crabs when I saw this fast motorboat comin' at me. They started shootin' when they were still outta range. I knew they were gonna kill me, so I jumped off the side with a scuba tank and a weight belt. They set my boat on fire. I watched it burn from under the water.

"It was so cold down there that I thought I was gonna die."

"Then what?"

"I waited. Just waited until they was gone. Then I swam to this tiny...what you call it? A little island. I was shiverin' so hard, and my chest hurt."

You could read the anger in his eyes. It was a certainty that we had to solve his problem before the government had to add capital murder to his crimes.

"What's the agents' names?" I asked.

"They called themselves Warren and Scott. Scott has a scar under his lower lip that comes down like a backward comma."

"What do they look like?"

"White dudes with short hair. Other than that one scar I don't think I could describe either one."

"Scott's the one with the scar," I said to make sure.

"Yeah, but I don't think they gave us their real names."

"Did they ever take you to an office or a real headquarters?"

"Maybe the first time, when we got arrested. But they put chains on us, and blindfolds. When Benita asked why we had to be blindfolded, they said it was because if we got out, they didn't want our gangs to know where they were workin' from."

"Man," I complained. "They got you comin' and goin'."

"Can we do anything, so I don't have to go to Uncle Raymond?"

That request, that threat, was stunning. I could imagine Benita telling her husband, my son, about what the streets knew of the man called Mouse. Ray would have no compunction about killing crooked federal agents. And there was all that cash Jesus had stashed away.

"No," I said. "I'll take care of it."

"You will?"

"Of course I will. You think I'd let them mess with my family?"

"I—I thought you would be mad."

"Naw. I don't like drugs. But people use 'em, and weed is prob'ly less of a threat than alcohol."

It was a pleasure to see the tension drain out of Jesus's face.

"Do you know anything else about these agents?" I asked.

"I'm pretty sure that one of 'em arrested this guy I know named Terry Lomax. He's a street dealer out in the Valley. White guy. When I told him about the scar on Scott's lip, he said that was one of the ones who busted him. He said the other name too, but I don't remember it."

"You wanna write down Terry's phone number?"

"Sure."

"And his address too, if you know it."

After he did this, I asked, "So, how you holdin' up, Juice?"

"Good, now that I'm talkin' to you. I feel stupid about what we did, but it's kinda cool stayin' out here. It makes me feel like I'm a cowboy or sumpin' in the Old West. And you know, Mama Jo is somethin' else."

"Essie okay?"

"She's fine. She knows that somethin's wrong, but she's not worried."

"You need anything?" I asked. "Money? Food?"

"No, Dad. You get us outta this and I promise that I'll never ask you for anything, ever again."

"They were dealing weed?" Amethystine asked me. "Tons at a time?"

"Probably just one ton at a go."

"Still. He's such a quiet, sweet boy."

"Man," I corrected.

"I guess."

We were on the chaise lounge set on the jutting terrace that looked out over the side of our mountain home. She was reclining against the raised cushion as I lay with my head resting between her legs.

"What are you gonna do about it?" she asked.

"Benita suggested going to Mouse."

"That killer you know?"

I nodded, feeling the strength of her thigh.

"You gonna do it?"

"No. I'm too old for that kinda shit, and Jesus is too young."

"So what, then?"

"Great thing about bein' a detective is that you don't need to know *what* before you have to act."

"What does that mean?"

"The boy and his family are safe where they are. So, now all I gotta do is see what I can see."

She leaned down and kissed the top of my forehead. Soon after that, I was peacefully asleep.

14.

I awoke upstairs, in bed, thinking that I was still on the lower terrace. I must have walked up there, but I couldn't remember the passage. That was a revelation for me. Over the entirety of my life, I had been aware of every step I'd ever taken. From the back ways of the bayou behind our one-room shack in New Iberia, Louisiana, to the forced marches with fifty thousand soldiers, headed toward Germany's destruction—I always knew, or thought I knew, exactly where I was headed. As a child, as a soldier, as a Black man walking down white streets, and Black streets too—I had to be aware of my surroundings and my actions, always. But Amethystine interrupted that litany, that endless catalog of mostly unremarkable steps.

"Are you gonna wake up, or do I have to hit you in the head with this pillow?" she threatened jovially, standing there, as real as anything, at the foot of the bed.

"What time is it?"

"Time for you to get up."

She was wearing one of my yellow dress shirts and her hair was a delightful mess.

"It's a quarter to eight," she said. "Do you have time to make me breakfast?"

"I thought it was the woman supposed to make the meals."

"Not if the man is a great cook and she can't boil water."

"I love you," I said when I hadn't expected to.

She plopped down on the mattress, her hip pressed against mine.

"If I had my druthers," she said, "I'd marry you tomorrow and move to Italy, or maybe France. Not in a big city but the countryside, where the olive trees are a thousand years old, and the people remember Alexander the Great in their bones."

This last confession sat me up. I wanted to say something but all I could manage was to stare at her.

"But I know the kinda man you are," she continued. "You need to be absolutely sure, no matter what your blood is tellin' you."

Still silent, I wondered what she was saying behind what she said.

She leaned close to my face, kissed me ever so lightly, and said, "Don't worry, baby, I'll take it slow. I'ma go home tonight and wait for you to call me. I mean, after you make breakfast."

"I don't even have your phone number."

"That's okay, I put it in the Rolodex on the desk in your office downstairs, while you were out saving the world."

She threw the blankets back, revealing what my blood had been telling me. And then, after an hour or so, I went downstairs to make her breakfast.

When I got to the office, Clementine Bowers was seated comfortably behind Niska's desk. Clemmie was a dark-skinned young woman with dimples and blazing dark brown eyes. She wore a wig made into a complex hairdo that was deep brown and gold of color. She and Niska were about the same size and shape, but Clemmie dressed to accent her figure whereas Miss Redman did not.

"Hi, Mr. Rawlins."

"Hey, Clementine. Niska sick?"

"I don't think so. She told me to tell you that she was lookin' into that thing you were talkin' about, whatever that is."

"Did she say how long you would be takin' her place?"

"She said it was gonna be day by day. But I hope it's at least a few days. We need the money. My mama got sick and Mr. Henderson, down at the restaurant, fired her."

"For bein' sick?"

"She been outta work for three weeks."

"Oh. She okay?"

"I don't know. She won't go to a doctor, too scared he might say she got cancer."

"Cancer?"

"You know, she watch all them medical shows on the TV."

At my big desk I had to ball my fists and imagine being in a fight to get myself going again. That's when I picked up the receiver and dialed a number.

"Hello?"

"He there, Myra?"

She didn't stall this time. Three clicks and: "Suggs."

"Hey, man."

"Easy. What's up?"

"You get anything else on that home invasion?"

"No. No fingerprints, no witnesses, nothing. You find that woman, Lutisha?"

"No, but I'll call you the minute after I do."

"Myra looked up those names," Melvin said in a rush. He most always sounded like he was in a hurry to get on with something else. "That Santangelo's been arrested for public disturbance a couple'a times. And the James woman was once arrested in a gambling bust."

"What kinda gambling?"

"Poker. It was a private game at a rich man's table. They didn't press charges."

"Huh."

"That all you need?" he pressed.

"No."

"What else?"

"I need to talk to your wife, probably face-to-face."

Melvin was quiet for maybe six seconds before asking, "What for?"

"Her vast knowledge of unwritten lore."

"Huh?"

"It's just things she might know about, Melvin. Got nothing to do with anything she's done."

Mel's wife, Mary Donovan-Suggs, was the most complete criminal I had ever met, and that includes Mouse. There was nary a crime she had not committed, and no law, civil or canonical, that she hadn't broken.

"Okay," he said. "She's at work."

"Work? Mary?"

"I know, I know. She told me that she wanted to try out civilian life. Said that now we were married she should help with bringin' home the bacon."

"Where she work at?"

"She's a receptionist for these patent lawyers in Beverly Hills. I'll give you the number."

* * *

"Tyrell and Sloan," Mary's singular, husky, and sweet voice answered.

"Mary?"

After a short pause she said in a ridiculously professional tone, "Hello, Mr. Rawlins. What can I do for you today?"

"What you doin' for lunch?"

"Um, that depends."

"On what?" I was smiling by then.

"Where did you get this number?"

"From your husband, of course. It's on the up-and-up, you know, I wouldn't be foolin' around—he's armed."

Mary had a lovely laugh for a dyed-in-the-wool killer.

"It'll have to be a late lunch," she said. "I have a report to finish. Why don't you come over around two."

I liked Mary Donovan. She represented a state of mind that, though not innocent, was at least free.

The next thing on the list was the warehouse that Benita followed the bent agents to. This was in one of my least favorite places, Bellflower.

Warehouse 86 was on South Street, a block from Bellflower Boulevard. It was a big place that had many trucks coming in, to load or unload materials of all kinds. Cartons of goods, lumber, machinery, and other merchandise. There were quite a few workers moving around doing their jobs. They were mostly white, which was the custom of specialized unions in those days. I walked through the big doors that were open to truck traffic. Nobody seemed to want to engage me, so I wandered around, looking for the main office.

It was a huge warehouse, containing great towers of wooden

crates, some parked cars, crushed boxes, and hay bales along with shredded-paper stuffing that kept items from being jostled too much while being transported around the state, the nation, and even the world.

There were men working with forklifts and mechanized and hand-powered platforms, all of them white men. One or two of them noticed me.

"Can I help you?" a deep-toned woman's voice asked.

Despite the strength of the voice, I expected to see a petite blonde wearing a short skirt and maybe big-lensed prescription glasses with transparent frames.

I smiled and then turned to behold a heavily muscled woman in dirty white coveralls. Everything about this white woman was strong and rough, from her bristly blond hair to her thick and calloused hands. Her name tag read MILDRED FRANZ.

"Um," I said, her surprising appearance arresting me. "Excuse me, ma'am. Hi, my name's Ezekiel... Ezekiel Rawlins."

She smiled, probably at my good manners, and said, "Hello, Mr. Rawlins. How can I help you?"

"Um, I was wondering if I could speak with the plant manager."

"About what?"

It was rare for me to experience a civil tone in that town. And so the delaying tactic was no bother.

"I want to ask him if they ever rented out a portion of the plant for private use."

Mildred cocked her head, taking me in. Her eyes were bold and appraising, gazing at me like a hunter in the deep wood who carried a horn to scare off big brown bears so that she wouldn't have to shoot them with the Winchester that would, most definitely, be strapped across her back.

"What use would you have for a place like this?" she queried.

"It's my son, he's a fisherman," I explained. "Trawls for mackerel up and down the coast. Lately the hauls have been gettin' slim, so he struck up a relationship with these potters down south of Ensenada. They make terra-cotta plates and bowls, cups and baking dishes. They're willing to sell their work wholesale."

I had made up this fairy tale on the way to the town that many once knew as Hellflower.

"And what does your son plan to do with all this crockery?"

"His wife's been goin' around to gift shops and places that sell Mexican novelties, and quite a few of them have said that they'd like to move merchandise like that. So, he figures to bring in monthly loads and then distribute them from a warehouse."

"Why not get something closer to the water?"

"Too expensive. Makes more sense to use the freeway and cut down on the cost."

Miss Franz liked me. Not only her mouth but also her eyes were smiling.

"That sounds like a very good business idea," she said. "But this warehouse doesn't rent out space or grant any kind of access."

"Do you mind if I ask the manager about that? You know, sometimes no can become yes, in the right circumstances."

"That is very often the case," she agreed, still smiling. "But in this situation, you're talking to the owner. And I have no intention of renting out space."

Another revelation. This one I had to experience a hundred times before reality took hold.

"I'm so sorry, Miss Franz. You know, I'm always thinking that there's a man in charge. And also, that even a man boss, nine times outta ten, wouldn't be the kinda guy to get his hands dirty."

Now grinning, the warehouse owner said, "That's okay. I have the same problem. I'm so used to men being in charge that I often ignore the women who I should be talkin' to."

"Well," I said, "I'm sorry we couldn't have worked something out. But do you know anyplace else around here that might fit the bill?"

Looking me in the eye, she said, "The Bellflower business community is not the most welcoming crowd unless you're a paleface, if you know what I mean."

Before I could answer, one of the burly warehousemen walked up to us. He was about my height with a little extra around the middle. Even though he was younger than I, his red hair was receding and sprinkled with gray.

"Any problem, Millie?" he asked, staring at me.

"No, Roger, why?"

"Um, uh, I don't know. I just wondered."

"Everything's fine. You can go on back to whatever you were doing."

Roger hesitated and then wandered off.

"You see what I mean?" she asked.

"Only too well."

Having learned all that I could at the drug-drop warehouse, I went to my Dodge, which was parked at the curb across the street. Before the key was in the car door a man said, "Hey."

It was Roger again. His taciturn expression caused me to look around. He was technically alone but, across the street, standing in the maw of the warehouse, two of his friends were watching us closely.

"Hey," I responded.

"What you want with Millie?"

He was standing half a step too close, making me think again about performing a pre-tracheotomy.

"Nothing important," I replied.

"What?" he insisted.

"Hey, man, I come up to you askin' 'bout your business?"

Roger wasn't expecting any lip. He probably got used to being top dog before dropping out of high school.

"I just want to make sure you're not causin' her problems."

"That's funny, you don't look like HR."

"What?" was his favorite question.

"My business is my own. Now, if you wanna ask Miss Franz about what I did and did not say, you could do that."

Roger glanced at his friends across the street, showing me, if I didn't already know, that he was not alone.

I opened the car door.

"Hey, man," Roger warned. "I'm talkin' to you."

"Not no more," I said.

Half a block away I could see him in the rearview mirror, watching.

Traveling from Bellflower to West Los Angeles was a long drive to get nowhere. Beverly Hills was another white town. The only difference was the number of zeros behind the positive whole number on people's paychecks.

Tyrell and Sloan LLC was located on North Canon Drive near Burton Way. It was on the third floor of an ivy-covered five-story office building. At that time there was no need for security in places like that. Criminals, on the whole, preyed on their own, and in Beverly Hills, the police were never too far away.

The doors to the patent lawyers' office were made of light

green glass. I could see Mary sitting at a wide, modern desk, tapping away at an IBM Selectric. When I pushed the right-side door open, she stopped typing and turned her head.

The people I make it my business to study are those whom I care about or them who pose a threat. Mary was both. Her white skin was tan and her hair what they call a dirty blond. Her brown eyes were clear, hiding their duplicitous potential.

She gazed at me a few seconds before smiling.

"Easy."

"You know how to type?" I asked.

"Sixty-five words a minute with hardly ever a mistake."

"Where'd you learn that?"

"I'll tell you at lunch," she said, letting me know that her talent came from the other side of the tracks.

"Mair," a man's voice called.

He came out from one of the two office doors behind Mary's desk. He was tall and well-padded; his natural hair looked like a wig on top of a jowly face that tapered toward the forehead. He was in his forties and surprised to see me.

"Yes, Mr. Sloan?" Mary answered.

"Um," the partner uttered. Then to me: "You're making a delivery?"

"No, sir," Mary said lightly. "This is my friend Ezekiel Rawlins."

"Oh. Oh, I see," Blindman Sloan said. "I see."

He turned away and went back into his office, closing the door.

"You ready for lunch?" my friend's wife asked.

"I could eat two horses."

Grinning at me, she stood up, showing off her form-fitting button-up-the-front tan dress and grabbing her off-the-rack, faux-leather, maroon-colored pocketbook.

* * *

"Do you mind if we walk?" she asked when we were on the street.

This is an unusual request in Los Angeles, no matter when it is posed. Anywhere you want to go is too far away, and a man without a car is the Southern California definition of a loser.

"Not at all," I told her. "You feelin' all cramped up in there?"

"Drives me crazy. Them callin' me Mair and always touchin' my arms. I stopped carrying my knife 'cause I was worried I might stick one of 'em."

I laughed out loud, getting a little attention from other pedestrians.

"How've you been, Easy?" Mary asked.

"Good, good."

"How's Amy?"

"You know, I decided not to see her anymore." I don't know why, but I just didn't want to share the idea that Amethystine was back in my life.

"Oh, still? You know, I see her now and then. She says that she wants to get back with you. And Amy's the kinda girl gets what she wants."

"No argument there."

We chatted idly until getting to a solitary door to a nondescript, maybe-office-building on Camden below Wilshire.

The door opened onto a slender stairway. Up two floors, through another door, and we were in a small restaurant with maybe a dozen little tables. Two other couples were there.

A middle-aged man with a salt-and-pepper beard stood behind the host podium. He had olive skin and eyes that refused to be any one color.

The man said, "Mary. So good to see you."

"Hi, Gregor, this is my friend." I noticed that she didn't give me a name.

"So good to meet you," he greeted, coming around the lectern and grabbing me by the hand.

His big hands were both padded and strong—worker's hands.

"Can we have the table by the window?" Mary asked him.

"Sure, sure. Take it." His accent was from another land—it wasn't French, German, or Italian. If I were to guess, I would have said the music of his words came from somewhere in Eastern Europe.

After we sat, another black-haired, olive-skinned man, this one younger, came to greet us. He bent down to kiss the left side of Mary's face and then smiled at me. Mary ordered for us and the young man went away.

"So, Mr. Rawlins, what can I do for you?"

I wasn't quite ready to get down to business, so I said, "This is an out-of-the-way place. And they seem to know you well."

"They're Albanians, by way of Greece. Old friends. I always come here to do business when I'm on the west side. I meet here with your friend Jackson Blue every other month or so."

"How you even know Jackson?"

"Amy introduced us."

I'd forgotten that Amethystine knew Jackson before we met.

"What kinda business you and Mr. Blue do?"

"I provide him with information about patents that come across my desk and those that are logged in the triannual publication that all reputable offices share."

"I thought Melvin said that you were trying out the straight life."

"I am," she declared. "Pretty much. I mean, I'm just sharing ideas with a corporation that can make money for the inventors. Nobody's getting ripped off."

I smiled and asked, “So, you ever meet with any members of law enforcement?”

That question summoned up Mary’s poker face.

“Why?” she asked softly.

“I’m tryin’ to get a line on a couple’a crooked BNDD agents.”

“You want to do business with ’em?”

“They’re leaning on a friend of mine.”

“Oh. No, I don’t know anyone in particular, but I could look into it if need be.”

“It do be, indeed.”

“Okay then. I can get into it today.”

After giving the agents’ false names and bare descriptions I asked, “So, um, what can I do for you in return?”

“Don’t you insult me, now, Easy Rawlins. I owe you more than anyone. I mean, even with Mel it’s usually a even trade-off. But you have saved my ass more than once, and when I offered you that ass you turned me down.”

“I never meant to insult you, girl.”

She gave me a forgiving look and then the feast was served.

The meal was family-style, served all at once. Moussaka, chicken souvlaki, grape leaves stuffed with rice, and something I’d never had before, tomato fritters. It was amazing.

About halfway through the meal Mary said, “I wasn’t insulted. That’s when you first met Amy. And let me tell you, if it wasn’t for you, I woulda fucked that girl myself.”

15.

In the mood for a well-deserved break, I drove out to Santa Monica after lunch. On weekdays there were always empty parking spaces near the beach. Barefoot, I walked for an hour or so through the moist sand down near the shore. There was a lot to think about and nothing to do. Amethystine was on my mind, like a line of music from a nearly forgotten song. I could come up with a word or two but wanted more.

On the way back to the car I bunged myself into a phone booth.

A woman's voice answered, "Stenman Service. How can I help you?"

"VIP51," I replied.

"Yes, ummm, let me see, oh, there it is, Mr. Rawlins."

"Hi. I'm sorry I can't place the voice."

"Char," she said. "Char Bostick. I just started last week."

"Welcome."

"Thanks. Um, let's see. There's a message from Niska Redman. She left a phone number."

"Hello?" There was a little tremor of excitement in her voice.

"You rang?" I asked.

"I bought a Cohiba cigar for fifteen dollars."

"You smoke it?"

"Sure did. How did you know?"

"That's what I woulda done."

"It made me a little nauseous, but I still loved it."

"So, tell me what happened."

"I got all dolled up. That's what they say in the old movies, right?"

"It is," I allowed patiently.

"He was the only salesman there. I told him that I was getting the cigar for my dad. I said I wanted an El Laguito, that's the first kind of cigar they ever made for Castro."

"Where'd you learn that?"

"I went to a cigar store yesterday and talked to them about Cohibas. There was this one guy named Fyure who knew all about 'em. You know Castro first thought about starting the company when his bodyguard gave him a cigar that a friend of a friend of his made."

She was talking a mile a minute, so excited that she had to remember to breathe.

"Then what?" I asked.

"Huh?"

"What happened when you talked to Delroy?"

"Uh-huh, right. Um. I was all dolled up and, and — I smiled a lot..."

"Calm down, Niska. If you get too excited, then you're liable to make a mistake."

"Yeah. Right. It took a minute. He had this beard and was wearing glasses. But I could tell by his eyes that it was him. He was nice, and he talked to me about my father. And then he asked me if I wanted to get lunch, and I said I had to do something, but I'd like to sometime. And he asked about dinner tomorrow night and I said yes."

"A beard and glasses," I repeated. "Tell me the last name he was using again?"

"Magi."

"That was on Anatole's list?"

"Yeah, but he only used it when passing bad checks. He didn't ever go by that name."

"So, somebody might be after him."

"Other than me and the police?"

"Maybe the police. Maybe somebody else, somebody he's scared of. Can't be sure, but that's what I'd bet."

"Why?"

"The glasses and beard seem kinda extra cautious for somebody committing crimes like the one you're looking for him for."

"Wow."

"What's your next step?"

"Go to dinner and have Doreen come in halfway through."

"Hm. Okay. Make sure you talk to me before you do anything."

"What for?"

"Your plan sounds good, but on your first job, the hardest thing to get right is the execution."

"I don't understand."

"Which is why we need to talk."

I made it down to South Central soon after sunset. When I got there people were beginning to leave the Brotherhood of Free Negroes Everywhere. They were at the end of their workday, heading out on the long migration home. The church had been painted a pale shade of lime green. There was nothing for me to do until the place was empty, so I went to a pay phone across the street and called Jackson Blue's office.

First, I got his assistant.

"Mr. Blue's line."

"This is Easy Rawlins. Mister, right?"

"Yes, sir. Did you want Mr. Blue?"

"What's your last name, Mister?"

"Strong."

"Now, that's a name."

"Thank you, sir."

"Pass me on through, Mr. Mister Strong."

"Hey, Easy," Jackson said, loud and clear.

The parade of people leaving the deconsecrated church had slowed.

"Mr. Blue."

"What ya need?"

"Nothing. I had to kill some time and so I called."

"Waitin' on that hot date?"

"That was day before yesterday. Right now, I'm tryin' to vet a client."

"You don't trust his ass?"

"I don't trust nobody's ass."

"Hey, hey, that's the way. What's wrong with the client?"

"Everything from the dirt on his shoes to the oily wad of cash in his pocket."

"Man, I sure do miss them days," Jackson opined. "You know, when we was in the street kickin' up so much dust they could not ever find us."

"Except when they did," I cautioned.

"Except when they did," he agreed, with a touch of sadness.

"What's wrong, Jackson?" I asked, realizing that this question was why I had called.

"I'ont know, brother. Things is just too easy."

Across the street a man came out of the big double doors at the top of the granite stairs, stairs that parishioners had used for many a Sunday before the dissolution of the congregation of the Church of the Savior. A woman met the solitary worker down at the curb. They shared a friendly kiss and then walked away, arm in arm.

"Don't you deserve a rest after all the mess from back when we were young?" I asked.

"Yeah, but, you know, it's hard to appreciate what you got if there ain't nuthin' to protect it from."

Another solitary man had come out and was working at the locks on the door, securing them.

Evening was coming on.

"You got a wife and child, Blue. That's what your job is now," I lectured, trying to channel the mountaintop philosopher, Erculi Longo.

"I know. I do. But what gets to me is just the thought of hangin' out at some pig's-feet juke joint and Little Walter or Son House playin'. People laughin' and drinkin', dancin'. Women who know just what you need right then and there. Not tomorrah, or the day after that, right gottdamned then."

The man finished with the locks and went over to the left side of the church, where there was a parking lot with a solitary Pontiac, waiting.

"I tell you what, Blue," I said. "If I need any help with this job I'm on, I'll call ya."

"You will? Really?"

"Talk to you later, man."

Ten minutes after hanging up, I stepped away from the pay phone, concentrating on my next move. That man who'd driven away in the Pontiac was probably the last worker of the day. He might have been the one I'd talked to earlier. Deep desert darkness was falling from the sky and my senses were peeled to detect any sign of life.

It was that blind focus that got me into trouble.

"Turn out your pockets, niggah," a voice that sounded like an out-of-tune stand-up bass with a bad cold said.

I turned to the left, toward the source of those words, hiding with that movement the fact that I was sliding my hand into my right-side jacket pocket.

"Say what?" I asked, feigning innocence.

"Say what?" he mocked. "You heard me, mothahfuckah. Turn out your goddamned mothahfuckin' pockets, 'fore I break yo' neck."

Instead of answering I looked away, down the street.

"Ain't nobody gonna save you, niggah. Ain't nobody gonna come."

His words somehow scared me even though I wasn't really scared.

Big, Black, and ugly, he'd been cursed with a face not even a grandmother could love. He had fists made for fighting, and you could tell by his scarred sneer that he liked making people hurt.

That scornful leer was relishing my defeat when I swung the fist of my left hand out in an arc that landed its big knuckle on his diaphragm. He oofed and then genuflected. I took the right hand out of my jacket pocket, my fist grasping a solid aluminum set of brass knuckles.

I hit him again and again and again, cracking bones, knocking out teeth, planting deep blows that just had to be causing internal bruises to his torso and arms. When he fell onto the pavement, I knelt down next to him, fully intending to keep the beating going.

I'd hit him on his left cheekbone when a voice said, "He had enough."

The words came from an old, very old man, whose rheumy eyes held no judgment. He was simply telling me that I had already dished out whatever my attacker deserved.

I stood up and away from the mugger, staring down into the old man's eyes. I wanted to apologize, but that didn't seem right. No words would fit that moment of communication between us.

The mugger groaned, moving slowly from side to side, at last sitting up. Finally, he rose to his feet, blood streaming from his mouth and other busted-up parts of his face. His posture was crooked, and his face grimaced in pain. He glanced at me and the old man for only a second before moving away. Trying to run, realizing he couldn't, he shambled down the street. He could barely stand up under his own power, so he made his way leaning up against storefront walls and fences, headed back to whatever den he used to lick his wounds.

When the mugger made the end of the block, the spell of silence broke.

"You need a ride home, sir?" I asked the old man. It was a warm evening, but he wore an old tweed coat that came down to his knees.

"No, I don't need no ride. I only live a couple'a blocks from here."

"I could walk wit' ya."

"No, brother, no," he said, waving the four fingers of his left hand like a tightly woven fan. "I got the Lord on my left side, where my heart is at, and..." He patted the overcoat pocket on the right side, adding, "a snub-nosed twenty-two on my right."

Some people, hearing about the violence I used, might think that I took unfair advantage of that mugger. But, as ugly as he was, he was also young, no more than twenty-five years. Past fifty, I've known for quite some time that fighting is a young man's sport. That's why I carried the aluminum knuckles. One day I'll give up the streets completely and live on top of my mountain till the lights go out.

I cracked the lock on one of the back doors to the clubhouse. Inside I used a penlight to guide me.

For all the changes they had made to the church, it still had the solemn and silent feel of a house of God. It felt chilly despite the summer heat outside, and there was a scent soaked into the wood that was pleasant though not sweet.

Mary, the mother of God, gazed down on me from a stained-glass window that was at least twenty feet high. She held out one hand as if blessing me on my mission. The illumination came from the sidewalk streetlamp that stood before the failed church.

I was suddenly very tired. I wanted to sit down, to lie down and rest, before continuing my desecration. Then I laughed, imagining lying down on some bench and sleeping till the next morning when the brothers of freedom came in to find me.

I had to pry open the dead bolt to the membership office door.

Luckily the file cabinet therein was not locked.

Sifting through the manila folders, I found the file concerning Santangelo Burris. It wasn't a very thick file, but it contained enough pages to keep me from remembering or writing down all of what I needed. Rummaging through the membership official's desk, I found a leather pouch in a lower drawer that had $386 in a tin cashbox, and a small .32 revolver in the pencil drawer. I took both. The money so that they'd think I was a simple thief and the gun in case my would-be mugger had friends.

My Dodge was parked four blocks away. I was walking down San Pedro when a woman approached me.

"Mister," she said in a beseeching tone.

Somewhere in her thirties, with light sienna skin, she wore a turquoise-colored T-shirt and navy-blue pants, both fabricated from tight spandex. Her figure was a little more than those tight clothes could contain comfortably, but the whole package delivered the idea she intended.

"Mister," she said again.

"Yeah?"

"You got a dollar?" The words came across more like a simple question than a request.

My reply was supposed to have been *What do I get for that dollar?*

Then she would have said, *A smile and a handshake.*

I would have wondered aloud what I'd receive for ten dollars, and, after that, the real conversation would develop.

But I wasn't interested in that dance right then.

I took the wad of cash I'd taken from the BFNE and pressed it into her hand. When she saw what I'd given her, her eyes opened wide.

"Take it, sister," I said.

"I'ma feed my kids with this," she promised.

"Give 'em a kiss good night from me."

She got up on her toes to kiss my cheek, in order to take both my gifts with her.

16.

Sitting alone in my lighthouse-like mountain home, I studied what the BFNE thought they knew about Santangelo. He'd told them that he'd moved to Los Angeles from La Marque, Texas, not Pistol, having been born in St. Louis. His mother was listed as *unknown,* his father too. Santangelo's acceptance for admission to full membership was still under review after four years because a couple of members of the admissions board thought that his anger represented some kind of instability. This seemed strange to me, because the original members of the BFNE back in the 1830s were men just like Santangelo. Today they might have been dentists and lawyers, shopkeepers and bank clerks, but back then they were desperate men forced to buy their freedom, or to steal it, from the men who held the entire race as inferior.

As far as I was concerned, the only important details in the file were his address and phone number.

I considered dialing Mr. Saint Angel's number but decided that, unless we met face-to face, he'd never answer my important questions.

So, instead: "Stenman Service. How can I help you?"

"Hey, Julie."

"Hi, Mr. Rawlins. How are you tonight?"

"Still breathin'."

"You got pencil and paper?"

"Right here on the table."

"Okay. First, you have Niska Redman. She's going to meet Delroy for lunch tomorrow. She said to make sure you know it's lunch, not dinner, and Doreen will be there to make the identification. You get that?"

"I did."

"Okay. A woman named Ama, Amat, Ama-thigh…"

"Amethystine."

"Yeah. That. She said that she wants to go mountain climbing again when you have some free time."

"Got it."

"Mr. Jones called. He said you two have got to get together, that it's important. He doesn't have a phone, so you'll have to meet him at Maynard's Coffee Cart tomorrow morning."

"How many more?" I asked.

"Just one. A Miss, or maybe Mrs., Alice Fab-ri-cant called and said that Geraldine is staying with distant cousins, the Ellenbogens, and that they need you to help them communicate with the child. Here's the address."

After writing it all down, I asked, "That it?"

"Yes, sir."

"Thanks."

"Hello," she said in a sleepy voice.

"I wake you?"

"Uh-uh. I was just, um, resting my eyes."

"Okay then, when and where?"

"Delroy called and told me that tomorrow is his day off, so

lunch would be better, for some reason, and he wanted to meet at a place called Clooney's Diner, that's on Wilshire."

"I know the place. What time is the date?"

"Twelve thirty."

"Okay. How long's Whisper gonna be gone?"

"Until next week sometime."

"Then you, me, and Doreen should meet at the office at eleven, no, no, make it eleven thirty."

"You don't trust me to handle a lunch on my own?"

"If I didn't trust you, I'd be the one meetin' Delroy."

"Okay," she said, only half convinced. "Should I keep Clemmie on the front desk?"

"Of course. You'll be out doin' detective work."

Later, I went outside with the three dogs and played fetch for an hour. The little guys got tired after ten minutes or so. They spent the rest of the time around my feet chewing on dried-out cowhide. But, like his wolfen ancestors, Valiant was tireless. He ran back and forth, barking and baying like a bloodhound. He retrieved that stick again and again till my throwing arm went numb.

After the dogs had eaten and fallen into a heap at the door next to the terrace, I went upstairs and made the call.

"Hello?" Amethystine Stoller purred into my ear.

"Hey."

"You get my message?"

"I did."

"So, when are we gonna get to it?"

"I'm workin' right now, juggling jobs like a full rack'a bowlin' pins."

"Do you wear a circus costume when you do that?"

"Always."

"Always?"

"Yeah."

"Even with me?"

"Probably."

"You know, it doesn't have to be that hard, Easy."

"So they tell me."

I was up at 5:00 a.m., dressed by 5:09, and on the road at 5:29.

By 6:31 I was at Maynard's Coffee Cart, down around Seventy-Sixth Place and Central. Fearless Jones was already there, perusing a copy of *Jet* magazine.

I bought my coffee from Maynard, who spent every morning, except Sunday, selling coffee and doughnuts to whoever needed them.

Maynard was a short guy with good eyes—eyes, he claimed, that could see everywhere all at once. Medium brown of color, he'd spent some time in prison for a felony that he never talked about. May, as we called him, hailed from Austin and had come north at the age of fourteen, the day after his father was beaten and stomped to death for talking back.

"Is that you, Easy?" Maynard asked.

"In the flesh."

"Fearless told me you was gonna be here. I bet him a dollar that you wouldn't come."

"Com'on, May, why you gonna do me like that? I come to see you . . . sometimes."

"You haven't been here in four months. Too busy bein' a fancy detective on the west side'a town."

We laughed and then I went over to Fearless, who was

reclining on a concrete bench that seemed to have no other purpose than to provide seating for Maynard's Coffee Cart.

"Fearless," I said.

"Easy." He sat up to make room for me.

"Paris Minton told me that you was down Texas."

"I took the overnight bus day before yesterday after Earline Pickens called."

"Earline? I thought you guys didn't speak anymore."

"We don't."

"Then why she call you?"

"Orem Diggs."

"What's a Orem Diggs?"

"He's what the white hoodlums call a—a middleman."

"Middle'a what?" I asked, even though I knew the answer.

"If somethin' need to be done but it ain't in yo' family, then Orem the man that makes it happen."

"And what does Earline say he's makin'?"

"She know a guy who know a guy who Orem aksed to tell 'im 'bout you."

"Me?"

Fearless nodded. He was long and lean, black as a man could get. If we were standing upright, we'd be eye to eye, but if the measure was courage, then I'd be down to Pygmy size in comparison.

"What's this Orem want with me?"

"I don't know exactly, but it's some kinda hoodlum shit. And you know it's serious 'cause it would take a sitiation of life and death for Earline to look for me."

Women loved Fearless. He was courteous, truthful, the

baddest man in almost every room he ever walked into, and his intelligence was emotional, not intellectual. His eyes and hands, and his words, all spoke to what almost any woman was feeling.

The problem with all that love and affection was when those same women couldn't get Fearless to be what they wanted him to be.

One day, a few years before, Earline told Fearless that he was the only man that she ever truly loved. When he didn't say those words back, she threw him out of her house and her life.

"Okay," I said, thinking that my plate was already full. "What do I need to do about Orem Diggs?"

"I'd lay low if I was you."

I had rarely heard Fearless suggest retreat. He'd participated in three wars and the only gear on his utility belt was attack.

"He's that dangerous?" I wondered.

"He ain't scared'a you and so he'll do whatever he please. I don't know if goin' up against him would be worth the aggravation."

"What kinda aggravation we talkin'?"

"The kind where a whole bunch'a blood gets spilt."

If Fearless cared about you, he became the closest thing you'd ever know to a guardian angel. To ignore his advice would always be the wrong choice. But I was in love for the first time in a long, long while, and that would not be denied. Love made me brave, foolhardy, and wrong.

"So," my friend asked. "What you gonna do?"

"I got a couple'a jobs right now, Fearless. I can't drop the ball on them."

He shrugged, gave me a grin, and said, "Okay. I'll stick with ya, then."

"It's that bad?"

"Or worser."

"You got a car around here?"

Shaking his head, he said, "I slept last night on Paris's bookstore floor. I walked to here from there."

"Okay. But I got a place or two to get to before we get serious."

The next stop was a small house on Alcott Street, near Casio—a block south of Pico Boulevard. I pulled to the curb in front of the cottage-style home.

"I probably should go in here alone, Fearless."

"That's okay. I got a call to make."

"Good. I don't think it should be more than a half hour."

"See ya then."

It was a nice property. Six feet back from the curb, sporting a manicured lawn, it was a perfect little box with a pointy roof, its teal-green walls fringed by bushy blue dahlias.

A small white woman answered the doorbell. She was in her forties, most probably, and shaped like a pear. The faded gray-and-green dress she wore was what Eastern European Jews called a schmatta. I thought of that because this was a Jewish neighborhood.

"Yes?" she asked timidly. "Can I help you?"

"Ms. Ellenbogen?"

She gasped silently, I assumed from hearing her name spoken aloud.

"Y-y-yes?"

"I'm Ezekiel Rawlins. The social worker, Mrs. Fabricant, told me to drop by," I said, and then added, "For Gigi."

"Oh. You."

I smiled and nodded. "Yes. Can I see her?"

"Oh." She backed away from the door and I strode in, feeling like some kind of brigand or barbarian in the process of razing the town.

The living room I entered was small, maybe twelve feet by ten. There was a sofa and a sofa chair set against each other at a right angle.

"Teddy," the small woman called out.

"What, Trude?" came a man's voice from a doorway on the opposite side of the sitting area.

It was a surprise seeing him come in. He was very tall, thick-limbed like a lumberjack, and clean-shaven. He wore a lime-green T-shirt and blue jeans. His walnut eyes wondered about me while I speculated on how such a big man negotiated that tiny home.

"Yes?" he asked me.

"I'm here to see Gigi."

It was like the murder mansion all over again. Gigi ran out from somewhere and slammed into me. She held on tight, my own private barnacle. I lifted her into my arms again, holding her to face me. There were tears in her eyes.

"Uncle Easy," she dubbed.

"Little Gigi."

"Did you come for me?"

"Not this time. But soon."

"You're the one that that woman Fabricant sent?" the lumberjack asked.

"Yes."

"Are you sure?"

"Am I what?"

The question did its job. I could see realization dawning in Teddy's eyes. Why else would I be there?

"Oh," he said. "Okay. Yeah."

Cradling Gigi with my right arm, I asked either one of the couple, "Are you related to the family?"

"Her mother was my second cousin, once removed," Trude, probably Trudy, said. "When she, um, you know…"

Gigi laid her head against mine at that moment.

"…well, anyway, that's why Mrs. Fabricant brought her to us," the woman called Trude concluded.

"Is she supposed to stay here with you?"

"No," Gigi said sternly. "I'm gonna go with Uncle Easy and live with him and Auntie Lutie."

"Can I talk to her alone a minute?" I asked the couple.

"Outside, in the backyard," Teddy suggested. "There's a picnic table out there."

And, I thought, you could watch us through the back window.

It was a working-class neighborhood with small houses that had small yards out back. The patio was defined by the rear of the house, the wall of the garage, and two chain-link fences that were overrun by passion fruit vines. The flora reminded me of the internal greenhouse belonging to the murdered cattle baron.

"You want to sit in a chair, sweetie?" I said to the child who had adopted me.

"No."

"Okay."

I sat on one of the folding aluminum chairs with the ghost girl on my lap.

"Have Teddy and Trude been nice to you?" I asked the child.

"I don't like them."

"How come?"

"They don't do anything."

"Do they feed you?"

"Yeah."

"Do they hurt you?"

"No."

"But you want a better place to live."

"I want to live with you."

"Hm." I had a notion. "I'm gonna have to think about that."

"Really?"

"It might not be exactly what you want, but something. Okay?"

"Okay."

"Now can you do something for me?"

"What?"

"I'm lookin' for your aunt Lutie. But I don't know where to go. Is there anyplace she goes that she told you about?"

"Um..." The serious expression on Gigi's face was adorable. She was trying so hard and coming up with nothing.

"She—she likes playin' for money with seven cards," she said at last. "Um, yeah, seven."

"Three cards?"

"No, silly, seven cards," she said, giggling.

"Seven?"

"Uh-huh."

"You're sure?"

"That's what she said," Gigi huffed in faux exasperation. "She told me that playin' cards relaxes her and—and helps her think about things."

We talked a little longer. She reminded me of when I was younger, having one-sided conversations with Jesus and later conversing with Feather. I liked taking care of kids. When I told her that

I had to go out to look for Lutie, she accepted that with a stern nod.

Fearless was waiting for me in the car. I hopped in and drove the six blocks to my office.

Clementine Bowers was at the reception desk, doing nothing that I could see.

"Hi, Mr. Rawlins."

"Hey, Clemmie. This is my friend Fearless Jones."

"Hi, Mr. Jones."

Fearless stepped forward and offered a hand. For some reason this gesture charmed the temp.

"When Niska and this other girl get here, send 'em on back," I said.

"Okay."

In my office, I explained about Niska's training as a detective and a little about the job she'd undertaken.

"She wanna be like you, huh?" Fearless asked.

"Yeah. What you think about that?"

"I think women should be policemen, paratroopers, presidents, and priests. That way the world would work better."

"Why you say that? You think women are better than men?"

"Not bettah, different. And if somebody think different is half'a the world, then they should be a part'a what make the world go round."

It was a good argument. I had nothing to add.

"So, we gonna he'p Niska," Fearless offered, "and then we go see about Orem Diggs?"

"You think that's the best way to go about it?"

"I think so."

"I thought this guy was so dangerous."

"He is, but that's when he comin' up behind ya," Fearless said with a smirk. "Face-to-face we could parley."

There was something about his crooked grin…I would have asked about it, but just then Niska and her client, Doreen, walked in.

Both ladies were dressed up. Niska wore a tight blue calf-length dress that I might have expected Clemmie to wear. Doreen had on a dark green minidress and a necklace with a single pearl hanging from a thin gold chain.

Doreen was a white woman, pink of skin with a broad face that belonged on a larger body. But for the while she was young and slender.

"Hi, boss," Niska said. "This is Doreen Anton."

"Nice to meet you." We shook hands. "This is Fearless."

"Hi, Mr. Jones," Niska said while Doreen shook his hand.

"Hey, baby," Fearless replied.

Niska said to me, "I thought you were coming in at eleven thirty."

"Yeah. Fearless and I had some business in the neighborhood, and we came here after it was over. Why don't we go get breakfast and talk over what you guys gonna do."

17.

After breakfast and strategy, it was time for us to execute Niska's seemingly simple plan. The four of us went to a bus stop a few blocks away from the restaurant Delroy had invited Niska to—Clooney's Diner.

Taking a deep breath, Niska walked across the street and then down toward the restaurant.

After ten minutes or so, Fearless and Doreen followed me to another bus stop bench that was catty-corner across the street from the eatery. Fearless was elected to go in and scope out the scene. It took him seven long minutes to return.

"Where you been?" I asked him. "I was about to come in after you."

"The call of nature," he replied. "You know, when you ask nicely, they usually let you use the facilities."

"You see 'em?"

"Yeah. You could too, if we go down to the far end of the windah."

"Time to go," I said to Niska's client.

She went.

* * *

Fearless and I positioned ourselves in front of Clooney's, a step away from the plate-glass window that stood as its front wall. We faced each other and pretended to be talking about something intense. That way, Fearless could peer over my shoulder and keep an eye on the target and the girls.

Clooney's called itself a diner, but really it was an upscale restaurant with tablecloths and everything. The waiters wore dark two-piece suits and white shirts and paid close attention to the diners in their sections.

Ten minutes after Doreen went in, I asked Fearless, "What they doin'?"

"Still talkin'."

"Maybe he's turning over a new leaf," I suggested.

"He looks scared. Wait, he's gettin' up, looks like he walkin' back to the toilet."

"Let's go, then."

We hurried down the utility alley at the side of the office building that housed the restaurant. This is because when Fearless had pretended to go to the toilet, he checked for a back door that Delroy might use.

D.M. was coming out of that door just as we arrived.

The alleged professional con man had a slight build and stood about five ten. His beard was a sparse and stringy black thing, but the hair on his head was lustrous and thick. He wore gold-colored trousers and a gold sweater over a dark blue dress shirt.

He was trying to move past us when Fearless placed a splayed hand against his chest.

"What? What? What?" Delroy asked.

"Where you goin', Del?" I asked, my demeanor sentry-like and stiff.

"Who are you guys?" His eyes were wide as saucers.

"Brothers," I said. "Niska's brothers."

Upon hearing this, Delroy visibly relaxed.

"I gotta get outta here," he said.

"Did you pay Doreen back the money you stole?"

"I didn't—I didn't steal any money."

I could see why women might like the man calling himself Magi. His face, under that travesty of a beard, would have been attractive on a man or woman.

"Okay," I said. "Maybe you didn't. Maybe she's lying. But I'm gonna have to talk to you both, face-to-face, before I know for sure."

"No," he contradicted. "I have to go."

That's when Fearless socked him on the jaw. Considering Fearless's strength, the blow was no more than a tap. But Delroy slammed against the wall and then slid down onto his butt.

"Keep him here," I said to my friend. Then I retraced my steps all the way back to Clooney's front door.

"Can I help you, sir?" the maître d', a small man in a very dapper straw-colored suit, inquired.

I glanced at the table where Doreen and Niska sat.

"That's my party there."

"The reservation was for two."

"Then why are there three drinks on the table?"

By that time Niska had seen me. She and Doreen came over to the maître d's podium.

"Excuse me," the straw man said to the ladies. "Have you paid your bill?"

"Here you go," I said handing the dandy man a twenty-dollar bill. "Come on, girls, we got to go."

* * *

At the back door again, Delroy was on his feet. The flesh under his left cheekbone had swollen considerably.

"Oh, baby, what did they do to you?" Doreen cried, rushing to him, bringing up her hands to cup his jaw.

They?

"He wasn't cooperating," I told the co-ed.

"You didn't have to hurt him."

"Hurt him? We probably saved his butt."

"What are you talking about?"

"Delroy here is not worried about you or your money. He's on the run from somebody else. Somebody that won't worry about him bruising or bleeding or stopping breathing altogether."

"What's he talking about, baby?" Doreen asked the man of many names.

Delroy looked at me and asked, "Manny send you?"

"Who's Manny?" Doreen asked.

"The boogeyman," I supplied.

Back at my office, the five of us sat around the conference table installed there.

"Okay," I said to Delroy. "Tell us the story."

The womanizer's eyes were pleading for the world to fall off its axis and lose him in disaster.

"I don't want to talk about it in front of her," he strategized.

Sitting by his side, Doreen put her hand on his shoulder.

As she witnessed this extraordinary response, the truth slowly dawned on Niska's face.

"I'm not going anywhere," Doreen stated.

"No," I said. "You are not. None of us are. Del here is gonna tell us why he's running and then we're gonna make some decisions."

"I'm not sayin' anything," the temporary prisoner claimed.

"Oh yes you are, because if you don't, I'm going to have Clemmie out there call the cops. She's gonna tell them that we have a man accused of multiple felonies under citizen's arrest at WRENS-L Detective Agency."

I'm quite sure that the con man would have preferred three minutes of the full fury of Fearless's fists to being put in a cage, one where some guy named Manny had access to many eyes and ears.

"I don't want you to do that," his maybe-ex-girlfriend challenged.

"Doesn't matter," I said, dismissing her wants.

"I'm the one paying you."

"True. But the cops want lover boy here for many more crimes than just takin' your little money."

"I want you to let him go," Doreen said, her words soft, like fire.

"You got my detective here involved in some shit, and I'm gonna scrape it off."

Delroy and Doreen were defeated.

"Um," he said. "I mean, uh, how can I be sure you don't tell somebody?"

"You can be sure I will tell, if you lie," I said, managing to get in a note of finality on the last syllable.

Delroy received that note.

"What you wanna know?" he asked.

"Who is Manny?"

"He's a—he's a crook."

"Like you?"

"That's not fair," Doreen complained.

"He's like a, you know, a gangster, like," Delroy admitted.

"And what's his beef with you?"

"I knew this girl who works at a downtown branch of the Bank of America, and she—and she told me about this guy named Feder who would come in on the third Friday of every month and make a withdrawal without filling out a withdrawal slip."

"How much?" I asked.

"Always more than fifteen and less than twenty thousand."

"Dollars?" Niska said out loud.

"So, what did you do to Mr. Feder?" I asked.

"I followed him for two weeks, scoped it out. He was this old guy who always walked the same way after getting the money. He always went to this park and walked between two bungalows where there wasn't too many people."

"So, you and your girlfriend were in on it together," I concluded.

"No. She told me about it because she was worried that she was doin' somethin' illegal. I told her that I was gonna follow the guy and see what he did."

"She didn't know?" Doreen asked. "What kind of heifer doesn't know when she's stealing?"

"Because of the bank manager, honey. He told her that it was bank business. He made her a senior teller. That was before I met you, baby."

I interrupted the tender scene, saying, "Let's get back to the bungalows, Del."

"On the third Friday I didn't follow him. I went to wait behind one'a the bungalows, and when he walked by, I hit him in the head with a security baton and took his briefcase 'cause he always put the money there."

"You stole it?" Maybe Doreen was seeing the light.

"Yeah."

"And what about the bank teller?" I asked.

"What about her?"

"Did she know what you did?"

"She prob'ly figured it out."

"Probably?" Doreen hissed.

"I didn't talk to her again."

"Because," Fearless Jones intoned, "that guy, that Manny, would have gotten to her by five o'clock."

"Manny kill her?" I asked.

"I was worried that he did," Delroy whispered. "I called her phone a week later and when she answered, I hung up."

"But Manny got your name from somebody," I surmised. "Whatever name it was that you were using. He kept asking around, tellin' people what you looked like and what names you used. It took him a while, but finally he caught on to the name Martin Durer. Somebody, some girl I bet, told Manny's people where they could find you. But your antennae were up and you bolted with Doreen's grandparents' ninety-two hundred dollars."

Delroy turned to Doreen then.

"Listen, D," he said. "It's true. The only reason I ran away from you was that some guys had been lookin' for me at the rooming house I was staying in. I had to run... to protect you."

She took his hand.

The shock on Niska's face was proof that she was learning an important lesson.

Delroy looked into each face around the table, ending with me.

"So, what are you gonna do?" he asked me.

I took my time, pondering a thief's fate.

"You can't turn him in," Doreen said. "I'm paying for this—this investigation. Now it's over. It's done."

Ignoring Doreen, I said, "You ask me what I'm gonna do, Delroy?"

"Yeah."

"Nuthin'."

"What's that mean?"

"I don't wanna get involved in your business or Manny's."

"You want me to pay your fee?"

"No. I want you to leave." I turned to Doreen and asked, "Now, what about you?"

"What about me?"

"Either you dodge a bullet, or you take the next step down."

She gazed at me, examining my words as if they were on a contract presented by the devil himself.

"Come on, sugar," she said to the man temporarily named Delroy. "My car's downstairs."

Minutes later, Fearless, Niska, and I were still seated at the table.

"I don't understand what happened," Niska said. "Did—did she hire me because she wanted to get back with him?"

"Probably not," I told her. "I'm sure she thought that she wanted her money back. Maybe she dreamed of turning him in to the police. But, you know, love's a powerful drug. Once she saw him, that was it."

Fearless leaned back in his chair and looked up to the ceiling.

"Why didn't you take the money?" Niska asked.

"Because that would have involved you in an aspect of the case that you're not ready for and that I don't have the time to take on."

Niska bit her lower lip and then smiled.

"That was fun," she said.

"Go on home, honey," I advised. "Take a few days off and think about all this. Clemmie's mama's out of a job, so she needs a few days' salary."

18.

"You got a crazy life, Easy Rawlins," Fearless said. "You sure do."

It was just him and me at the conference table.

"I don't know about all that, Mr. Jones. This thing with Niska was just Detecting One-oh-One. It's only now that the trouble begins. And this time you the one brought it to me."

"Bet ya dollars to doughnuts you the one called Orem on yourself."

"I don't even know the man."

"You armed?" he asked, dismissing my claim of innocence.

"No."

"Then get so and let's go."

While I checked out my .32, Fearless made a short call on my desk phone. I didn't hear what he said but, then again, I didn't care.

I was behind the driver's wheel again, Fearless riding shotgun. He was studying a street map, giving me directions.

"Turn up here on the left, Ease. Yeah, there."

We'd made our way to a kind of no-man's-land six or seven

blocks north of downtown. There were businesses with apartments on the upper floors, convenience stores next to failed endeavors with boarded-up windows and doors. It was a cityscape almost totally devoid of people, like a specially designed film set waiting for the actors and film crew to arrive.

We turned on a little street named Charles Terrace. Going up the sharp incline, I was about to ask Fearless where we were when he said, "Pull up here, man."

There was a long sky-blue Cadillac parked about twenty feet up the hill. When Fearless and I climbed out of my car, the Caddy disgorged four men.

The men were Black, wearing dark suits that were designed more for official functions than for any office job. After they took a few steps, I thought I recognized one of them.

"Joe?" I called.

"Mr. Rawlins," hailed Charcoal Joe, one of the most powerful gangsters in LA.

"What are you doing here?"

"Your friend called me," he said, motioning his head toward Fearless.

"He what?"

"Well, you know, Easy," Fearless said, almost shy. "You said that you wasn't gonna back down. So when you was in that house, I called Joe."

"How you guys even know each other?"

"Who in this town don't know Fearless Jones?" Joe asked.

"But why would you come? And there you got three men behind ya."

"I like you, Easy," Joe confessed. "You been good by me and so . . . here I am."

"Okay, long as you here, why don't you tell me what you think about this Orem Diggs."

"Diggs is your fish outta water tryin' to learn how to breathe."

"Um," I uttered. "Maybe you could try tellin' me about him in words that I can understand."

"He's from Cincinnati, wanting to make a place for himself here in the sunshine. Been hookin' up with people so rich they might be able to benefit from help like his."

That was the best I was going to get, so I didn't ask any more.

Joe introduced me to his gunsels, but I don't remember any of their names. One of them took point and led the way up Charles Terrace until we got to a street with no street sign.

"This way," he said, and the group went behind him.

It was a dead-end street plugged by a singular building. Not a business, house, or apartment building, not a utility or factory. Not a store. But, for all the things it was not, it was familiar, the kind of structure that would have had a place at any time in history. It would have been right at home in Pompeii, back in the days just before the eruption.

The entranceway had no door, just a more or less rectangular maw, the edges of which appeared to have been gnawed on by some great toothed beast. The interior of the first floor, swathed in gray shadow, was indefinite and vague. When a man in a crayon-blue sports jacket and black pants appeared there, I moved a hand toward my gun pocket.

"Can I help you?" the white gatekeeper asked the Black gunsel who had led us to his door.

"Rufus Tyler et al. for Mr. Orem Diggs."

I was surprised at the formality of the sentence.

The guardian was lean and pock-faced, with skin that had

darkened from too much drinking with maybe a dash of sin mixed in.

He said, "I don't know no Rufus Tyler," sneering indifferently.

"Maybe he knows him by another name," the guide suggested. "Charcoal Joe."

The sentry decided then to count our number.

He nodded, still sneering, and said, "Wait here."

Moving away, he faded into shadow, and we waited. It felt as if there was a countdown in our collective mind, ticking off the seconds before something ugly was bound to happen.

But before the dreadful event could occur, the man returned and said, "Follow me."

Once inside the dead-end edifice I realized that the familiarity of the architecture was that it was most like a burned-out and looted building in a war-torn city. Even the paint seemed to have been blasted away, and there was dust a quarter inch thick frosting the floors. I had prowled through many abandoned premises like it—from Berlin 1945 to Watts 1965. I could almost smell the smoke and moldering flesh.

At the end of a long hall there was a surprisingly wide stairway. Following the flights up four floors, we came to a set of double doors that were new, made from finished oak.

After you, the criminal Charon said with a hand gesture and a bow.

"No, motherfucker," our articulate point man replied, "after you."

The blue-coated guide counted our number again and then complied. He pushed the doors open and walked in, seemingly without a qualm.

* * *

This room, like the doors we came through, was neat and clean, with white walls and a carpeted floor, a high ceiling and sparkling-clean glass windows that let in a sun that had been extinguished for the rest of the disaster zone.

Maybe ten yards on was a big mahogany desk, behind which sat a white man somewhere in his forties. He had a wide face, flattened a little at the ears. His brown hair was neatly coifed, but it was also wiry, giving the impression that, at any minute, it might spring into disarray.

On either side of the substantial desk stood two men dressed in dark suits like Joe's soldiers.

"You have to give me your guns," the man in the blue sports jacket said.

"You would not like the way in which you receive them," Joe's well-spoken representative rejoined.

"Charcoal Joe," the man behind the desk announced.

Joe moved to the front of our squad while the leader got to his feet and came around the desk. They approached each other, meeting and shaking hands at the dead center of the office floor.

Diggs's men moved forward and so did we.

The board was set.

"It's a pleasure to meet you," Orem Diggs greeted. "I've been wanting to do this for quite a while."

"Everything in its own time," the south side gangster intoned. "Everything in its own time."

Orem smiled and inquired, "What can I do for you, Joe?"

"Easy," Joe said while looking our host in the eye.

"Yeah," I said, moving up to stand next to him.

"Tell Mr. Diggs what it is we're here for."

I said, "A little bird told me that an Orem Diggs was lookin' for me and that he wasn't smiling."

"Who are you?" Orem asked. "And who's your little bird?"

"My name is Ezekiel Rawlins," was all the answer I had as to the source of my interest. "I wanna know what your business is with me."

The gangster's eyes sharpened. He studied me in a way that was commonplace for men who made their living outside the scriptures of law. His expression exhibited scorn, contempt backed up by potential violence, mixed in with a desire to acquire knowledge that he had no obligation to reciprocate.

"There's a woman name of Lutisha James that I would have words with," he said at last.

"About what?"

He didn't like being questioned, but his expression seemed to suggest that this was a singular situation.

"I'm looking for a thing that she might know the whereabouts of."

"What thing?"

"A piece of paper."

"Did you kill that family?" I just had to ask.

"What family is that?"

"The one in Bel-Air."

"I haven't killed nobody," Diggs said. Then, turning to Joe: "Is that why you're here? Those people belonged to you?"

"Anybody else you know after Lutisha or this paper?" I asked.

"Why?" the gangster replied. "What's she got to do with murder?"

"That's what I'm here to find out. I don't get behind the slaughter of old people, innocent children, and most women."

I didn't mean to sound so angry in my reply. When men like

Diggs heard anger pointed in their direction, they got their hackles up.

"Answer him, Diggs," Charcoal Joe said in a velvet tone. The kind of black velvet that lines the interior of a coffin.

That was the moment of decision. Diggs was a dyed-in-the-wool bad man who made his way west like all the other prospectors, looking for gold. He was a bad man, but Joe had roots in the city that no one else could equal.

Orem glanced at Joe, then exhaled, realizing that he would be taking on an opponent above his weight class.

He said, "I don't know."

"You don't know if anyone else is after her?" I asked.

"Right."

"How about why they want her?"

He proved he was brave by hesitating before saying, "The paper is a deed that a man named Sasha, now deceased, gave to someone, and that someone gave it to Lutisha before the injured party could get to him."

"Why give it to her?"

Orem chuckled and said, "Because Lutisha James is both a woman to fear and a woman to trust."

"What's the deed to?"

"I don't know."

"So, some guy named Sasha gave her this deed?"

Orem studied me again. This time it was less like a predator, more like someone considering a move in an important game of chance.

"Sasha gave the deed to some guy named Hannibal. I guess he was the one supposed to get it to her."

"Who's Hannibal?"

Shrugging his shoulders and holding up both hands, he said, "You tell me. Is that all?"

"Only one more question."

"Shoot."

"Who did Sasha steal the deed from?"

Smiling broadly, he said, "Waynesmith Von Crudock."

Shit.

19.

After sending his backup men off, Joe joined Fearless and me on a drive down to the Pacific Dining Car on Sixth Street. There was always a place ready for Joe there. He'd helped one of the managers with a problem at some point along the way, earning himself a permanently open table toward the back of the restaurant.

Joe and I ordered prime rib and Fearless asked for a Roquefort salad along with French fries and a side vegetable plate.

"What's up, Fearless?" I asked.

"What you mean?"

"No meat? No chicken? Not even some shrimp?"

"Naw, man. I met this white girl up at UCLA told me all the bad things meat does and how they basically torture the animals before butcherin'."

"UCLA?" Joe said. "What you doin' there?"

"I was—I was—I was," he said, thinking his way into an answer for the question. "I was livin' wit' this girl name of Helen Darcey. She cooked every night, know what I mean? In the kitchen and the bedroom. I was happy as a pig in shit. Then, one day—"

"She wanted you to move in and maybe get married," I supplied.

Fearless threw up his hands. "You know how I am, Easy. I get calls at any time for things people need. I ain't no detective or nuthin', but I'm on the go. I really liked Helen, man, but she wanted a house and a car and a man come home every night when it gets dark. Every night."

"And when it get dark is when you get goin'," Joe said.

"Yeah, you boaf right. Anyway, I got this room down on Avalon. It wasn't big but I don't need a whole lotta space. There was this two-burner stove in there, and every time I look at it, I'd think about Helen and her fried chicken. Man...I could take that gas stove all apart and put it back together again, but I couldn't boil water right. So I saw that there was a extension class at UCLA that teach anybody how to cook. So I signed up."

"That don't say why you only eatin' vegetables now," I said, slipping into the language of my upbringing.

"Naw, man, like I said, that was because'a Delilah."

"The white girl?"

"Uh-huh. I mean, the first day I got to the class the teacher says that we got to buy this two-hunnert-page book and read it. You know, Easy, I can make it through a letter, read the bettin' sheet at the races, but a whole book? Uh-uh."

"But you stayed in the class, right?"

"Yeah. After class Delilah aksed was I gonna buy the book. I didn't wanna ack like I couldn't read or nuttin' so I went with her to the campus book store. Book was fifteen dollars, fifteen. She didn't have it. So, I said that I'd buy the damn thing, and we could read it together. I figured that she'd keep it when I stopped comin' to class. But she wanted to meet at the lie-berry the next day and, well, you know—one thing led to another."

"And now you're a vegetarian."

"There you go."

"But if you wit' this Delilah, then why was you down in Texas?" I asked.

"My uncle died, and I had to help with the breakdown of his farm and shit. Anyway, the class we go to don't meet this time'a year."

We three, who some might call serious men, talked about things like the price of gas, TV shows, and even the stock market. When it got down to dessert, Joe turned serious.

"Why you lookin' for Lutisha, Easy?"

I told him about Santangelo and the murders in Bel-Air.

"What's in it for you?" the elder crook wondered.

"Tryin' to do what's right," I said.

"What's right? You save that shit for blood fam'ly, sometimes in-laws, and maybe a girlfriend. But you ain't expected to owe sumpin' to some stranger walk in off the street."

"What can I tell ya, Joe? You just saved my life, so I damned sure ain't gonna call you a lie."

Joe moved his head around as if his collar was tight. Then he stood up to take off his arsenic-gray suit jacket. He removed the garnet-red cuff links from each wrist, rolled up the sleeves, and then dismantled the top two gold button shirt studs of his dress shirt.

"You haven't asked," Joe said. "But I'm'onna tell ya what I know about this woman you lookin' for."

"You know her too? Damn. Feels like everybody knows Lutisha James. Everybody but me."

"She serious business," Joe claimed. "Only time I ever heard her name outside'a some scheme or scam was that song Sonny

Terry wrote on her. I knew her back when I started workin'. She was the girlfriend of Catfish Garland."

"Who?" Fearless and I asked.

"Catfish. He ran gamblin' an' girls and did some larceny on the side. I kept his books, mostly in my head.

"Anyway, 'fifty-one 'fifty-two he met this woman was runnin' all kinds'a property outta Chicago. I'ont know if she stoled the shit in Chi, but it come by crates outta there."

"That was twenty years ago," I commented.

"Yes, it was, and she was fine. She knew her words and her numbers, but what made Lutisha special, what she taught me, was how to question what you see and hold that up to what you believe."

"How that work?" Fearless asked.

"Way back then," the gangster replied, "I hated white people. If I saw a white man, or had to talk to one, I was ready to fight. One night, when me and Lutie was up late drinkin' and breakin' down a load she had hauled in from back east, she told me to talk to this white man name of Niles. I said I wouldn't do business with no white man. When she asked me why not, I said 'cause you cain't trust 'em.

"I remember that night as clear as if it was yesterday. She was pullin' a case of stolen watches out this crate. She stood up tall and said, 'You do business with Curt Bingham, don't ya?' I said I did. And she says to me that Bingham had been buyin' from her to sell to Catfish for years.

"I knew that Catfish had introduced Bingham to Lutie and so it was bad form for him to do a go-around like that. Lutie told me that Niles hadn't cheated anybody she ever knew.

"I got it. I learned a lot from that woman. And she could play them cards. There are casinos today that have a permanent ban on her because she could read the dealers better'n they could her."

"The way people talk about her," I said, "it's like she's evil incarnate."

"If you wanna call a pack'a hungry dogs evil, okay," Joe allowed. "But the way I look at it, she ain't no more evil than a hawk's claw or a tornado bearin' down. Rather than judge her, you'd do better to stay out the way."

I tried to imagine how sharp a woman or man would have to be for Charcoal Joe to treat that individual like a peer. I mean, he looked on Raymond Alexander as an unruly child.

Giving up on useless speculation, I turned to the more significant problem at hand:

"Waynesmith Von Crudock," I stated.

Joe met my stare and smiled. "What about him?"

"That's what I'm askin' you."

"He rich. Could be the richest, really. An' the way I hear it, he play rough."

"Crazy?"

"If you worked in a carwash an' told me that you were gonna buy a ticket from TWA so you could fly to Paris to spend a weekend with your mistress, and you believed that shit, you would be crazy. But if Crudock told me that, I'd just wonder why he didn't fly his own jet."

That's the way Joe talked. He wanted you to feel the nuance of what he meant.

"You know how I can get to the man?" I asked, hoping that that was all the information I'd need.

"Get to him how?"

"You know, walk up to the front door and knock."

"He ain't no dime a dozen like Diggs."

"Neither am I."

Joe shrugged and grinned. "I'll ask around. If I get somethin' I'll pass it on through Fearless."

A while after that the restaurant manager brought a black telephone on a long cord to our table. Joe thanked the man with a twenty-dollar bill and then made a call, telling whoever was on the other end that he was ready.

The well-spoken man who had led us to Orem Diggs's place showed up soon after.

"Take care'a yourself, Easy," Joe said, before walking off with his gunsel. "Luck don't last forever."

"Neither will we," I said.

Joe laughed all the way down the long hall.

"You want me to come along wit' ya while you look for this Lutisha?" Fearless asked after we cleaned off the last few crumbs on our plates.

"I don't think so, Fearless."

"Why not? Everybody need somebody to back him up."

"I guess. I'll call ya if need be."

"Okay. Don't forget."

"I won't. You wanna come wit' me to the mountain, man? I mean, a proper bed should be better than some bookstore floor."

"Nah. Thanks anyway. I'ma call Paris an' get him to pick me up. He said he wanna talk to me about sumpin'."

When I left the downtown restaurant, it was my intention to drive home. But on the way I started thinking about my mortality.

Most people wouldn't understand when I say that Amethystine might signify my demise. I don't mean that she'd shoot me like she did her ex-husband's uncle. I don't even mean that she would turn against me someday and side with my enemies. What I do mean is that she would, and did, impact my soul in such a way that I began to feel my manhood so intensely that I could start to take chances that most fools would avoid, even young fools.

That thought in mind, I decided to drive to the address that the file of the Brotherhood of Free Negroes Everywhere had for Santangelo Burris. He lived on Hubert Avenue just a block or so from Olmstead Ave. It was a small pink cottage behind a sprawling apartment complex. There I encountered another door ajar and no answer to knock or ringer.

I should have left and gone home. Maybe Amethystine would be there to greet me. But how could I love her right if I was afraid of a simple entranceway to a pink cottage?

The front door entered a fair-size living room. The oyster-blue curtains, tangerine rug, and lemon walls made the place look frilly, even girly. But the bloody visage of my client dispelled that illusion. He was lying on the floor, leaned up against the far wall, taking gasps of air like Charcoal Joe's fish out of water, and nearly out of time. There was blood all down his gray T-shirt, snot and saliva from his nose and mouth. The spilt blood had hardened in places, telling me that he'd been in this condition for some time. He was holding on to his dick through rough jeans.

"The detective," he said, maybe to some imaginary friend who came to keep him company at the end.

I got down on a knee beside the dying man.

"Who shot you?" I asked.

"White man."

"Which one?"

The perplexed look on Saint Angel's face made me regret the attempt at humor.

"Do you have the deed?"

He shook his head sadly.

Feeling a little guilty, and not knowing why, I said, "Lie still, brother, I'll call the ambulance."

"White man. He wore—he wore a dark and light jacket, like a, like that game, you know."

I asked the operator to get me an ambulance.

"Man fell through a glass windah and is bleedin' a lot," I claimed.

After making the emergency call, I went back to the dying man and took the wallet from his pocket. He roused, trying to stop me, but the big bad boar had become as weak as a little piglet.

I searched the house but found nothing.

I had put everything away by the time the paramedics arrived. The problem was—the police came with them. I identified myself to the cops, saying that Santangelo had retained me, that I was there to make a report and found him in that condition.

They didn't believe any of that.

I wouldn't have either.

20.

County jail, the only official place worse than the California penal system. County jail, where they stack prisoners one on top of the other and then leave them to figure out the pecking order. The same county jail that welcomes drunk drivers, those who fail to pay child support, and unemployed parents who shoplift milk; it also sequesters murderers, perverts, and gang members, especially gang members.

County jail. That's where they put me. I could have been up at my house, my house that had an actual mountain stream flowing through. My home where I could leave the door unlocked and open wide and never would I get burglarized. My home where there lived a killer dog who would die to save me.

"Hey, bruddah," somebody said, a little sing to his words.

I had to control my response to the auditory stimulus. In county jail you needed to be ready to fight to the death at the drop of a hat. But you also had to be judicious. Not every stimulation meant war.

"How you doin'?" I replied.

"Okay."

The man speaking was probably my age, though he looked

older, Hispanic, probably Mexican, with faded brick-red skin and dark eyes that studied me almost lazily. He was seated on one of the comparatively few bunks, which told me that he held sway in that overcrowded cell. He patted the space next to him. This gesture said that he was the one who was going to vet me.

I accepted the invitation. There was no other choice.

"What's your name?" he asked.

"Easy. Yours?"

"Carlos. Carlos Ortega. What they got you for?"

"I was," I said, trying to figure out what to say and how to say it, in that specialized and volatile environment. "I went to a guy's house to tell him some things. Door was open and he was bleedin' on the floor. I called an ambulance. They called the cops, and here I am."

"The man your friend?"

"No. A client."

"What kinda client?"

"I'm like a—a private investigator. This guy hired me to find his aunt."

"Find her for what?"

"His grandmother, her mother, who lives down in Texas, hadn't heard from her for a while. I guess she was worried."

"And him lookin' for his aunt got him shot?" Carlos asked. He seemed honestly interested.

"I sure hope not." I was speaking truth in that man-made hell.

"You gonna ask him?"

"I'm pretty sure he didn't make it."

Looking around, I saw that other men in our cell built for twenty that held forty-five, many of whom were also Hispanic, probably Mexican, were watching me. These were specialists in maintaining the pecking order.

"That's too bad," Carlos said. "They gonna blame you?"

"They might. But I'm not too worried."

"Why not?"

"Well, first, I didn't shoot the man. Second, I really am a private investigator, so they don't have any reason to not believe me. And lastly, they won't find a weapon, at least not the one that shot him."

"You're so cool. Don't nuthin' bother you?"

I laughed easily. "Well, Carlos. Sometimes you got to face what's in front of you. When it comes down to that, there's not much time to be bothered."

Carlos made the slightest motion with his left hand, and the men who were watching turned away.

After that, the jail cell bossman interrogated me, asking many questions about my profession; how did I start looking for people, did I ever work for the police, how much can you make being a detective, what happens if, when you find the missing person, there's been a crime committed?

I answered his questions more or less honestly. When he asked if I worked for the police, I said no, that sometimes they might be looking into some case that held my interest too, but never had I taken money from them to find anyone.

It was a pleasant conversation. A good way to take my mind off the beating I could have received and might still receive in that cell.

"Why you askin' all this, Carlos? You wanna be a detective?"

I expected a laugh, but instead he got serious.

"My father, his name is Rafael. He's from Sinaloa, out in the country where he farmed tomatoes. He's an old man but he still knows his family and his prayers."

"You're lucky. My dad died when I was eight."

"Sorry to hear that," he said, his eyes connecting with mine. "My father is a good man. He taught me much."

"So, I take it, he's missin'?" I asked, wanting to get down to the real reason he called off his soldiers.

"Yeah. Me and him take walks around the neighborhood a few times every week. He likes to take walks, have a beer, and look at the girls. But now they got me in here trying to figure out if they could, you know, prosecute me for something a friend of mine might have did. And so, my dad don't have nobody to walk with. He usually waits for me, but now I don't know when I'm gonna be home and my sister tells me that he's gettin' kinda restless, you know? He has his mind, but he forgets. He knows his name and where he live at, so usually he can make it home with no problem."

"Not the last time?"

Carlos's nod was almost a bow. That was to show respect.

"He went out three days ago and didn't come back. My people are lookin' for him but he's not at any of the usual places."

"Where's your father's house?"

"On Hamel Street in East LA."

"He talk to people around there on his walks?"

"Yes. He has many friends."

"Gimme the address and I'll see what I can do."

"How much?"

"I think we both know that you already paid me."

Not long after that, a phone call I'd made when I was being processed bore fruit.

Two guards came to take me out of the cell.

I shook hands with Carlos, taking a slip of paper that contained pertinent information about his father.

* * *

The uniformed escorts took me to a part of the jail I'd never been to before. It was like a lounge for the guards and their superiors. Off from the lounge was a room they had for special circumstances. In that room Anatole McCourt and Melvin Suggs were waiting.

"Easy," Melvin said, jumping up and shaking my hand.

"You want coffee?" Anatole offered.

"Sure. Yeah."

"Why don't you take a load off, Easy," Melvin suggested. "They never have enough places to sit in those cells."

I sat and Anatole placed a paper cup of black coffee before me.

"Damn," I said. "Shit must be hip-deep for both'a y'all to be here."

"We need resolution on this Bel-Air thing," Melvin admitted. "The chief is callin' me five times a day."

It was maybe 3:00 a.m. by then, a long day.

"You know I'm too old for this, don't you, Melvin?"

My friend cracked a grin, but Anatole was serious as an undertaker.

"At least you're gettin' older," Melvin's number two informed him.

"I don't know who did it," I said. "That's the truth. I think I might find out before it's all over, but as it stands, I can't tell ya what I don't know."

"What can you tell us?" Anatole pressed.

"The guy they arrested me for maybe shootin' is named Santangelo Burris. He hired me to find his aunt, Lutisha James, like I already told Melvin. He said it was because her mother, his grandmother, who he said lives down in a town that don't exist, wanted to talk to her. After lookin' into it I think maybe she got hold of a deed or somethin' like that, that some rich man prob'ly wants."

"What rich man?" Mel asked.

"I'm not sure." I put a spin on these words because Melvin was a living polygraph machine.

"What does that mean?"

"Deeds make you think of somethin' legal. I mean, ain't no bank robber gonna wanna steal a deed."

"You don't think it's some crazies did this?" Anatole asked.

"No."

"Why not?"

"Because I think whoever did it was there lookin' for Lutisha James. That's all I know about right now. If you want more, you got to gimme a couple'a more days."

"We don't have days," Anatole complained.

"Then tell the chief and newspapers that the crime happened but you're sure that it was a robbery. Mel said that they took a safe. The man was rich. Makes sense that someone'd break in his house and steal and kill."

Anatole got to his feet, exhibiting his disfavor. I didn't show the right kind of respect he thought a senior officer of the law deserved.

I half expected him to take my bitter cup of coffee and pour it over my head.

Melvin sat back in his chair, pondering the value of my suggestion.

After a minute or two the senior officer said, "You need a ride home?"

"Not all that way," I said. "But maybe to my office."

"How you doin' with that other thing, Easy?" Mel asked on the ride out to West LA.

"The way I hear it, the two BNDD agents that are after my boy are in business for themselves."

"Where'd you hear that?"

"Around."

"From your son?"

"No."

"No?" asked the living polygraph.

"No."

Over the years since we'd met, Mel and I had become close. We both had secrets and, even though the police captain wanted to stay on the straight and narrow, he also understood the love of family. So he dropped the discussion about Jesus, and we rode in silence until he stopped in front of WRENS-L headquarters.

"I think I'll take you up on the advice, Easy," he said before I disembarked. "It don't feel like a hippie thing."

"No," I agreed.

Hitting the couch in my office at around five in the morning, I slept fitfully but long.

"Mr. Rawlins," she said, shaking my shoulder. "Easy."

"Hey, Niska. I thought you were takin' the day off."

"I did too. But Clemmie called me and said that when she went back to the bathroom, she saw that you were here asleep. I came in and told her she could go home, and that she'd still get paid for today instead'a me."

That was enough to get me to a seated position.

"What time is it?"

"About two fifteen."

"In the afternoon?"

She nodded.

"Whoa. I must'a been tired."

"I know. I told Clemmie to turn off the ringer and just use the light to answer. I only woke you up because I know you're on a job."

"What happened with Doreen?"

"I called her, and she said she was dropping out of school and that her and that boyfriend'a hers was leavin' town."

"That was a great lesson for you. 'Cause ya know you can't always trust that you and the client gonna be on the same page."

"I can see that now," Niska agreed. "You know, if you had asked me, I would have said that Doreen would have been thinking exactly like me. But then I realized that if I fell in love with somebody, I might do the same damned thing."

"Yeah," I agreed. "Understanding people's flaws instead'a what we think is right and wrong is the only way to go."

"So, I'm doin' pretty good?" she asked.

"Mostly."

"Mostly? What have I done wrong?"

"Goin' to that cigar store, goin' to meet Delroy Whatever at that restaurant, comin' out back after Fearless hit him upside his head. Then, after all that, you find out that the boyfriend has robbed a bank robber."

"Yeah?" she questioned, showing that she still didn't see anything wrong.

"Lookin' at all that, are you frightened?"

Taking my question in, she considered and then said, "I guess not."

"That's what's wrong."

After that Niska went back to the front office and I took a shower. That woke me half the way up. I made coffee in my office percolator and drank it, wondering when the fright of my night in jail would descend.

The interoffice buzzer on my phone sounded and I answered, "Yes, Niska?"

"Amy's on line two."

I pressed the button for line number two and said, "Hey."

"Hi."

"Where are you?"

"At your place."

"I thought you were gonna wait till I called you."

"You didn't come home last night," was her reply.

"Yeah. I got arrested."

"What? Why?"

"I made the mistake of trying and probably failing to save a man's life."

"Well, why are you at work? You should come home."

Home. That word in her mouth seemed to brush over me like the tongue of some bestial mother.

"I got work to do and no time to lose. You gonna be there this evening?"

"Are you comin' home?"

"I sure the hell hope so."

"Okay, then. I'll be here."

More than a long rest, better than coffee, even outdoing a brisk shower, talking to Amethystine exhilarated me, brought me back to life.

Dressed in my best dark suit, I came out to the front office and pulled up a visitor's chair to Niska's desk.

"You look nice," she said. "You goin' t'see Amy?"

"If only," I lamented. "How you doin'?"

"Okay. I understand what you mean about me not bein' scared. If I had come across those men that were, I mean are, after what's-his-name, I don't know what I woulda done."

"Or," I said, holding up an educating finger. "If Delroy was the paranoid sort, he could have shot or stabbed you because you might'a been workin' with the men after him."

"I didn't even think of that."

"Don't worry, girl, in this business a healthy sense of distrust and fear builds up over time."

"I hope my next job will be more clear-cut."

"That reminds me. You speak Spanish, right?"

"I do."

"Fluently?"

"Near about. Why?"

"I met a guy in jail name of Carlos Ortega. He's probably some kind of gang leader but we didn't really talk about that. Carlos has an elderly father name of Rafael Ortega who lives at this address on Hamel Street out in the barrio." I put the slip of paper with all the information on her desk. "Rafael went out for a walk three days ago and lost his way or something. He's a friendly old man, so stores, gas stations, maybe ladies who hang out on their porches might have said hello to him."

"Okay," Niska said. "I could go out there tomorrow morning, and Clemmie could come here."

"Sounds like a plan. Why'ont you go on home now and rest up. I won't need you anymore today."

21.

Back behind my grand desk I made a call.

"Mr. Blue's line," the well-dressed executive secretary answered.

"Hey, Mister, it's Easy for him."

"Hello, Mr. Rawlins. I'll pass you right through."

"Easy," Jackson hailed. "You got a job for me?"

"Not yet, Jackson. I just need a little information you might have."

"What's that?"

"Where are the best seven-card stud parlors in LA?"

Jackson didn't even have to think. He told me that they were all in Gardena and then rattled off the names of the three best.

He loved games of chance.

"They keep me honest," he liked to say.

The next call was a number I had to look up.

"Books and Things," Myrna Salt, bookstore owner, Paris Minton's wife, answered.

"Hey, Myrn."

"Hi, Easy, how you doin'?"

"Good as Fearless on a bad day and Paris on a great one."

"Fearless on a..." she quoted, abortively. "And Paris the other side. You sure know them. Which one you want?"

"Fearless there?"

"He out back diggin' up the lawn for me to make a vegetable garden."

"Could you get him, maybe?"

The next voice I heard was Fearless's.

"You need me, Ease?"

"Parked my car out in front of a dying man's house last night. I called the ambulance, they brought the cops, and my ass ended up behind bars."

"You need me to get your car?" he asked, completely unperturbed by my brush with the law.

"I sure would appreciate it."

"You in a rush?"

"Naw. Where I'm goin' next, I could take the Lincoln. Extra key is taped to the inside'a the back left wheel guard."

"Okay, gimme the address and I'll get Paris to take me when he can. He likes to drive. We'll drop it off at your office."

The first place I went to in Gardena was the Dreamland Casino. It was a big round building on a street of restaurants, a large used-car dealership, and an open-air vegetable market.

I went to the front door, feeling good in my dark suit.

"Yes?" said the greeter, a very tall and skinny white man in tux, tails, and a top hat, all black.

"Comin' to lose my hard-earned wages," I said with a grin.

"Not here, brother man," Top Hat said.

"You not open?"

"We're open. You're just not comin' in."

It took me a minute to absorb his words. Because no matter

how long it is that I've been Black in America, it always throws me off when I confront Top Hat's kind of prejudice. This ridiculous red-faced man had decided or been instructed to keep certain people out of the establishment based on the color of their skin. This was more absurd than Red Face's suit. At that time Gardena had a Japanese mayor, and this man was still saying that I couldn't walk in through a casino door.

"You heard me," Top Hat insisted.

I had heard him. Once again, I wanted to fight, to make noise. But you can't spend your whole life fighting. I mean, I guess you could, but that would end up being a short life indeed.

The next stop was Martinel's Gambling House. They let me in there. I bought three hundred dollars in ten-dollar chips and sidled up to their seven-card stud table. I played my heart out. The only thing I got for it was a free martini from a lovely waitress who had never heard of a woman named Lutisha James.

Jackson Blue's last suggestion was Harold Stein's Emporium. It was the largest place. I knew from the minute I walked into the establishment that at Harold Stein's my luck was going to turn either very good or very bad. This because the first thing I saw was a platinum-blond-haired Black woman playing seven-card stud. There were five players, including the dealer, surrounded by an audience of watchers. It had to be a good game, the kind of match that excited the dreams all gamblers lived for—hoping, that with the odds stacked against them, they would persevere and come out on top.

There was a one-armed bandit that I could play while watching the game unfold. It was an expensive slot machine that took only silver dollars. I bought a hundred of the Liberty-headed suckers and started to feed the machine. I lost and won and lost while watching the middle-aged blond-haired Black woman play. The hair of her wig hid part of her face and, also, she wore sunglasses. These incidental details didn't bother me. I didn't know what Lutisha James looked like anyway.

Her play was magnificent, folding at just the right moments and then winning either by holding superior cards or, even better, by subtle bluffs and well-placed bets. The house couldn't beat her. The other men at the table couldn't beat her. Nobody could defeat that woman, not that night.

Looking at her, I knew that this had to be Lutisha James. It was almost like we were old friends who knew each other on a first-name basis.

Her chips piled up into precarious little towers. The pit boss had come over to watch. There were cheers for every hand that Blondie won.

Enjoying the show for about an hour, I finally ran out of betting cash, like all the other lifelong losers. I then went to get another tray of silver dollars. There were two people in front of me, but they were served soon enough. Still, by the time I got back to the slot machine, Blondie was gone.

I went to the cashier's window, but she wasn't there. I asked the cashier had she come there, and he said, "Yeah, collected her money and split."

I went over near to where the restrooms were, hoping that she'd gone in there to hide the money in her corset or maybe under her wig. But after ten minutes, no one even faintly resembling the woman came out.

I couldn't believe it. She was right there and then she was gone. I was definitely losing my edge.

* * *

I hung around maybe a quarter of an hour longer. I was sure she wasn't coming back, but what else could I do?

Realizing there was no answer to this question, I took my leave from Harold Stein's Emporium.

The desert darkness had fallen once more, and the large parking lot was filled to capacity. I had to walk up and down a few lanes before seeing my midnight-blue Lincoln. Approaching the WRENS-L company car, I could see through the window that someone had taken up residence in the shotgun seat. I tried to think if I'd locked the doors. I knew that I'd done the driver's side but couldn't remember leaning over to press down the passenger-side lock. When I got closer, I could make out the blond wig. That brought a smile to my face. Somehow Blondie knew that I was there for her, and she wanted to know why. I unlocked the driver's door and scooted in behind the wheel.

"How ya doin'?" I said to my welcome but uninvited guest.

The moment the door closed, she produced a .22 revolver.

This was the second time in only an hour that I'd underestimated the woman. I broke out in a cold sweat, hairs all over my body standing on end.

Being in a gambler's state of mind, I figured that the odds were against my survival.

Taking off her sunglasses, she said, "Easy Rawlins," in a way that was familiar both in her mouth and on my ears. This was no stranger from Texas.

I peered intently at her face, and a whole lifetime of memories flooded through. I remembered helping an older girl carry her shopping bag and then refusing to accept her offer of a tip. So, instead, she gifted me three fresh grapefruits and two store-bought cigarettes. I recollected waiting for the end of her shift at her late-night place of employment, where she took in stolen goods, always paying thirty-three percent of the street value. At the tender age of fourteen I went up against a full-grown man, trying to protect her. All I got was stabbed. There I was, on the ground, bleeding from a shoulder wound, and happy that she had pulled out a pistol, shooting that man to death. Later that night, in a makeshift living space down by the Galveston docks, I was still bleeding but at the same time being made love to by Anger Lee. It was a blood ritual that bound her forever in my heart.

"A-A-Anger," I stuttered, trying, once more, to will my heart back down into my chest.

"Yeah, baby, it's me."

She sat up straighter with an emotionless smile stitched across her face. I could see in that disguise how she'd hidden her identity from the world.

"You remember when we got kicked outta my room at Toolie's speakeasy and you and me snuck up into the horse barn them white people owned?" she asked, reminding me of that night and a thousand other stories we'd shared in the months we knew each other.

"The Parkers," I said.

"Yeah, that was their name. That old guy, the one called Nate, he heard somethin' out there and ran out with his scattergun. Shit, we run outta there, screamin' so loud that he didn't even remember to shoot." She laughed, reminding me again of the children we'd been.

"I..." I said.

"What, baby?"

"Whatever happened with you?"

"I rode a Mississippi riverboat for a while and then moved to East St. Louie. Sold stolen merchandise and then I started gamblin'. I went to prison once for killin' some fool tried to love me with his fists. After I got out, we moved down to La Marque, my two kids and me."

"You got kids?"

"Oh, yeah. Hannibal and Santangelo."

"Santangelo is your son?"

"Yeah. You know him?"

"He the one hired me to find you, told me that he was your nephew."

"Saint did?" She actually seemed surprised. "I—I thought you just happened in on me. You know, I been in LA long enough that I always expected to run into you one day."

"No. He hired me to find you."

"Oh. He did? Huh."

"What's this all about, Anger?"

"I don't know, Easy. I mean, I knew you was around. Now and then, when I passed through LA, I used to see your friend—Mouse. He talked about you but he didn't know about us. I heard that you was a detective and shit."

"Why didn't you call me?"

"No reason, really. As far as I was concerned you was a part'a the past."

"All right," I said, accepting her judgment. "Then why did your son come to me claiming you were his aunt and that he needed me to find you?"

"I have no idea. Saint didn't even know that I knew you. I guess it coulda been Hannibal. Maybe he told Saint about you."

"Hannibal?" I asked, hoping for more detail.

"Yeah. He's my other son, the good one."

"Anger."

"Yeah, Easy?"

"Could you please put that gun away?"

She looked down at her gun hand. This seemed to cause some kind of inner turmoil. Her lips moved but she didn't say anything. Her free hand clenched and then she shoved the pistol back into her purse.

"Somebody shot Santangelo," I said, once the pistol was safely away.

"You?" There was a deep feeling imparted to that one word.

"A white guy," I said softly, while shaking my head to the accusatory tone.

"Is he all right?" the mother in Anger asked.

"I don't think so."

"Take me to him. Take me now."

I called Melvin at home. He told me what hospital Santangelo was in. He said that he'd call ahead to make sure we got in to see him.

Santangelo Burris was laid out on one of those mechanical beds with a tube up his left nostril and one down his throat. There were three IVs dripping their holy waters into his veins.

"Oh my God no!" the hardest woman I'd ever known hollered in despair.

She ran to the side of his bed while I pushed up a chair for her to sit in, next to him. She settled in, holding his hand and muttering invocations to God, his angels, and probably even Lucifer if he'd listen.

It was a holy moment. Mother and child at the end of their journey. After a while Anger ceased her mumbled pleas. She just sat there, holding Santangelo's hand and gazing at him. Spread across her face was the naked pain of all the mothers who ever felt for children they could not save.

I backed up against the slender window that looked in on the two. It felt as if my job was to be the witness to the saddest event that could befall a woman.

We stayed like that for hours. The room was almost absolutely silent, except for the hissing of the respirator that struggled to keep his breathing even. When the sun finally began to make its presence known in the sky outside, a large-bodied, pale-skinned, redheaded nurse made her way to the other side of the bed. She felt around for Saint's pulse, and, after maybe two minutes, she stopped.

"He's gone, ma'am," she said to Anger.

"What?" Anger replied in the most fragile voice I'd ever heard.

22.

We sat across from each other at a corner table of a twenty-four-hour diner situated down the block from Temple Hospital. It was the first time I could study the grown-up version of the woman who had branded me with the truth about love and death. She'd doffed the wig, revealing salt-and-dark-chocolate hair. Her skin was dark, and her face still had the sharp-angled beauty of youth. She was older than I by three years, but there was a vitality there that could never be subdued, only killed. Her hands were balled into hard fists trying to choke out the hurt in her heart.

"Who did this to my baby, Easy?"

"I don't know, Angie," I admitted, calling up the memory of a nickname I hadn't used for nearly forty years. "It's like I said: Saint hired me to find you. I went down to that SRO you stayed at in Compton, the numbers parlor in Hollywood, and asked everybody I could think of. I finally got to the poker club because'a somethin' that Gigi said."

"The child?" She raised her head, up above the swamp of misery. "How you get to her?"

I didn't want to, but I told the woman called Lutisha James

about the Bel-Air murders and the little girl's and the ancient woman's survival.

"Killed them?" I'm pretty sure that she was asking her God, not me. "Why?"

"I don't know."

"That's crazy. It's insane to kill them folks."

Gazing into each other's eyes, I think we could have stayed like that for hours. But as much as Anger was a part of my orphaned life, I still had a job to do, even though the client was dead.

"Anger."

"Yeah, baby?"

"Following your trail, it seems as if, I don't know, you seem to be hiding, running from something, someone."

She was gazing absently across the early-morning restaurant.

On the other side of the dining hall there was a very large white man in either hospital or restaurant whites sitting next to a gorgeous copper-colored Hispanic woman, decked out in fine clothes as if she had just come from some upscale nightclub. She looked bored but he was happy, chattering away.

"Anger," I said again.

"For the past few years, I been movin' from place to place, goin' from one job to the other. Maybe I don't need to no more, but it's habit by now."

"Do you think that whoever it is you runnin' from might'a killed Gigi's people?"

"What?" she asked in a pestered tone, jerking her head back as if my question was a mosquito bombing her ear.

"Do you think the people after you are the ones that killed Gigi's people and—and Santangelo?"

"You sayin' you think I got my son killed?" Her words, as the

Bard once said, were sharper than a serpent's tooth. But I couldn't worry about that.

"I'm askin' you who you're running from so we can find out who did it."

Anger wanted to use those strangling hands on my throat, I was sure of that. It took her a very long moment to overcome the rage. But she did get over it.

"I did something a while ago, Easy. Because'a that the police been on me."

"Here in Los Angeles?"

"Naw. Back east. It was business as usual till somebody ended up dead."

"And the cops are after you," I stated.

"Cops, federal marshals, I don't know, maybe even the FBI by now. They want somebody to pay. That's why I'm in LA movin' every couple'a months or so. I don't know who all is after me, but I can tell ya they ain't slaughterin' no house full'a civilians."

The fancy Spanish lady and the blubbery man were actually talking now. She was telling him something and he was listening intently.

"So Santangelo was really lookin' for you," I said. "I mean, he made it clear to me that he didn't know where you were."

"Saint's a lovin' son. He is. But he ain't got no discipline. If I told him where I stayed at, everybody would know. I only stayed in touch with Hannibal. He the older one and his lip is always zipped."

"So does Santangelo know where Hannibal is?" I asked, keeping up the use of the present tense for Anger's sake.

"Usually. But the last time Hannibal talked to me, on the Orchid's pay phone, he said that he had got hold'a sumpin' important and he wanted to get it to me. But he was worried about bein' followed so he gave it to Saint for safekeepin' and told him that if anything happened that he should get the thing to me."

"Was this thing a deed?"

"I don't know. Hannibal said it was in a green envelope. Maybe a deed."

"And did anything happen to Hannibal?"

"I don't think so. No."

"So you're in touch with your older son."

"We don't talk too often. But every week or so we put ads in a neighborhood newspaper, the *Pico Post.* That way we could tell each other we okay and maybe a thing or two more. And—and—and he got a girlfriend named Violet, Violet Welles. If sumpin' happened to him, she woulda told me through the *Pico Post.*"

"So," I said, trying to untangle the mess. "Hannibal got somethin' he wanted to get to you, but he was maybe in some trouble, so you think maybe he gave his brother this letter an' asked him to try and pass it along?"

"Maybe. Like I said, Hannibal knew that I had stayed at the Orchid."

"And you sayin' it was just blind luck that sent your other son to me in order to find you?"

"No!" the blubbery man said aloud, responding to something the petite woman had said.

"No," Anger echoed softly.

"So he knew that I knew you?"

"Hannibal did. I talked about you to him one night when we was drinkin' wine, years ago now."

"So Hannibal got the envelope," I said, talking to myself as much as to her. "For some reason it was too hot to hold so he gave it to his brother to bring it to you. But by that time you had talked to Hannibal, and you knew that Santangelo was in the mix, and you might be in trouble, so you took a caretaker's position at the cattle rancher's Bel-Air home. But then you moved outta there because one night you was thinkin' and you realized that somebody might work out where you had gone to."

"That's it," Anger said. "Pretty much. People know me in LA as Lutisha James. I usually come out here every winter. You know these Texas bones don't like no cold."

Anger shivered from the thought of freezing temperatures.

"Then how did Saint know to get in touch with me?" I wondered aloud. "You think Hannibal told him?"

"Prob'ly did. He's Saint's older brother and he wanted to make sure the envelope got to me."

"But it didn't," I said to be certain.

"I guess not."

"He went out to the Orchid like Hannibal told him to and you weren't there, and then he remembered to come ask the detective man to look."

"Damn!" the blubbery man shouted.

There was a loud crashing sound. The man had gotten to his feet and overturned the table he and the petite woman were sitting at.

"I don't give a goddamn what some greaser says!" the man shouted. "Fuck him!"

"Richard, stop," the young woman said, loud enough for me to hear it but still not at the level of a scream.

I didn't care what was happening over there. There were enough people around who could help, if help was needed.

As I made my silent pact of noninvolvement, Anger grabbed her purse and blazed across the dining room. By the time she'd gotten to the blubbery man, she was wielding that eight-inch knife I'd been warned about.

"Step the fuck back, niggah!" she shouted at the white man.

He moved a hand in the general direction of my childhood love, and she swung that blade. The way he pulled that hand back, I was pretty sure that she had nicked him.

"Get the hell outta here, fool!" Anger commanded.

Screaming like a frightened woman, the blubbery man ran for the door, grasping at a hand full of blood.

Witnessing this scene had a profound effect on me. It was as if I had never left the Fifth Ward, never went into the army, moved to California, aged forty years, or learned a goddamned thing. There are some things that we never learn and other things that we can forget in the twinkling of an eye.

Anger had her arm around the young woman's shoulders. She was whispering to her. I came up to them then, the rubber sole of my shoe slipping a little on the dollop of red blood Richard had dropped on the green linoleum floor.

"We should go," I suggested to Anger.

"You need a ride?" Anger asked the young woman.

"Please," she replied, nodding.

We dropped the young woman, Conchita Alfaro was her name, at the Pathways bus station. When we asked her what the problem was with Richard, the blubbery man, she told us that she was going out with him for a few months but had decided to go back to her old boyfriend, Hector. She didn't want to tell Hector about Richard because they both had bad tempers, and she just wanted to be happy.

"Don't we all," Anger Lee / Lutisha James lamented.

"Don't we all," I agreed.

* * *

Lost in our own private thoughts, Anger and I were sitting side by side in the front seat of the company Lincoln, parked at the curb out in front of the bus station.

"Is there someplace I could take you, Angie?"

The sound of her nickname brought a smile to her lips.

"I cain't think'a anywhere," she said.

"Can't you go stay with Hannibal?"

"Hannibal in just as much trouble as me," she said. "I wouldn't be surprised if he left the state."

But I would have been surprised. There were people who would have killed Anger, and those who would have saved her, but precious few who would just walk away.

"How did your good son get into this shit?"

"I cain't really explain it, Easy, but I know it had sumpin' to do with his job."

"What job?"

"He work at a place called the Creative Mind."

"What's that?"

"Where people go to study their lives so they could see their opportunities in a different light."

"How's that work?"

"I ain't got the slightest idea. I make my own opportunities an' then use my knife, or my gun, to keep 'em. But Hannibal is part'a the younger generation. That's what started all this shit."

"How's that?"

"Some guy come into his office and said that he was tired'a workin' for businessmen no better'n thieves."

"What did your son say to that?"

"He said that that young man, Sasha is his name, he said Sasha should use all his knowledge to start a honest business on his own. They worked it out that he could start a import-export business from relatives he got in Europe. It was goin' pretty good, until one day Sasha come in with this paper that he said was proof that his bosses was stealin'. He wanted Hannibal to take it to the authorities to do sumpin' right. But I raised that boy good enough that he knew he had to at least think it out before actin' a fool."

That was a lot, more than I could process in front'a that poor man's Greyhound.

"So you got no place to go?" I concluded.

"Not really. But, you know, I got a few dollars. Must be some SRO got a room."

"I know a place."

At a pay phone in the bus station, I called Fearless Jones at Paris Minton's bookstore to ask if he could make a reservation for Anger. I said to make her name Carlinda Newgate. He called back five minutes later to say it was done.

Then I drove Anger to the N&T Hotel on Grand Street. It didn't look like a hotel, nor was it registered with the Chamber of Commerce. This was an ultra-private residence for kings and millionaires, ex-presidents, ousted dictators, and lapsed communists who had abdicated, taking the lion's share of the state budget with them. Fearless was registered as a bodyguard for the N&T and, therefore, was given a deep discount if there were any rooms empty.

Parked out in front of the unremarkable entrance of the residence, I turned to say so long to one of my oldest friends.

"You can stay here as long as you want," I told her.

"Okay," she replied, her voice maybe light with gratitude.

"You know any way I could find your son?"

"Not really. We ain't talked in a couple'a weeks, like I said.

I know he got a apartment somewhere in West LA, but I told him that I don't wanna know the address. You know, loose lips and all."

"Is there anything I should know about him? I mean, anything at all."

"Well, after all this time I don't know if it's important anymore."

"What?"

"Hannibal is your son."

23.

"Easy," Amethystine said, holding my head against her breast.

We were reclining on the love seat next to the terrace, looking out over West LA all the way to the expanding darkness of the nighttime ocean. I was exhausted and so worn-out emotionally that I was having trouble just talking.

"Huh?" I grunted.

"What's wrong, baby?" she cooed.

"Can we talk about that later?"

"Okay. But can you at least tell me where you've been the past couple'a days?"

"Sure. I—I helped a detective in training find a man that had seduced and then robbed his girlfriend. In the process we discovered that the man, who went by a dozen names, had robbed a bank robber. The girlfriend forgave him and took him back again. Then I went to see some gangster name of Orem Diggs who'd been hired to grab me and make me talk about a document that I never even heard of. Then I had dinner. After that I went to a guy's house to talk but he'd been shot. I called emergency, they called the cops. I was arrested and taken to the county jail, where a guy, another inmate, hired me to look for his father. I got outta jail, took a nap, then went to three poker parlors, lost five hundred dollars, and found the woman I been searchin' for, for days. She wanted to shoot me, but I got her to put away her gun, then I told her that the man I saw get shot was her son. We went to the hospital but soon after he died. That's everything that's important.

"Oh. Oh, yeah. Except that it turns out that the woman I was looking for was a one-night stand from forty years ago, and on that night we made a son that I never knew about."

"Oh my God," Amethystine said on a hollowed breath. "Your son is dead?"

"No. That was her other son, the bad one."

"That poor woman."

Sleep overcame me and stayed on course with no incursion from the worry or fear that I should have felt.

After that night I was convinced that something I'd often been told, but never believed, was true; that love is the most powerful and therefore the most dangerous human emotion. I came to this conclusion because, lying there with Amethystine, with us touching each other carelessly, and breathing the mountain air, I was unconcerned with the turmoil, danger, and utter helplessness of my life. I didn't care because I had something that wound its way around the core of my being going all the way down to the soul. I was as deeply satisfied as a timber wolf is, baying at the moon and being at one with everything in his domain.

I awoke completely refreshed at 4:53 a.m.

Two hours later I was seated at the table ledge of the second-floor kitchen, drinking my fourth cup of French roast, thinking about all the things I had to do.

"Hi-i," Amethystine said, making the word into two syllables.

"Hey."

We shared a long kiss and then another.

"You gonna take the day off?" she asked.

"No time for that."

"So, what now?"

"Now I track down Anger's son, and mine. I think he holds the key to a problem."

"What problem?"

"I don't exactly know. It's got somethin' to do with a deed, a rich man that wants that deed, and people dyin'."

"You want me to come with?"

"No. I'd like it if you stayed here. The guys guarding this place feed my dogs when I'm not around, but you could keep them company."

"Now I'm a dog walker?" she asked, full of humor.

"If I could be the mutt."

The Creative Mind: Different Alternatives for New World Living had its office on Sunset Boulevard, a few blocks east of Doheny. The building that housed the new age company was twelve stories high. The Creative Mind occupied the top three floors. It had a special elevator that went only to floor ten, the outer wall of which was made from glass. Taking the express lift, I read a little write-up etched upon a chromium plaque: *The Creative Mind is a nonprofit corporation dedicated to helping people achieve their dreams. We are here to obliterate the humdrum, the nine-to-five, the drudgery of working to make other people rich, other people happy. In this travesty's place we aim to offer the potential joy of living, a life that gives back.*

The doors slid open, and I entered a world where oil and vinegar just had to be the best of friends. That much was apparent in the people who occupied the lobby. The outer walls of the upper floors were glass, tinted a faint green. The reception area ran the length of the front of the offices and had a ceiling that was three floors high, giving a feeling of what I can only call largesse.

Populating this futuristic, and definitely capitalist-leaning, nonprofit enterprise were long-haired, mustachioed, braless, patchouli-scented, multicolored, smiling, actually grinning employees who looked as if they were on a permanent break…from life. Some men wore colorful pants rendered in psychedelic patterns, and there were women in pants, miniskirts, maxiskirts, and some with single sheets of bright fabric wrapped around them and pinned.

There was a front desk of sorts, positioned in the farthest corner against the window. A woman sat there. She was wearing drastic dark purple makeup and a black dress. Her nameplate—yes, she had a nameplate—read SUNSHINE EOS.

She was a Black woman, the color of maple syrup, with eyes that seemed a little large.

I walked up to her desk and said, "Excuse me…Miss Eos?"

She gestured to a chair next to her marbled violet-and-cream desk, which seemed to be carved from fanciful stone.

"Yes?" she asked, not smiling.

"I'm looking for a directory."

"For what?"

"I'm looking for a man named Hannibal," I said, realizing that I wasn't sure about his last name.

"Mr. Lee?"

"Yes. That's right."

"Do you have an appointment?" There was the faintest hint of an English accent in her articulation.

"Do I need one?" I wondered aloud, looking around at the chaos of the entrance hall.

"Of course you do. Why would you even ask that?"

"It looks like a—like a nightclub in here."

That got me my first smile.

"Oh," she said. "No, no. That's just the design."

"Um," I said, looking confused.

"The president of the Creative Mind, Mr. Hamsho, made the entrance a room where people could take their breaks. That way when visitors came, they would be put at ease, feeling like this was going to be a good time."

"How would they know that it wasn't just a big party?"

"Usually, when visitors make an appointment, they are told to ask at the desk against the window."

"That's a different way'a doin' things," I admitted. "You from England?"

This was the first time the stern Miss Eos showed surprise.

"Why do you ask?"

"The way you talk."

"You hear that?"

"Yeah."

"My father was a lifer in the army. We were stationed in London for six years when I was a kid."

It really felt like I was at a party, meeting someone and chatting.

"To the left of the elevator," she said then. "All the way to the corner. There you'll come to a door to the stairway. You go up to the top floor, turn right, and Mr. Lee's office is three doors down."

"What's he like, your Mr. Lee?"

"You've never met him?"

"No. His mother suggested this meeting."

"Oh. He's never spoken about his mother."

I had nothing to say about that.

"He's a very nice man," Miss Eos told me. "He deals with everybody the same way and he doesn't ever lose his cool."

The door to Hannibal Lee's office was closed. I knocked and then knocked again. I tried the doorknob and then walked in.

The back window looked out over the Sunset Hills. There was no desk, just a few chairs, a locked file cabinet, and a foldaway table no larger than a TV tray. Upon this tray was a pink slip of paper that read *Emily Haas from Von Crudock Enterprises.*

I had just put the pink slip in my pocket when someone asked, "Can I help you?"

She was plain-faced, tall, in her twenties, of Asian origin, at least racially so; I suspected that she was from Chinese stock, but I've been wrong about assumptions like that as many times as I've been right.

"I was looking for Hannibal, Miss . . . ?"

"Rosetta."

"Well, Miss Rosetta—"

"No, just Rosetta."

"And my name is Easy. Ezekiel, really. I was looking for Hannibal."

"For what reason?"

"He's my son."

That claim stood my inquisitor up a little straighter.

"You're Hannie's father?"

"I am."

"He's never mentioned you before," she said, studying my features closely.

"His mother and I broke up a long time ago. I just came back into the picture recently."

"Oh," she said, biding her time while considering the landscape of my face. "Um. He's not in today, Mr. Lee."

"My last name is Rawlins. His mother and I never got married."

"Oh. He's still not in."

"Hm. Do you know how I can get in touch with him?"

"Not really," she fibbed.

"Oh. That makes this tough. You see, well, Hannibal's brother had an accident and he's, well, he's dead."

It was like being back in the casino, playing against the house. I kept raising the ante hoping that the bluff would take me over the top.

"Oh no," Rosetta lamented. "What happened?"

"I'm not sure. Hannibal's mother told me that Santangelo had some kind of accident and was taken to Temple Hospital, where he died."

"Oh my God."

"I know. I really would like to talk to Hannibal."

Rosetta hesitated and then came to a decision.

"You look a lot like your son," she said. "I think it'd be all right if I gave you his information."

Rosetta provided Hannibal's address and phone number, but I decided not to call. I wanted to make sure that I was looking into his eyes when we first met.

The address was an apartment building on the fifteen

hundred block of South Stanley Drive near Saturn Street. It never felt strange calling Hannibal my son. His mother might have been a cardsharp, a killer, and a thief, but she was not a liar. He was my blood, I never had a doubt about that.

The apartment building looked somewhat like a Spanish castle in miniature. The brick-red plaster walls were all curved. I went through a circular patio into the front door and up the sinuous stairway to the third floor, apartment C. I knocked, of course, waited, knocked again, and then I cracked the lock with a screwdriver that I brought along especially for this circumstance.

Hannibal's apartment was impressive. The floors were sealed pine and there were plants of many kinds set in the bay windows looking down upon Stanley. Everything was neat and swept, dusted and in order. The bookshelf had two encyclopedias and one fat dictionary, books by W. E. B. Du Bois, Booker T. Washington, Malcolm X, James Baldwin, Langston Hughes, and other writers, both Black and not.

This time I heard the door.

I turned in time to see a willowy and yet striking young Black woman walk in. I was hoping she hadn't noticed the damage to the lock. She exhibited no fear, even though I was nearly two times her weight and half a foot taller.

"What are you doing here?" she demanded.

"This your place?"

"I asked you a question."

She was very dark-skinned, wearing a bright yellow cotton dress that buttoned all the way from the knees to the collarbone. Her face was heart-shaped, her lips generous, yet twisted into an unfriendly welcome. And she had no-nonsense eyes.

"My name is Ezekiel Rawlins," I said, as if that should mean something.

"And what are you doing in this apartment, Mr. Rawlins?"

"And your name?"

"Violet," she uttered reluctantly.

"Violet Welles?"

Her name in my mouth threw the bantam inquisitor off a little.

"Yes," she said. "Now you answer me."

"I am Hannibal Lee's father."

"That's a lie," she said, pointing at my face. "Hannibal's father is dead."

"His mother tell him that?"

"He the one told me."

"Well," I conjectured, "that was probably just wishful thinkin'."

That created the second crack in her resolve.

"I am very much alive," I continued, "and I need to see my son."

"Hannibal is not here," she said, looking around the room to prove the point.

"He's not at the Creative Mind either."

"I don't know what to tell you, Mr. Rawlins."

"You his girlfriend, Violet?"

"We're friends."

"If you're close, then you probably know that Hannibal's in trouble. There's people after him and he needs my help."

More cracks.

"Sorry, but I don't have anything for you," she said, a worried crease appearing in the middle of her forehead.

"Okay. You don't know me and there's no reason for you to trust what I say. So if you hear from Hannibal, tell him that his father's alive and his brother, Santangelo, is dead."

"What?" she gasped.

"Shot dead in his house over there in Leimert Park."

"No."

"Tell him that that deed he got from Sasha could get him killed too. I'm gonna write down my number, and if he wants, he can call me."

24.

On the south side of Pico Boulevard, a few blocks east of Hauser, there was a bar called the Blue Reindeer. I went in there, the only customer, at just past noon. I had a drink, though it was too early for alcohol, and the cigarette that I usually allowed myself only in the morning. The bartender didn't know why the bar bore that odd name; she'd only worked there for the past year.

"What's your name?" the forty-something server asked. She was white, with fair posture, and on the tall side, wearing just the pattern of a white slip over which there was another, semitransparent, stiff lace dress, dyed in delicate yellow and green.

"Easy," I answered.

"I'm Madeline."

"Pleased to meet ya."

"You live around here?" She had about her what seemed to be a faded glamour. A beauty queen from a long-ago life.

"I used to," I said. "Why?"

"You look familiar," she answered with a shrug, looking me in the eye as if expecting me to answer.

"Excuse me, Madeline, but I have to make a call."

* * *

On the pay phone I called the number that Emily Haas had left for my son.

"What?" a gruff male voice growled.

"Julie there?"

"What? No. There's no Julie here." He hung up.

I considered asking Madeline for another drink but nixed the thought. Instead, I redialed.

"What?" answered Billy Goat Gruff.

"I'm—I'm sorry to bother you, sir," I said, trying to sound timid. "But Julie's my daughter and this is the number she left us to call. Do you know where my girl is?"

"No Julie here." He hung up again.

On the third call I asked, would he please tell me whose number I was calling.

"Listen, motherfucker," the man said. "If you call here again, I'm gonna find you and I'm gonna tear you a new asshole. Hear me?"

That time I was the one who hung up.

Back at the bar I ordered bourbon, neat.

Sipping the sour mash and sucking down a Lucky Strike borrowed from Madeline, I pondered my next move.

Finally, I decided on George Baron Dunkirk.

George worked at Bell Systems, affectionately referred to as Ma Bell. He was a supervisor of some sort, pretty high up. A white guy, maybe fifteen years my junior, he'd had a run of bad luck a few years before. His wife left him for a new man, in her eyes a better man. Her name was Dorinda, and she'd met J. J. Lothar at a supermarket. J. J. asked her how he could tell when a cantaloupe was ripe. An hour later, at a little coffee place on La

Brea, Lothar told Dorinda that he was a salesman at the May Company department store. Handsome and strong, with a friendly laugh, he neglected to confide that he was a career criminal who wanted to own or control everything he could see or imagine. J.J. took Dorinda and the three kids and then he, through the former Mrs. Dunkirk, demanded that George set him up to sell special phone systems to corporations. He didn't want just a job, but a way to embezzle Ma Bell, one of the largest monopolies that ever existed.

It was Jackson Blue who brought George's problem to my attention.

"He's a good guy, Easy," Jackson said. "And he done a lotta work for me and Jean-Paul. If you could help him out, we'd both really appreciate it."

J.J. had threatened George with all kinds of torture, but the only thing that the good Mr. Dunkirk worried about was the safety of his ex-wife and their children.

As a rule, I stayed away from jobs of that kind. George was a natural-born sad sack; nothing could save him from that. But his job intrigued me. Any in at the phone company could come in handy in my line of business.

I asked Raymond to go talk with Lothar. I usually didn't bring out a big gun like Mouse to deal with riffraff of J.J.'s ilk, but the things he threatened to do to George and the way he turned Dorinda against him made me mad. I honestly think that if Mouse had killed him, I wouldn't have minded.

But Ray was the more levelheaded one that time. He asked one of the white gangsters he worked with about Lothar. Once the details were obtained, Ray said to the mobster that a friend of his would like it if J.J. was asked to leave Los Angeles. Two days later Lothar was gone for good. I'd like to think that he left

Los Angeles under his own steam, but, then again, like I said, I didn't really care.

"Bell Systems," a woman's bright voice declared.

"George Dunkirk, please."

"One moment."

"Mr. Dunkirk's line," an equally cheerful male voice said.

"I'd like to speak with him, please. My name is Rawlins."

"Hold on, Mr. Rawlings."

I had long since given up correcting strangers about the pronunciation of my name.

"Hello," a man said in what I can only call a pillowy voice.

"George. Easy Rawlins."

"Oh," he said nervously. "Hello, Mr. Rawlins. How are you?"

"Fine," I said, and then got down to business. "I have a number for you. Two, as a matter of fact."

"Go on," he murmured in a hushed tone.

I gave him both the bar's pay phone number and the one I pretended that he'd asked for. The first number was the number to call me back, while the second one I wanted him to look up. We had devised that system just in case someone was listening in. You could never tell with Ma Bell.

"I'll call you back later," George told me.

No one had heard from Lothar in three years. Dorinda was so heartbroken that the children had to come to live with George. He'd met a new woman, one who didn't mind his mundane life. And I had a license to correlate any phone number with a physical address.

It was going to take a while before George called back. First, he'd have to send out a computer inquiry and wait for a paper reply.

Then he'd go across the street to a phone booth, where he could call me without worrying about being eavesdropped upon.

So I decided to make some headway on other jobs in the interim.

"Mr. Blue's line," Mister announced.

"Easy for him."

"Yes, sir, Mr. Rawlins, I'll pass you right through."

"Hey, Easy, what's happenin'?" Jackson asked in a voice that was comparable to a tenor clarinet.

"You still want some street action, Jackson?"

"Sure. What you got?"

"You ever hear of a Waynesmith Von Crudock?"

"I know who he is. Why?"

"You think you might be able to arrange a meeting with him?"

"I'm sure. Everybody wants a word with P9. What you need?"

"Talk to the man about real estate. Tell him that P9 would like to start buyin' and you heard that he's got some holdings."

"Real estate. Pretty sophisticated, huh? Maybe I should bring Jewelle along with me. You know she got a property mind."

"Yeah, maybe. But you got to be careful, I hear Crudock's kinda tough."

"That's okay, Easy, you know I been dealin' with men like that since I cut my teeth, sleepin' in the street."

When I got off with Jackson I said to the bartender, "I'm gonna get a call on your pay phone in a bit, Madeline."

"As long as it's short," she said.

"That's a lovely dress," I replied.

"Oh. Thank you."

"Yeah," I added. "Dyed lace over white silk is what I'd imagine Marie Antoinette would wear."

That bought me a ticket to converse for the next three-quarters of an hour with the weathered debutante.

We talked and talked. The longer we did, the more her posture straightened. Her face took on a glow, bringing to my mind the thought that so many people lived their lives not being at all what they wanted. This certainty echoed with the mission of the Creative Mind.

Madeline was from Michigan, competed in a beauty contest out there. She came in second, but still, a talent scout from Hollywood gave her his number if she ever wanted to throw the dice. She took a Greyhound bus and used that number. The scout, who called himself Noone, did his best to get her work. She did a couple of commercials and general events where pretty girls were needed.

"I finally gave it up," she said.

"Why?" I asked. "You got that kind of appeal that starlets have."

"Maybe a little," she admitted. "But they work you hard for every minute they pay you for. Real hard."

Then the phone rang.

"Hello."

"Mr. Rawlins?"

"Hey, George."

"I got an address for you."

The phone George checked on belonged to a Gretchen Miller, who lived in a small house on Ayres Ave. in West Los Angeles. I parked across the residential street and down the block, under a big carob tree that threw a dark shadow.

There was a toy red wagon lying on its side in the front yard.

Now-dead blades of grass had grown up through and around the child's conveyance in better times, when someone still remembered to water the lawn; or, maybe, the vegetation throve during the rainy season the previous winter. The windows were all shut and shaded. There were three dark sedans parked in a line in the driveway, running from the backyard to the front.

I sat there for hours.

Now and again big rough-and-tumble men would come or go. The men reminded me of soldiers, deployed in enemy territory that their army had occupied but not completely suppressed.

That's the real work of a private detective. We sit and observe, take pictures through windows and from behind trees. If you were any good at the job, you'd spend this time creating scenarios that would clarify your way.

There was a long way to go. I wanted to protect my family, new and old. There was Anger and our son, Jesus and his brood, and even Carlos Ortega, an incarcerated survivor looking for his dad.

After four or five hours, when the sun was going down and I hadn't taken one positive step toward the resolution of any case, except Niska's, I drove away from the faulty domestic facade that hid a squadron of enemies who had their sights set on the son I had never met.

All that was okay. I was becoming familiar with my targets. And they had no idea about me.

25.

Big and bearlike, Cosmo Longo lumbered out from the sentry's hut at the bottom of the mountain I called home.

"Mr. Rawlins," he greeted.

"Mr. Longo," I hailed. "What's goin' on up the hill today?"

"She is gone," he said.

It was a warm evening, but a chill ran over my scalp.

"Ama—Amethystine?" I managed to say.

The hirsute guard smiled and said, "She told me that she left you a note in the kitchen and that she would be back tomorrow."

I was a little lightheaded and unsteady just standing there.

"She is beautiful," Cosmo said, reading my mood.

"How you doin', Big C?" I asked to change the subject. "Your father told me that you been goin' down to the beach on your days off."

"I like the ocean," he confessed. "It is, how you say, vass?"

"Vast, with a *t* at the end."

The towering Sicilian grinned.

"Sometimes I swim out a mile, more. There dolphins swim, and sharks sometimes too, I think. There is no more freedom than the ocean. It is a place where everything else is small."

* * *

Amethystine's note, written with a No. 2 pencil, was on the dining ledge on the second floor. Sitting on one of the high stools, I considered the block print, which was so neat and precise, as if she had been straining to pass on meaning far beyond the words she wrote.

> Hi baby,
>
> Sorry I'm not here to meet you. Pearl called from up at their school. She needs some feminine products and a big sister's love. I'll stay up there tonight and then be back to you by noon tomorrow.
>
> Okay?
>
> I love you.
>
> Amethystine

Rereading her note at least eight times reminded me of my teen years spent in love with Anger Lee. Every breath, back then and right now with Amethystine, was imbued with the subtle vibrations of that love, that obsession.

Prince Valiant came into the room and hopped up, draping his forelegs across my lap. His big head lay there.

Love gets love, Theressa Edgington used to say. She was an old woman, a neighbor of mine who lived on the first floor of a tenement we both lived in, in the Fifth Ward. *Love gets love, baby. Because it shines like a beacon and strikes like lightnin'. You can see it and hear it, feel it an' smell it on the air.*

The answering service had been kept busy taking messages for me. Jackson Blue had been able to get in to see Waynesmith Von Crudock. Mary said that she had information for me too. The last message was from Hannibal Lee. He'd merely left a number for me to call.

I decided to contact the lady first.

"Hello," Melvin Suggs answered. "Who is this?"

"Damn, Melvin, you gonna interrogate me on your private line?"

"Can't this wait till tomorrow, Rawlins?"

"It could, but them patent lawyers don't like me too much I don't think."

"Patent? Oh, you callin' for Mary?"

"I am indeed."

He banged the receiver down on something hard. After that, I heard him calling his wife.

"Hello?" she said sweetly.

"He's such a brute," I joked.

"But he's my brute," she said, after a laugh.

"So, what you got for me?"

"The BNDD agent with the backward punctuation scar under his lip is Drake Simmons. His title is investigator, but I couldn't find out any more than that about him and the agency."

"No, no, that's more than good enough. Where'd you get it?"

"I know a dude on the highway patrol, a dispatcher. He said that the BNDD did a joint operation with the CHP a while ago. Simmons was the federal contact. My guy there said that the chief was dissatisfied with the results of the investigation, but my contact didn't know why."

"Thanks, Mary, this gonna help."

"I still owe you, Easy. Call whenever you want."

"At the lawyers'?"

"No. They fired me."

"Why? You not a good secretary?"

"They didn't like the company I keep."

* * *

"Easy," he said in my ear.

"How you know it was me, Jackson? You got some gizmo on that phone tell you who's callin'?"

"I got seven phones, Ease."

"Seven phones? You only got two ears."

"Between me and Jewelle and my son, that's six ears."

"And one phone too many."

"No, no, no, no, no, no, Easy. Each phone has a purpose. My business line and personal line; Jewelle's business and personal; our family line, doctor's line, and finally there's you."

"Me? I got my own dedicated line?"

"Yeah, man."

"Then how come you never said my name before when I called?"

"'Bout six months ago I changed all the numbers around, got Mister to tell everybody we in touch with that the numbers have changed. We would still get a stranger callin' on your line every once in a while, but nowadays it's most usually just you."

"Damn."

"You wanna hear about Waynesmith?"

"Shoot."

"When I had Mister put a call through to Von Crudock he got right on the line. And when I talked about real estate, he said come on out, so I did—"

"Where?" I interrupted.

"A place on La Cienega, a restaurant and bar called Shorts. When me and Jewelle got there, I told him that Jean-Paul was lookin' to expand his real estate portfolio in Southern California. You know we got all kinds'a reports sayin' that the land is gonna quadruple in value ovah the next fifteen years."

"That all sounds good. What was he talkin' about?"

"He said that he's puttin' his money in the canyons around LA an' buyin' up orange and lemon groves around the outer borders of the valley. You know, cheapest investment for greatest profit.

"But that wasn't nuthin'. Then he said that he'd heard that we got a computer system keep tabs on everybody in the world that was in any way involved with a policy issued by P9. I told him that I was the one set up that database."

"Oh," I said. "And what did that mean to him?"

"He wanted to know about a woman name of Shelly Dormer. He says that this Dormer woman is the owner of a lot out in Culver City and that he's very interested in talkin' to her, and if not her, then to her heirs.

"What you think about that?"

I had asked Jackson to have a conversation about business in general because if I had to speak to the man, I wanted him to think that I knew something about what he was into. But now…

"Did he seem excited about findin' this woman?" I asked.

"Excited? Shit. It was like his dick been hard for the whole month his woman been gone."

"Jackson!" Jewelle shouted from somewhere near at hand.

"Sorry, baby, I was just talkin' to Easy, you know," Jackson said to her. And then to me, "Yeah, man. You wanna get to him, tell 'im you got a line on this Dormer chick."

"Thanks, Jackson. Thank you. That's gonna be some help."

"Cool. Hold on, Easy, Jewelle wanna shout at ya."

I was already deep in thought about the information that Jackson had mined.

"Easy?"

"Hey, Jewelle. Thanks for keepin' Jackson in line."

"That man is a mess."

"What can I do for you, darlin'?"

"I don't need a thing, Easy. But I wanted to tell you that I had a friend who did business with Von Crudock."

"Oh? Who's that?"

"Lindhoff, Bertrand Lindhoff."

"What about him?"

"Bertie was a nice guy if you remembered never to do business with him."

"Why's that?"

"Bertie felt that if you lost sight of the ball, then the ball was his. So, he got into a deal with Von Crudock. They were building a shoppin' center or sumpin'. Bertie called me one day and said that he saw a loophole in their contract, so he was gonna take the project over. He wanted me to provide workers that Von Crudock didn't have his hooks into. They were thirty million dollars in, and he was gonna end up with it all."

"So, what happened?" I asked, though I didn't have to.

"Bertie disappeared. The police came and asked me about it. I told 'em I didn't know a thing."

This was no surprise. I'd seen the mercenaries on Ayres and what had happened to my son's brother.

"Thanks, J. I'll be careful."

"What's going on with you, Easy?"

"About Von Crudock?"

"No. Your voice."

"What's wrong with my voice?"

"It sounds, I don't know, kinda forceful, like you about to bust out your skin."

"I'm at home, honey. Must be the altitude. You know, they say it affects the larynx."

"Hm, if you say so."

"I do. If you don't mind, can I holler at Jackson one more time?"

It was a relief to get off the line with her. I often forget the deft perceptivity that Jewelle possesses.

"Ease," Jackson said.

"Do me a favor, Jackson. Look up that Shelly Dormer and her heirs in your files, but don't tell Von Crudock."

"You got it."

"Hello?" a woman answered. A woman who had the crisp and authoritative voice of Violet Welles, my son's friend.

"Easy Rawlins, callin' for his son," I replied.

"He's not here."

"You expect him back?"

"Sooner or later."

"Come on now, Violet. Why you got to be like that?"

"Is there anything else?"

"Yeah. Tell him that the same folks killed Santangelo are after him. I know who they are."

"Who?" Violet asked, the angry tone draining from her voice.

I told her my phone number, twice, and then hung up.

I decided to make lasagna for dinner using three kinds of cheese, including ricotta, a tomato-based pasta sauce that I made once a month just in case my fancy turned Italian, and thick-cut pepperoni for the meat. I'm a fast cook and within thirty minutes my lasagna dish was ready for a 350-degree oven. I like the lower temperature for an hour of baking.

The meal had been cooking for a quarter hour when the phone rang.

"Hello?"

"This is Hannibal Lee," he uttered, with words clipped and his baritone fully under control.

Those four words imposed a temporary silence on me. That was my son calling. The child of my blood.

"Anger tells me that you're my son." Even though I was deeply moved, I saw no reason to pussyfoot with the man.

"I'm callin' because you said that you knew who killed my brother."

"That's why *you* called. I called you because of that and also because your mother claims my paternity."

"I don't care about that."

"Okay," I said and waited.

The seconds slid by.

"So, what do you want to ask me?" he said at last.

"I want to meet you, face-to-face."

"That's not possible."

"Anything is possible, no matter how unlikely."

That halted Hannibal again.

"All right. Tomorrow morning at eleven. The Penguin Club."

"What's that?"

"You never heard of the Penguin Club?" he accused.

"No. Where is it?"

"Down on a Hundred Twenty-Third. On the east side. You turn right at One Twenty-Three goin' south on Central. It's the first empty lot on the left. You can't miss it."

"Eleven o'clock," I said.

"Eleven," he replied, sounding as if he were correcting me.

I pulled up to the curb at 123rd in front of the empty lot at 10:31 the next morning. I remembered the big blue house that was once there. It was three stories high and proud-looking, an old place where a single family had lived at the beginning of the century. By the time I first saw it, the urban mansion had been subdivided and was then home to at least five families, only to be burned to ashes in the Watts Riot, August 1965.

The empty plot of land was covered with what looked like scorched earth. A light-gray-and-yellow dirt, rock-hard soil that wouldn't give a micromillimeter under a man's shod weight. Running the width of the back of the lot was a weathered wooden fence, maybe twelve feet high. At the far end, in front of the gray weathered fence, maybe eighteen cars were parked.

Driving to the back of the vacant field, I parked and got out.

From the street the fence looked solid, with no breaks. But up close there was a rope handle toward the center. I pulled on the hemp loop and the door gave way.

"Who is that?" a man demanded.

"Ezekiel Rawlins," I declared. "Here to see Hannibal Lee."

There was a moment of silence, and then from around the trunk of a solitary oak came a man in black slacks and a square-cut milk-chocolate-brown shirt. He had a mid-caliber rifle hanging down from the crook of his right arm.

"I heard'a you," the light brown Negro allowed. "They say you hang out with pimps and pushers."

"You just standin' there, makin' up shit, right, brother?" was my reply.

"Say what?"

"Have we met?"

"I, uh, don't think so."

"Then you should have the sense to know that people talk every day. They say all kinds'a shit. Don't mean it's true. Don't mean it's anywhere near right. And here you are, spreadin' rumors 'bout your brother just like the white man want you to."

I knew what kind of place I was in. I knew the words they used.

The high-yellow Black man considered a moment and then nodded.

"Follow me," he said.

On the other side of the wood wall was a slender swath of grass.

"Why you need to have an armed guard at an open door?" I asked my guide.

"It's not usually unlocked," he said. "I keep watch on the lot, and when I saw you, I took the bolt off the door."

"Oh."

Beyond the strip of lawn there was a huge privet hedge, at least as high as the fence. The sentry led me to the center of the hedge and then through a man-size gate that had been overgrown with the dense cover of dark green and oval leaves.

The other side was a real surprise. It was a three-story white house, but instead of the back it was set up like the front. There was a generous porch and welcoming front door.

"Whoa," I declared.

"What's wrong?"

"What's the other side look like?"

"That's the back'a the house, on One Twenty-Fourth. Beyond that there's an eleven-foot cinder-block fence to keep us secure."

"Like a fort, huh?"

The rifleman grinned in reply.

He led me up the stairs and past the front door.

The first floor of the Penguin Club was a large, open area where there were couches, chairs, and tables set here and there. Maybe a dozen club members were seated, deep in conversation, reading, writing, or just thinking. Everyone was Black.

"He's on the second floor," my armed guide said.

"What room?"

"They'll tell you."

The staircase was wide, with each step cushioned by royal-blue-and-maroon carpeting. The oak-wood banisters were well maintained and there were framed portraits on the walls: Black men and women from every century since the beginning of the Great Enslavement.

"How can I help you?" asked a woman seated behind a black desk. She was young, like almost everyone else at the Penguin Club. Her light brown hair was curly and teased out into an Afro.

"Hannibal Lee."

"Down the hall to your left," she said, looking me in the eye. "It's the cream-and-cranberry door."

The door of red and white was halfway down the hall and closed. So, I knocked.

"Come in."

It was a small room, tastefully done in burgundy and wood-dark brown. There was a long slender window that looked over the houses to the east. Set before that frame were two deep red padded chairs, facing each other.

My son was an inch taller than I and dark-skinned like both his parents. His face had character—formed, I believed, by years of decision-making in the face of hard times and distress. In a similar uniform to the sentry down below, he wore black slacks along with a fancy green, square-cut short-sleeved shirt. There were two marks up near the bridge of his nose, telling me that he wore glasses, sometimes.

"Have a seat," he offered.

I chose the chair to the left of the window. He settled across from me.

"I'm very happy to meet you, son."

"That makes one of us."

"Oh, come on now, man. It's not my fault that I didn't know about you."

"You could have looked."

"No, I couldn't have. When your mama left Texas, that was all she wrote for me. She didn't say how I could write, call, or get on a bus to her. And, as far as I knew, she wasn't pregnant the last time we met."

Hannibal's face didn't change from its stolid expression, except for his eyes. They seemed to be focused on some inner question.

"How old are you?" he asked.

"Fifty-two last September."

After a brief calculation he said, "That's impossible."

"Why?"

"Because that would make you fourteen when I was conceived."

Our eyes met. I didn't look away.

"Is that true?" he asked.

"You wanna see my driver's license?"

He wanted to, but didn't press.

"You were a child," he averred.

"I'd been on my own since the age of eight. Your mother had from the age of ten. The word *child* wasn't in our vocabulary. I loved her more than I'm willin' to remember. And she cared for me. Only thing I could think was that she thought I was too young to be a father to you."

Hannibal mixed all those words in the cauldron of his mind. I assumed they jumbled up quite nicely because he couldn't say any more about me abandoning him.

"What's this about my brother?" he asked instead.

"Santangelo hired me to find a woman named Lutisha James."

"My mother."

"That's what it turned out to be. The name I knew her by was Anger Lee."

I told him the rest of the story and he listened closely.

It took him a minute or two to digest the complex tale. Then he said, "I was the one who sent Santangelo to find you."

"So you already knew about me?"

"I knew your name, and that you were my father, by blood. But I didn't know it all."

"When I talked to your brother, after they'd shot him, he said that a white man, probably wearin' a jacket looked like a checkerboard, was the one that did it. I went out lookin' for you because whoever killed him, I figured, had you in mind too."

"Okay," he said, trying to regain the superiority he felt when I'd walked in. "Now you told me."

"It's not just the warnin'. You need to come with me. I can protect you."

"You expect me to trust you?"

"Did you send your brother to me?"

"Yeah, so?"

"Then you must'a been told by your mother that I was a man to be trusted."

From there my son went through an internal dialogue. I imagined him thinking of questions, or accusations, and then coming up with the answers I'd give.

Finally, he said, "Where would we go?"

I explained where my house was, reiterating that I wanted him to come there with me. Then I said, “But first you should call Violet and tell her to stay away from anyplace they could find her.”

“You think they’re after her too?”

“They’re after you. And if twistin’ her arm would bring you out, I’m sure they wouldn’t mind.”

26.

"I don't need your help," my son said in rebuke. "Whoever it is after me, they don't know where I am. And even if they did, I'm protected here."

"I doubt if they knew where Santangelo was at, before they needed to."

"Then why didn't you help him?" Hannibal accused.

"I didn't understand the deep shit you guys were in at first. I took your brother at his word. Nobody told me about Sasha and the deed he stole, about you and the Creative Mind. I thought I was lookin' for a middle-aged woman who liked to play the numbers sometimes, a woman who needed to call her aged mother."

Hannibal wanted to dislike me. I could see that in his eyes and sour lips. But I couldn't blame him.

"I'ma ask you again, Mr. Rawlins, why should I trust you?"

"Because your mother told you, you could," I said simply.

Anger Lee was a force of nature; I knew that when I was a child, and Mouse had underscored that fact with his remembered blues poem. My son knew this too. His mother was not to be ignored.

"Where is she?" he asked.

"I put her in a safe place. She has my number, and she will call. She will call me lookin' for you."

That was the clincher. Hannibal was connected to his mother the way a serf believes in his queen.

"I want to get Violet and bring her with us," was his condition.

"Call her, then."

We left through the back/front of the Penguin Club, through the dense hedge, and out from the great wood wall. My senses were at the very highest alert, like they had been in the days of World War II, when every step could have been your last, either by land mine, sniper, or bayonet in the back. I was so aware because of my son, his danger, and the intense passion I felt for Amethystine Stoller. My hypersensitive hearing picked up a car door's lock cracking open, a gravelly step, and the clank of something metal on metal...

"Get down!" I yelled, jumping on my son, dragging him to the ground behind a light green Chevrolet.

The shots had started on our way down. Hannibal grunted. I pulled out the .32 revolver stolen from the BFNE. Maybe half a dozen more shots rang out. I lay flat behind the automobile and, aiming from the space underneath the car, shot three times.

A man grunted in pain, so I rolled to the left and shot twice more at the four legs of the two men who had come out of nowhere. When I stood up, I saw that the man I'd shot in the shins was leaning on his friend and being dragged away. I had only one bullet left and a powerful need to make the right move.

The would-be assassins tumbled into a late-model Cadillac, popped the motor, and drove off unevenly, the car moving like a drunken mare in the first days of spring with green oats fermenting in her stomach.

"Come on!" I shouted, dragging Hannibal to his feet. He was bleeding from the upper part of his left leg.

I dragged him to my car, got him in the passenger's seat, and went around to the driver's side looking everywhere at once. I turned the engine over and took off.

"Did the bullet go through?" I asked him.

"I don't think so."

"Put pressure from both hands on the wound. Press down hard, hard!"

A mile or so from the Penguin Club I pulled into an alley and turned my attention to Hannibal. Ripping the fabric of the pant leg apart, I studied the wound. If you rubbed the blood away, for a moment you could see the round hole that the bullet made.

"Ain't bleedin' too bad," I said.

"Looks pretty bad to me."

"Yeah," I admitted. "It's not good, but I seen bullet holes where the blood's pumpin' out. This shot didn't hit no major vein or artery."

"You're bleeding too," Hannibal observed.

"What?"

"Your face."

The rearview mirror revealed a leaking streak just below the right cheekbone. I took a blue rag from the glove compartment and dedicated three minutes' pressure to stop the wound from dripping. I didn't really care about the blood, it's just that I didn't want to be driving around like that. A cop seeing a bleeding Negro behind the wheel of a Lincoln Continental would turn on the siren and call for backup.

"I need a doctor," Hannibal said, almost as if talking to someone he expected to care about him.

"I got one for ya."

* * *

We made it all the way from Watts to my mountain. I drove right up to the guard hut and called from the window, "Help."

Cosmo rushed out from the lean-to shed.

"My son is shot," I said.

The Sicilian guardsman didn't ask about the son he didn't know I had. He just pulled Hannibal out of the driver's side and helped lug him up to the funicular.

"I'll come with you," he told me.

I didn't argue with the man.

Amethystine met us at the front door, a big smile on her face until she saw what was happening.

"Bring him to the couch," she said to Cosmo. Then, to me: "What happened to your face?"

"Same thing happened to your butt."

She gave me only the briefest grin and began to examine the flesh wound.

"Not now," I told her. Then: "Cosmo."

"Yes, Mr. Easy?" he asked while laying my son out on the chaise lounge next to the terrace.

"Go to Orchestra. Tell her that we'll need Dr. Lambert and that it will have to be kept in confidence."

Without another word, the ocean-loving bodyguard left.

Hannibal lay on the settee, obviously in pain.

"What about Violet?" he asked.

"Yeah, yeah. Right," I said. "You'll have to write down the address for me."

"I'll get pencil and paper," Amethystine offered.

While she went to my office, I pulled up a chair next to Hannibal.

"How's it feel?"

"Like your face looks," he said.

"It's not a bad wound. We get the bullet out and you'll be fine."

When he grimaced, I had the urge to take his hand, but I resisted.

"Why they wanna try an' kill me?" he asked.

"I guess they figure that even if you have that deed, it'll get lost without you to shepherd it."

"That's why they killed Santangelo?"

"Probably."

"Kill somebody over a piece'a paper?"

"Piece'a paper that must represent a whole lotta cash."

"Who's doin' all this shit?"

"You don't know?"

"The guy you were talkin' about, that man Sasha, he worked at a place called Clint Investment and Research Corporation. He's an accountant. He's the one came across that deed."

"Deed to a plot of land in Culver City," I said. "Signed over to a Shelly Dormer."

"Yeah. How did you know?"

"Dollars to doughnuts, the man who owns your Clint company is named Waynesmith Von Crudock. He plans on makin' a killin' from whatever that document says, right after puttin' you in the ground."

Amethystine returned with the writing materials and Hannibal wrote down Violet's name, phone number, and address.

I brought him the downstairs phone that we had on an extra-long cord.

"Tell Violet that I'll have a guy named Fearless Jones pick her up and bring her here."

Not long after Hannibal finished the call to his girlfriend, Dr. Irene Lambert came to the door.

"Orchestra said that somebody had been shot," she said to me when I let her in.

"Yeah. It was an ambush, but we can't talk to the police about it."

The doctor was in her early sixties, slender and tall. A white woman, she'd been in practice for more than a dozen years when, in the late forties, she was arrested and charged for performing unsanctioned abortions on women and girls. Orchestra Solomon, the owner of our mountain, paid for Irene's legal fees and gave her a home on the mountain after her conviction. Lambert had been stripped of her right to practice medicine, and then she was fined a great deal of money, everything she had. So I wasn't worried about her turning us over to the police.

She gave Hannibal an injection that put him out. Then she went about removing the bullet while I held his legs still. She sewed him up and gave us a bottle of antibiotic pills that he was to take over the next ten days.

After the doctor left, there was only Amethystine and me standing over my sleeping boy.

"He looks a lot like you," she said.

"He does?" I really didn't see it.

"Yes, sir," she said. "How's your wound?"

"It burns a little, that's all."

"So it isn't making you feel weak or anything?"

"No. I'm fine."

"Then why don't you take me upstairs and make me a little one like this big one here?"

27.

Making love to Amethystine blocked out everything that had come before. It was as if I were a kid again experiencing the world for the first time: colors, textures, breath. The feelings were so strong that it felt somehow impersonal, like I was drifting through another man's dream.

"What you thinkin'?" Amethystine asked.

"That I'm happier than I should be."

"Why not be happy?"

"Where I come from, if you take a break of any kind from the job at hand, then the ground will crumble from under your feet, and you'll fall all the way down, into an early grave."

She sat up in the bed beside me staring hard, not at me but at the words spoken.

After maybe a minute she said, "I know. I know you better than you think, Easy. I do. From the first time in your office when I came to get you to find Curt. I knew right then that we were meant to be together. Or...maybe not definitely, but if the stars aligned, then we could make something out of—of—I don't know, that we could make something more out of what we are.

"Does that make sense?"

"Yeah. But at the same time, I got a thirty-eight-year-old son downstairs that I didn't even know about before two days ago. His brother been murdered and the same folks wanna kill him too. And here I am . . . happy."

"Here you are," she said, taking my hands in hers. "Here we are."

"Tell me somethin'."

"What's that, my love?"

"Where'd you get that bullet scar from?"

She took her time, watching me, maybe even glaring a wee bit. The wait was so long that I thought she wouldn't respond. This was, in some ways, a relief, because part of me really didn't want to know what happened.

"About a year and a half ago I met this guy," she said out of nowhere. "His name was Chandler, and he had a doctorate in modern philosophy. I liked the way he thought about things, the way he talked. We spent some time together. His parents liked me. They had money, I don't know where from. You hadn't called, and I was, I don't know, I was feeling like . . . lost. He took me to Paris over a long weekend. After that we spent time up north in Berkeley, where he was the youngest professor of philosophy that UCB ever had.

"But you know me, Easy. One day I woke up and realized that I was using him for filler in the space you left in my heart. I told him that I wasn't going to marry him, and he said that I would. So, I walked out. I mean, there's not a motherfucker on this planet gonna make me be somethin' other than what I am. Not one. Not even you could do that, Mr. Easy."

I smiled at myself, enjoying the way she told her tale, making me a part of what happened.

"What does any of that have to do with your scar?" I asked.

"As I was walking away to my car, he shot me."

"Shot you?"

"Uh-huh," she grunted in a tone that I could only call defiance. "I don't know if he was aimin' for my butt or what, but he didn't shoot anymore, and so I got in the car and drove to the hospital. Lucky I got some paddin' back there. They treated me and I came back down to LA."

"What happened to Chandler?"

"I don't know. The emergency room physician called the police, and I made up some story about bein' on Isabella Street in Oakland. I told them that I had been lookin' around for a friend of mine that lived up there and then somebody, I didn't know who, shot me."

I sighed broadly.

"What?" she asked.

"I don't know, baby. If somebody asked me right now, what should I do, I'd be at a loss. But I could tell 'em this: you are my woman, as long as it lasts. And here I am, between right here and some other place."

"You see?" she said.

"See what?"

"There Chandler was with his Plato and his Nietzsche. For him it was all just words. But you, Easy Rawlins, you got your feet on the ground, toes dug deep in the soil beneath your feet. I know exactly where I am when I'm with you."

My mother died when I was seven. I loved her more than anyone I had ever known up until the day I met Amethystine. I tried to jump into the grave they laid my mom in. For years I dreamed of going back there and digging my way down to her. My mother tended my cuts and scrapes, bathed me in a tin tub next to a chicken coop, told me that I was the smartest person she'd ever known. When she died a light went out.

I went downstairs to see the man my wild oats had sown. He was unconscious. Dr. Lambert had told me he would probably sleep for hours.

"What you doin'?" Amethystine asked. She had come up behind me, speaking those words as she leaned up against my back.

"I gotta go do somethin'."

"What?"

"A chore for my other son."

"What can I do?"

"Fearless is coming here with Hannibal's girlfriend, and I left my number with Anger, also called Lutisha. Can you be here for them?"

My best thinking is most often done behind the wheel of a car. I don't even have to be driving. Just sitting there, I feel powerful, like some barbarian god on a throne of skulls seeing everything I need to and deciding on what had to get done.

The first and most important problem was Waynesmith the rich man. He was after my family. I was safe from most dangers on my mountaintop but not from Von Crudock or cancer. He wasn't a criminal in the eyes of the law because he had never been, and would never be, convicted of a felony. But that didn't mean he couldn't receive punishment. Mouse would kill him if asked to. I mean, that would be human justice. Von Crudock had had both me and my son shot that very day. Murdering the man would be both justified and expedient. But maybe there was another way. My driving mind told me that I should at least try to find a nonlethal alternative.

* * *

The city of West Covina was a long drive from my home. But the journey, I knew, would be worth it. Nestled in the bosom of the San Gabriel Valley, the small municipality was a subject of the County of Los Angeles. I got there around sunset and, after consulting my forty-page Southern California map, I made my way to East Thackery Street. There I came upon a faded house that was in dire need of a paint job and a gardener. It was a big house that sat upon a hill of writhing weeds.

I parked out front and scaled the uneven stone pathway to the front door. The doorbell made no sound that I could hear. When I was just making up my mind to knock, the door slowly opened, revealing an older gray-haired white lady with a soft-skinned face and lantern-like green eyes.

"Yes?" she asked on a wisp of a voice. "Can I help you?"

"Hi," I said brightly. "I came to ask a young man name of Terry a question or two."

"What kind of questions?" I noticed that her right hand was reaching beyond the door jamb.

"My son, Jesus, is trying to figure out this problem he got, and he told me that Terry knew at least part of the answer."

"You're Jesus's father?" she asked, pronouncing his name the way the Spanish did.

"Yes."

"Why didn't he come?"

"Benita, his wife, and their daughter, Essie, are down with the flu, so I told him that I would come."

"Why didn't he call?" Her voice was getting stronger.

"He couldn't remember the number and didn't have it written down."

"He could have called Information," she suggested.

"I dialed four-one-one, but there was no Terry or Terrance Lomax listed."

I didn't like the way she was looking at me.

"I don't know," she said, dubious.

"I understand, ma'am. Your boy's been in some trouble and you're thinkin' that I might have brought some of that here to your door. But I'm not here to mess things up. Just the opposite. Jesus helped me figure out something I could do that might help your Terry avoid spending time in a federal penitentiary."

"You're Jesus's father?" a young man's voice asked from behind the woman.

"Yes," I said, looking up into shadow.

A frowning young man stepped forward. He was white and tall, thin and black-haired. Despite his lean frame I got the feeling that he was pretty strong.

"What do they call you?" he asked.

"Easy. Easy Rawlins."

My answer elicited a smile.

"It's okay, Grandma," he said. "He can come in."

The elder stepped back from the door, her right hand formed into a fist around the barrel of a Winchester rifle.

"Don't worry, Mr. Rawlins. She won't shoot you unless I ask her to."

"Terry?"

"Yes, sir. Come on in."

Terry led me down a narrow hallway into a dark kitchen. There was an overhead light shining, but it did little to illuminate the room. The gas stove was old and black. The air was scented with mercaptan, the rotten-egg scent added to natural gas. A heavy wooden table dominated the space. The waxy finish was peeling away from the tabletop, which was also scarred and dented.

"Have a seat," my young host offered. "Can I get you somethin' to drink?"

"No, thanks. I just wanna talk a little."

Terry had the kind of thin face that made you think of the outcome of generations of inbreeding, but his eyes, like his grandmother's, burned with untamed intelligence.

"How's T.J. doin'?" he asked.

"Who?"

"Jesus, your son."

"Oh. Never knew people called him that. At home we call him Juice for short. He's not too good. The BNDD is lookin' for him."

"Oh. Oh yeah. He said that he was in trouble with them. That why you're here?"

"Yeah."

"You told my grandmother that maybe you could help me with my legal problems."

"Yes," I said, sitting up a little straighter.

"Why you wanna help me?"

"I don't, but it just so happens that the way I plan to get Juice outta trouble will benefit you."

"How?"

"The BNDD agents that have charges pending against you are also putting pressure on my son. I know that one of them is named Drake Simmons. If I can identify the other guy, I think I might be able to implicate them both in a thing. Once that happens, Jesus will be cut loose from his problems and anybody else being prosecuted and persecuted by those guys will, hopefully, have their charges dropped."

"Implicate in what?" Terry asked.

"You don't have to worry about that, son."

After gnawing a bit on his lower lip, the strong-shouldered, lanky kid smiled and said, "Okay. T.J. says that you're cool, so why not? The man who arrested me is a dude name of Agent William Banks. He's with the BNDD, like you said."

"What they get you on?"

"I was drivin' three keys out to Laguna Beach. They stopped me, took the stash, and then charged me for one key. That what they did to T.J.?"

"Somethin' like that."

I drove all the way back to my office before making the requisite calls.

"Hello, who is this?"

"Me, Mel."

"You callin' my wife again, Rawlins?" he asked, only half joking.

"No, sir. This time I'm lookin' for you."

"You know I got an office."

"And that's the last place you'd want me sayin' what I got to say."

There passed a brief moment in which he could chew on my cryptic words. Then he muttered, "What you got?"

I told him about Warehouse 86 and the rumors regarding BNDD agent Billy Banks.

After I'd finished, Suggs went quiet for at least three minutes. I accepted this silence as a compliment. Mel was a brilliant tactician, and he was rarely moved to act solely on someone else's initiative.

"You sure this Banks is bent?" Mel said at last. "Dealing drugs."

"I am. And it's not just Banks. He's got a partner named Drake Simmons."

"He's an agent too?

"He is."

"And they use this warehouse out in Bellflower?"

"I'm pretty sure."

"This isn't some trick, now, is it, Rawlins? I mean some shit you makin' up to protect your own."

"No. I wouldn't do anything that had a chance of backfiring on my boy. It's all true. The only thing I can't tell you is when they're gonna be movin' the next shipment."

"I'll get back to you."

My answering service had a message from Niska. I wanted to get home, but that would have made for a late-night call to her.

"Hello?" a man said.

"Reggie?"

"Yeah. Who's this?"

"Easy Rawlins. Niska's boss."

"Oh. Hello, sir. You callin' for her?"

"I am."

"Okay. Niska," he said aloud, and then, whispering: "It's your boss."

"Hello," she said then. "Mr. Rawlins?"

"It is. You called?"

"Yeah. I went down to that street in East LA you said about, looking for the father of that man you met in jail."

"How'd it go?"

"I went with Reggie. I don't know if I ever told you, but his mother is from Mexico City. So, he came along, you know, to keep me company. We went to two stores near to where he lives.

They knew him and his father. One even saw him the day he disappeared, but they didn't know where he'd gone to. Then we just started talking to people out in front'a their houses. Two different ladies said about how much Rafael liked playing bingo. It's like the Mexican Lotería but you could win money. We found out where there was one bingo parlor in that neighborhood and went there.

"It was too early for it to be open, so we went to a movie and then had lunch. After that we went back to the bingo parlor and the lady there told us that Mr. Ortega met a woman named Rosa and that they had come back two more times. They said he liked her because she made food like he used to eat in Sinaloa."

"Wow," I said, truly impressed. "Did you find Rafael?"

"When the game started up, there was a lady that knew Rosa and she agreed to call. We gave Rafael a ride to his home so they could send a message to his son."

"I hope you told them that I sent you."

"We did."

28.

On the drive back to the mountain I thought about Niska and Amethystine. They had very little in common except for the thing Amethystine had said about me: Toes in the soil beneath my feet. That's what a detective had to have. She had to know her city, its peoples, dialects, and languages, its neighborhoods and histories, everything you could see and touch. A detective's mind had to be right there in front of her. Your city was your whole world. That's what Amethystine loved about me, and that same sensibility was what I was trying to impart to Niska.

Erculi was manning the entrance to the funicular that night. Motionless, he stood there, almost invisible in the earthen colors of his work clothes, leaning against a slender eucalyptus tree.

"What you doin' out here, Herk?"

Pushing away from the slippery bark, he said, "Your friend Fearless told Matteo that you asked him to bring a woman he didn't know. And then there was another woman."

"One too many?" I asked with a smile.

"Cosmo said that you brought a man with a bullet wound at noon. And you have that scratch across your face."

"Yeah," I admitted. "I was gonna call you as soon as I got in, Signor Longo. I swear I was."

He nodded and then I told him the broad strokes of the trouble I had brought to his mountain.

"Not so bad," he said when I'd finished.

"These are bad men, sir," I said.

"We have had trouble with worse."

"Okay. But don't take any chances. I like your sons."

He patted my shoulder and then sent me up the mountain.

It was about 10:30 when I went through the front door. There were lights on all over the bottom floor. And there were voices, even some laughter.

Beyond the entrance hall I could see that the foldaway long table we used for big dinners on the entrance level had been assembled in the middle of the large room. There were people sitting around the long bench in their folding chairs, eating and drinking, talking carelessly as if there wasn't a problem in the world.

Fearless Jones was there along with his cowardly complement, Paris Minton. Hannibal, my son, was perched next to Violet. They were sitting back from the table, holding hands—somehow seeming serious even in that gentle act. At the table's head Amethystine and Anger Lee were sitting side by side upon a short couch. Two matriarchs sharing a common throne.

When I entered, Prince Valiant and the smaller dogs leaped up and started barking their greetings and warnings.

"Easy," scrawny Paris greeted. "Home at last, home at last, thank God a'mighty."

"Paris, Fearless, Violet," I hailed.

I used both hands, waving at everyone else.

"So, you decided to come up here, huh?" I asked Anger after kissing her cheek.

"When I called, your girlfriend told me that Hannie was here and that he'd been shot. You know I'm comin' then."

Fearless and Violet had stopped off at my favorite, nameless soul-food stand to bring in barbecued baby back ribs, macaroni and cheese, potato salad, collard greens, monkey bread, and redeye gravy, all along with a variety of hot peppers and pickles.

I was ravenous, and so eating occupied the majority of my attention. Fearless had also brought beer and wine. He was treating this retreat as a holiday. It was no wonder women and children loved him so.

For the next couple of hours, we all talked and joked around, ate and drank.

Paris found one of my albums, *The Best of Sam Cooke.* That was our clock. We played the LP all the way through—twice. At the end of the first side Hannibal and Violet retired to the guest room on the third floor. When the second side had played, Amethystine went up to my room. Fearless and Paris called it a night at the end of the third side. They took Feather's room where there were two beds.

When Cooke started in on "You Send Me," there was only me and Anger left.

"You want a cigarette?" I offered.

"Yes, sir."

"Let's go up to the roof. I don't smoke in the house."

On the way up the stairs, we ran into Hannibal. He was sitting in the kitchen, drinking from a tumbler of water and reading a book that I had recently purchased—*How Europe Underdeveloped Africa* by the scholar-activist Walter Rodney.

"Hello, son," his mother greeted both formally and lovingly.

"Hey."

"We goin' up to the roof for a cigarette. Wanna come wit'?"

"What you readin'?" I asked as he rose, painfully, to his feet.

"You should know," he said. "I got it off your shelf."

"Yeah. I was just surprised to see that's the one you picked out."

"It's my field of study."

"Which is?"

"Economics and revolution."

"Where'd you go to school?"

"Princeton."

The crown of my three-story round house was where I smoked, grew roses, and, now and then, made clandestine phone calls from a special phone that no one could eavesdrop on.

I lit Anger's cigarette, Hannibal said that he didn't smoke, and then I lit mine.

"It's beautiful up here, Easy," Anger said. "You know I always knew you was somethin' special."

"Takes one to know one," I joked.

"So, this man is really my father?" Hannibal asked, the words feigning doubt.

"The best man I ever knew in all my life."

"You know," I added, "they say that the lowliest hyena female is superior to the best male in the pack."

Mother and son both laughed at that fact.

I brought out a few folding chairs and we sat in a circle.

There were a lot of stars in the sky that night, and a chill flowed over our shoulders.

"I'm sorry about Saint," son said to mother.

"It wasn't your fault."

"If I hadn't told Sasha about what I was gonna do, they woulda never known to come after him."

"Yeah," I agreed. "But you thought you were dealin' with a regular corporation, not no modern-day robber baron."

Hannibal clasped his hands and stared down at the concrete between his feet.

"Why aren't you asleep?" I asked him.

"Slept all day."

"But you need to heal, baby," his mother chided.

"Yeah, man. You wanna keep your strength for Violet," I put in.

"That wide-faced girl, that Amethystine, your woman, Easy?" Anger wondered, running on a tangent from my words.

"I guess so."

"You know she ain't nuthin' but trouble."

I thought of maybe half a dozen smart-ass rejoinders, but I knew how much she was hurting and so kept quiet.

After Anger stubbed out her second cigarette she asked, "Where you got me sleepin', doll?"

"There's a couch on the first floor with blankets on it."

"Okay," she said, and then turned to her son. "You need help goin' down the stairs, Hannie?"

He didn't answer, just stood up and put his arm around her shoulders.

A while after they'd gone, I went down to the kitchen, there to pour a single shot of hundred-proof bourbon. I wasn't tired, and even if I had been, there was too much going on for my body to consider sleep.

Somewhere around 2:30 the phone rang. I snatched it up so the ring wouldn't arouse any of my many guests.

"Hello?"

"Now I'm callin' you," Melvin said.

"That's why I stayed up, man. I was wonderin' when you'd finally get down to work."

"How's Amy doin'?"

"Why you ask me that?"

"Mary said that you guys were back together."

"What you callin' about, Mel?"

"I got three men on Simmons," he said. "We asked around about him. The FBI woke up a banker and had him look into his financials. We're pretty sure your information was right."

"You into Banks too?"

"Like white on rice."

"Or black on my back."

Having no rejoinder, Suggs asked, "Anything else?"

"I'm pretty sure that the owner of the warehouse, Mildred Franz, is not a part of all this."

"Why?"

"Too proud of her business."

"She coulda been playin' you."

"Maybe. But if I'm right, she could be a help to you."

"I'll look into it."

29.

I didn't sleep that night. Somewhere there was a shoe waiting to fall and I couldn't let the drop find me napping.

When the sun started to light up the sky, I made a call and then went outside and followed the blue-brick road from my place to the round platform that stood before the entrance to the funicular car.

Five ten, lean, and standing erect, sixty-something Orchestra Solomon was wearing an ankle-length dark blue dress with a nose-to-tail red fox fur draped over her shoulders. Beside her was Reynard Khan, her life companion. They were looking out over Los Angeles like proud property owners. That might be a little of an overstatement, but Orchestra did own a great swath of the city. She might have been even wealthier than Von Crudock.

"Good morning," I greeted my landlady and her friend. "Thanks for comin' out so early."

"Mr. Rawlins," Reynard replied, giving me a civilized, if slightly snooty, nod.

"I spoke to Erculi," Sadie said. "He told me that there might be trouble."

"I hope not. And I'm really sorry."

"Why not call the police?" Reynard wondered.

"I'm not sure if that's a good idea. It's about a disagreement with a man named Crudock."

"Waynesmith Von Crudock?"

"Yes, ma'am. You know him?"

"Nine years ago, he assaulted a friend of mine. He beat her and did other things, then kicked her out of his house, naked in the street. Her name is Belinda Soren. She came to me after the attack. I tried to get that bastard arrested. I wanted him to go on trial and to be convicted. But he got to Belinda somehow and the charges were vacated.

"I wanted to have him killed—"

Reynard coughed and then interrupted, "Enough of that now." The aged dandy was wearing a formally cut rose-colored suit that might have been in style during the Roaring Twenties. He wasn't interested in women as a rule, but he loved Orchestra. She was his muse and his patron.

"Von Crudock is the one coming after you?" Sadie asked me.

"Me, a son I didn't know I had, and the first woman I ever loved. A whole boatload of targets."

"I'll get Erculi to warn the other tenants and to help you."

"I hope that I'm just being overcautious," I said. "I mean, you'd have to be some kinda maniac to go up against a place like this."

"Some kind of maniac," Sadie repeated. "That's exactly what you're dealing with."

I made a breakfast of flapjacks, maple-cured bacon, grits, and fresh-cut pineapple. The whole clan came down to eat it. The feeling was festive the way I imagined old-time barbarians were before they went out to kill and be killed.

When the feast was over, I asked Hannibal to come up to the roof with me.

Struggling valiantly, he followed me up all the curved stairways set into the round walls. When we finally got to the top, he limped right over to the gated edge, appreciating the vast vistas of LA.

"You make enough doing detective work to buy a house like this?" he asked, looking out at the sprawling panorama.

"I lease it."

"You make enough for that?"

"It averages to a penny a year."

"How the fuck a poor Black man from the Deep South get a deal like that?"

"Same way a rich white man gets cancer."

It was a pleasure that my son, a man I had never met, was arrested by thoughts that most people would just pass over and forget.

"The people at the Penguin Club say that you're a crook," he said, adding a touch of condemnation to inquiry.

That made me smile.

"Any'a your fellow penguins know me?"

Hannibal gave me a half shrug and asked, "What you want me up here for?"

"I wanna know what it is with this deed your client took."

"Why?"

"Because that's my job. Your brother engaged me under a false pretense, but still, he hired me to find Lutisha James and I assume he wanted me to make sure she was safe. Right?"

"I guess."

"The problem is this rich man, this robber baron, who wants what he thinks you have."

My son nodded and then said, "It's a deed to a single lot where there's a one-family house. The owner was a woman named Shelly Dormer. You know all that already."

"I do."

"Well, the thing you probably don't know is that there was a limited-time rule exception to the sale. That is, the man who sold her the house could buy it back anytime before a seven-year period had elapsed. The deal was, if he wanted the buyback, he had to pay three times the purchase price."

"But he didn't execute that clause?"

"The man who sold the house to Dormer was named Klaus Eckman. He worked with a real estate syndicate named Desert Fox and, with no one else knowing, he attached the mineral rights of all the homes that the syndicate built to that one lot. That included almost all the oil under Culver City."

"Damn," I said. "That don't sound legal at all."

"There was some kinda language in the fine print about a discount given to every lot they sold. It was a sweet deal for Eckman, but then he died from a heart attack three years after the transaction. Dormer died a while after that. She had a cousin who inherited the house. His name was James Martin."

"Was?" I asked.

"He died almost a year ago," Hannibal said. "That's what started the ball rolling. You see, James had decided to keep up the payments and so the mineral rights were tied up, even if nobody knew it. The seven-year buyback clause had lapsed, and so the property goes to the Dormer line."

"Huh. So, your client, Sasha, somehow came across this deed?"

My son, the son of my blood, nodded.

"And how'd he find out all the rest?"

"It was in the files that Eckman controlled."

"And he told Sasha all this?"

"No. Sasha never knew any of them. He was hired by somebody, probably this Von Crudock you talkin' about."

"How does Waynesmith come into it?"

"Sasha told me that a wealthy man bought the company that Eckman worked for and then sent a crew of accountants in to find a copy of the deed on the address that Shelly Dormer owned."

"So, Von Crudock knew about the mineral rights?"

"I didn't know the name, but Eckman offered to sell the deed to somebody for millions."

"What about this cousin, this James Martin's heirs?"

"I don't know. But I do know that the property is currently in probate and the rich man, the one you call Von Crudock, wants to make sure that the rightful owner is not told of what the property controls."

"That could be worth millions."

"Sasha said billions. Desert Fox built and sold hundreds of houses around Dormer's."

"And Sasha thought that was wrong," I speculated. "Or maybe he wanted to cash in on it."

"By the time he got to me, all Sasha wanted was to stay alive," my son said wryly.

"He's dead?"

At just that moment, I heard a firecracker, then a whole pinwheel of fireworks going off.

Only, I knew that it wasn't fireworks.

Without another word to Hannibal, I ran slamfoot down the stairs to the first floor. When I got there Fearless was by the door with two pistols and my old M1 rifle in hand.

"Come on!" he shouted, and we were out the door.

When we reached the funicular, he handed me a pistol. I checked to see that it was loaded.

Fearless knew where I kept my guns because he'd come to my house to look out for the kids more than once.

"I don't know if we should take the elevator or maybe try and climb down," he said. "That glass box is a natural target."

"Climb is too steep and, anyway, the shootin' has stopped."

"They could be reloadin' or circlin' around."

There was a phone in the funicular car, put there in case there was any problem with the mechanism. It buzzed loudly.

Crouching low, I picked up the microphone and said, "Rawlins."

A voice came through the speaker embedded in the car wall.

"They shot my boy!" Erculi cried. "They killed Cosmo!"

By the time Fearless and I got to the base, the entire Longo clan had gathered around the sentry hut. Cosmo was laid up against his father, blood seeping from three gunshot wounds to his chest. Agosto, Matteo, and Gaetano stood around father and son, high-powered rifles clutched in their angry fists. Gaetano was bleeding from his left shoulder, showing no sign of pain. In the distance there could be heard multiple sirens, heading for our once-peaceful home.

"Agosto," I said. He was wearing dark clothes like all the other Longos. "Did you call for an ambulance?"

"Yes," he said. "Yes."

Fearless was already on his knees next to the grieving father.

"He's still alive, Erculi," my friend was saying. "The blood still comin' means his heart still beatin'."

Five men were in the dirt before the entrance to the gate that barred access to the funicular. They had come in two cars that had all their doors open. Each dead man had multiple gunshot wounds. None of them were still bleeding.

30.

Orchestra Solomon and Reynard came down to the base a few minutes before the official procession of flashing lights arrived. She took the time to try to understand what had happened. I did my best to orient her.

Then came the onslaught of ambulances, police squad cars, unmarked cars that brought a few detectives, and even a police helicopter that passed overhead.

The police captain in charge of the small army was tall and ruddy. His hair was cut in short military fashion and his face looked as if it had been chiseled from granite by an artist that wasn't quite up to the task. He started his inquiry with me.

"What's your name, son?" he asked, none too fatherly.

"Um," I said.

"What's your name, Captain?" Orchestra cut in.

For maybe three seconds the good captain reacted with silent offense at her aggression. But then he remembered who he was in the great scheme of things.

"Lonigan, ma'am, Captain Frederic Lonigan."

"Well, Captain, I've never met you, but your precinct should have made you aware that I have bodyguards who protect the entry point to the residences above. Today a group of armed men tried to shoot their way to the funicular. They shot two of my people and then were shot themselves." You could tell that Orchestra was feeling emotional, but she was still in charge, had been trained to be so since she was a small child.

"Um, well, yes, ma'am," the captain uttered reverentially. "But you understand that we'll have to question those who participated in the action. And also the witnesses."

"I suppose," she said, accepting his words with a touch of disdain. "Cosmo Longo has been seriously wounded and will be brought to the hospital with his brother Gaetano. Erculi, the father of the two, will go with them. You can talk to Agosto and Matteo under my supervision."

The good captain's face reddened but he didn't argue.

Orchestra invited him along with one detective to ride up to her house, where the interrogation could begin.

Erculi climbed into the ambulance that took his comatose son.

Other ambulances took Gaetano and the dead.

Fearless and I went back to my place, where we explained what had happened. I told Hannibal and Violet to stay upstairs.

"Don't want to get your names in their records," I told my son.

After that I made coffee and served it around the big table that was still set up on the first floor.

"That crazy man sent his people to do what?" Anger/Lutisha asked.

"He's after you and your boy," I said. "Before they killed him, Sasha must'a told his people that he gave the deed to Hannibal and maybe that included Santangelo too. I don't really know how your name got in the mix."

"That's crazy," my onetime lover said. "He already rich, now he gonna kill innocent people for a little more?"

I had no answer, but, then again, she didn't expect one.

"You think those killers still out there, Easy?" Paris asked nervously.

"Naw, man. Cops got helicopters lookin' all over. And you don't have to worry because once you outta here they won't be thinkin' about ya."

"Yeah, yeah, um, maybe me and Fearless should make our exit," Paris said, letting this suggestion hang in the air.

"We got to stay here, Paris," Fearless said. "Cops wanna talk to me and they prob'ly gonna ask you if you heard the shots."

"I didn't hear a gottdamned thing!" Paris protested, preparing his defense beforehand.

Maybe forty-five minutes later the doorbell rang.

It was my front door, so I opened it.

Standing there was a forty-something man wearing an olive-green suit. He was five seven at most, exuding an aura of steadfast confidence.

"Mr. Rawlins?" he asked.

"That's me."

"Detective Brian Kitagawa," he said, "here to talk to you and your family."

"Come on in. You might as well start with me."

My *guests* went upstairs to their various rooms and the roof. I set up two chairs next to the terrace. Kitagawa took out a notebook and a black mechanical pencil.

"You stationed in West LA, Detective?" I asked once we were seated.

"No. The Valley."

"Oh, that's why we never met before."

"You know many policemen?"

"My fair share."

"Why is that?"

"I'm a private detective, have been for twenty-three years. A lot of the cases I get involve working for criminal lawyers and those clients who don't think they've been given a fair break."

"I see," he said, giving the impression of keen objectivity. "And you were downstairs when the shooting started?"

"No. I heard the shots, but by the time I got down the hill the shootin' was over."

"But . . . you were armed."

"I'm a vet, Mr. Kitagawa. If I hear shooting, I pick up a gun. Your men took my weapons. So I think you'll see that they weren't fired."

"Did you recognize the men that attacked?"

"No, sir."

That answer, combined with the tone of my voice, called something up in the detective's flat expression.

"Was the attack a surprise?" he asked.

"If it wasn't, I don't think Cosmo or Gaetano would be in the hospital right now."

"I'm not asking about them."

"Maybe not, but I'm tellin' you that if I knew, I would have told them."

We parried back and forth like that for nearly half an hour. During that time the detective didn't take down one note.

While Kitagawa was questioning Fearless, the house phone rang. I ran up the stairs to the second floor and plucked the receiver from our wall phone.

"Hello?"

"How's it goin', Easy?" Melvin Suggs asked.

"Same old, same old."

The seasoned cop issued a harsh laugh that reminded me of sheet metal tearing.

"You know," he said. "That's what I always liked about you, Rawlins."

"What's that?"

"You keep your cool."

"I had an uncle once who used to say he kept his cool, so he would be ready for the time it was his turn to be put on the cooling board."

"Okay," he said, his tone telling me that he was through with small talk. "I got a dozen cops on the workers you said were at Warehouse Eighty-Six, Billy Banks and that Drake Simmons guy."

"You talk to Mildred?"

"Yeah. I sent Anatole over to her house. He thought the same thing you did, so then he brought her down to talk with me. I think she's got a crush on you, Easy."

"So, what you need, Mel?"

"Simmons and Banks drove out to a motel near the airport—"

"LAX?" I asked.

"Yeah. They went into a motel room wearing suits and came out in work shirts and jeans. They left the car they drove there and got into a wood-paneled pickup that was already in the parking lot. From there they drove onto the security grounds of the airport and then went into one of the property hangars where they keep the shipments being loaded and unloaded. They came out with three wooden crates on a hand truck and put 'em in the back of the pickup."

"What was in the crates?"

"Don't know yet."

"You don't? Why not?"

"We're not workin' this alone, Easy. There's four or five other agencies involved."

"So now you're followin' them?"

"Tried to, but because of miscommunication, we lost 'em. Luckily, because of you, we had people at Warehouse Eighty-Six. The truck passed by there and then went to a parking lot a few blocks away."

"So, you guys are gonna try and catch the people they're sellin' to?"

"That's the idea."

"And them makin' all those moves sounds like somethin' about to happen."

"It does. But I got the FBI, the CIA, and the Bellflower sheriffs all involved. An operation of that size and complexity is gonna cost a lot. I'd sure like to have some kinda assurance that something's happening before pushin' the button on it."

"Gimme a couple'a hours, Mel. I got to clean up this and that around here first."

"Sure, Easy. Make sure you say hey to Captain Lonigan for me."

"You know about that?"

"You askin' if I know about a shootout at the entrance to the home of the richest woman in California?"

"When you put it like that, I guess you do."

"You need anything?"

"I don't think so."

"Are there gonna be any repercussions for the department?"

"I really don't know."

I called Mama Jo's telephonic sentry, telling him when I would probably be out there. Then, while Kitagawa continued his interrogations, I wandered over to Orchestra's home.

It was a three-story block of a structure, reminiscent of an office building in a small town in the Midwest. No frills, bright colors, or oversize windows. Everything about her home was pedestrian—except for its size.

A man I didn't know answered the door. He was white, or, more accurately, a mixture of angry pink and muted gray, what passes for white in the modern world. Whatever color, he was built for battle. His suit was all blue, cut a little loose in case he had to move quickly. There was a bulge under the left breast of the unbuttoned jacket and scars around the knuckles of both hands.

"Yes?" he asked.

"Mr. Rawlins for Miss Solomon."

The butler I had never met took a moment to digest my request and then stood back and away from the entrance.

Everything about the Solomon house went against my sense of design. The rooms were small and boxy, painted in the passive hues of muted white, ecru, and pale blue. The weave of the carpeting was cut short, and the color was a uniform tan. There were original, almost primitive, paintings of early Americana origin hung at regular intervals and the ceilings were a uniform nine feet from the floor. The furniture was of sleek fifties design and the temperature was neither warm nor cool.

I was led to one of the many sitting rooms that made up the first floor of the home. There, the butler and I came upon Orchestra. She was seated on a blue chair in this chamber, sipping from a long and slim frosted glass that held a green libation.

"Ezekiel," she greeted, standing up from her chrome-and-maroon cushioned chair.

"Sadie."

"Would you like a drink?"

"I'd love one, but I have a lot to accomplish today, so no."

"You may go, Arnold," she said to the armed butler.

"Yes, ma'am," he said.

She watched him leave and then said, "Have a seat."

I took a blue chair near hers.

"This has been a terrible day," she confided. "I'm only happy that your daughter is away. I'd hate to see Feather affected by all this—this carnage."

"Look, Sadie, I take complete responsibility for this mess. And I'm willing to move out. The only thing I'd ask is if I could hold on to the lease for Feather. I know she would love to stay. She'll probably get married one day and have some kids—"

"Don't be foolish, Ezekiel," she said, interrupting my well-thought-out spiel. "You are part of our family here. And that Von Crudock monster; no one could predict what he would do. No, you are not leaving. We need you."

I would have moved out if she wanted me to. I hated having brought violence and bloodshed to our mountain home.

"What do you think of Arnold?" Sadie asked me then.

"Who is he?"

"I have a deal with a private security agency to have staff to fill in, in circumstances like these."

"But it was hardly two hours ago when it all came down."

"Erculi had Matteo make the call. That's part of the deal I have with him and his sons. A new crew came in to cover for those not here. The contract I have with their firm assures immediate replacement."

"You mean there's other Arnolds downstairs and at the other posts?"

"Yes."

"Hm."

"What are you thinking?" she asked me.

"I don't know. I'm pretty sure you can trust Erculi and his sons. They live here. But these stand-ins, I mean, they leave here with all your secrets and one day somebody offers 'em a boatload'a money...they might not be able to resist sellin' you out."

The mistress of the mountain stared hard at me and then said, "You see? No one else might have said that to me. I'll have Erculi change things around enough so that we can maintain security."

"I'm sure he would have done that anyway."

"You're probably right," she said after taking a sip from her gin, sugar, and lime drink. "But the difference is that you explain the problem where Erculi will just make the changes."

"Yeah," I said. "I sure hope that Cosmo pulls through."

Orchestra's eyes tightened in response.

Detective Kitagawa was coming down the blue-brick path as I was headed for home.

"Mr. Rawlins," he said out of politeness.

"Detective, you get what you need?"

"I don't know yet," he said, wincing a bit as if he were looking into a too-bright light. "It is very strange."

"You don't think they were just a gang wantin' to loot a rich woman's enclave?"

"I don't know."

He waited a moment, blessing this acknowledged ignorance with a short span of silence, nodded once, and then walked on.

A few steps farther on I met Paris Minton. He was scurrying along, looking all around for potential dangers.

"Easy," he said, unable to hide his nervousness.

"Where you goin', Paris?"

"I'ma get my ass away from here, brother. Fearless can stay if he want to, but all this violence get on my nerves."

"I understand what you sayin', but the shootin' is over and the shooters dead. So, what you worried about?"

"Police make me nervous, man."

"Why? You didn't shoot nobody."

"Plenty Negroes didn't do nuttin' been thrown in jail or hung from some tree. You know that's true."

"That's a fact, Mr. Minton. It is. But our greatest danger, the worst enemy, is lettin' that truth lead us down the wrong road."

"What's that supposed to mean?"

"Knowledge like that makes us feel guilty. And when you feel guilty you act like it."

That simple pronouncement banished Paris's fears for a time. This was due to his towering intelligence. His mind was telling him that I was offering a talisman of protection, if only he would heed it.

"What you mean?" he asked.

"Come on now, man. You know what I'm talkin' 'bout."

Paris Minton and Jackson Blue were both genius cowards. They could see so many potential dangers that waking up in the morning or going to bed at night, for them, was filled with trepidations. They were similar but Paris had it a little better because his thinking mind often eclipsed his fears. I could see in his face that he realized the problem. If he left right then, a whole squad of police would see him hurrying away from the scene of a crime. They would mark him for acting guilty.

It was a pleasure to watch.

"You got any good whiskey somewhere, Easy?"

"I don't suggest you drink and drive," I said.

"Naw. I ain't gonna drive. I think I'll stay around till Fearless need to go. He could do the drivin'."

Back at the house, nearly my entire extended family had gathered around the long table again. Amethystine was getting drinks; Fearless was telling war stories about the last days of World War II when he was tasked with the slaughter of a Gestapo bureaucrat named Gustav Blaustrahl. When Paris and I walked in, Fearless paused his tale and regarded me.

"So, what are they saying?" Mr. Jones asked.

"They don't know what happened."

"Do you?" Violet asked.

Before I could think of some lie, Anger stood up and said, "Come on with me, Easy."

We climbed all the way to the roof, sitting ourselves down at a low point of the outer wall. I offered her a cigarette and took one for myself.

For a long while Anger puffed on her cancer stick while watching me. Her way of smoking was to fill her mouth with the smoke, then pull in her upper lip and blow the vapors up her nose, inhaling deeply. There was an intensity to this process that was impressive.

"I can hardly believe it," she said at last. Her sneer was less a snarl and more a question.

"What?"

"What would you have said all them years ago if I aksed you to come run away wit' me?" she asked, her words reinforced by sincerity. "I mean, would you go on the run with me, leavin' all you knew?"

"The only thing real to me was you, honey. You know that."

"But you was just a child."

"Man enough to make Hannibal."

Anger's grin was love in my heart.

"I shoulda asked ya," she said. "I wanted to. I didn't wanna be alone out there. You know the only people made me suffer more than them Black men was they women. I got scars inside and out. And in all that time you the only one stood up for me. The only one. That's why I didn't take you wit' me."

"I don't understand."

"I never trusted nobody till you stood up to Edgar—"

"That was the man attacked us?"

"Edgar Jess," she said on a nod. "You put your life on the line for me. How could I take you away to where we would be in that kinda danger every mornin' and every night?"

It was my turn to be quiet.

There was a brown-and-red beetle scuttling across the weathered wood floor of the roof garden. That bug was headed for the flowers, worried about birds, shoes, shadows—and, all the while, looking for a mate.

"That's not why I wanted to talk to you," Anger said softly.

"No?"

"I been thinkin' 'bout Santangelo," she said. "Hannie told me that he give that letter-deed to him to get to me."

"Why didn't he get it to you himself?"

"He didn't know where I was, and when he talked to his brother, Saint said that he knew a way." Upon saying this, she reached into her brown leather purse and pulled out a red leather wallet. From this she took a small brass key. Then she handed the key to me. "There's a little post office box sto' on Western down around Venice."

"I know it. Mail and money orders, that's what the sign says."

"PO box twenty-one B," Anger added. "I didn't know that Saint was lookin' for me. But this mornin' I remembered that I give him that PO box address in case he needed sumpin'. You know Santangelo was always jealous at how close me and Hannie was."

"Why didn't you check the box?" I asked.

"I gave up usin' it a few months ago because, you know, it was time. That money order joint was the only sure way that Saint could get in touch with me. I bet ya he sent me sumpin' there. I bet he did."

31.

New World Money Orders, Mail, and Stationery was a bodega-style bungalow, wedged in between Lucky Star Liquor Store and Vanessa's Veterinarian Care, two blocks north of Venice Boulevard, on Western Ave. I went in, found box 21B, and retrieved its solitary piece of mail, a green envelope scrawled upon with Anger Lee's pseudonym and New World's address.

"Excuse me, sir," a woman said to my back.

"Yes?" I turned, putting on a smile for her.

"Is that box yours?"

"It belongs to a friend. Miss Lutisha James."

"Yes," the small, somewhat wide, white woman said. She had cheeks that crowded her eyes and wore a short, curly wig that sported gray strands of hair, here and there, among the predominantly black strands. "That's her name. Her rent on the box is seven months overdue."

"How much she owe?"

"Forty-seven dollars, twenty-one cent."

I took out my wallet, handing her two twenties and a ten.

"Oh," she uttered. "Well, this is very nice. Let me get your change."

Saying this, she went behind a modest lime-green Formica-topped counter, reached underneath to retrieve a tin cash box, and then carefully counted out my two dollars and seventy-nine cents.

Handing me the change, she asked, "Would you like to pay for the next month also?"

Proffering the brass key to the box, I said, "No, ma'am. Miss James has moved back down to Texas. She won't be needing this box anymore."

"Would you like to leave a forwarding address for her?"

"I don't know it offhand, but the next time I'm around here, I'll drop it off."

"Okay," the shopkeeper replied, saying, with her expression, that she didn't believe a word I said.

Benita met me at the bamboo scrim that hid the entrance to Mama Jo's domain.

"Hey," I said from the open window of my car.

"Hi, Easy," she said. When we were with Jesus, she almost always called me Mr. Rawlins. I never really understood why she used my nickname only when we were alone.

"Hey, Benita. So, you the welcome wagon, huh?"

"Essie and Juice is sleep, so I came out in case I had the answers you needed."

"Come on and sit next to me, then," I said.

She went to the passenger's side and got in.

"You and Jesus are about to be free from the BNDD men."

"How? I mean, I'd like to know, but, um, can we drive around a little bit first? You know I been cooped up in that tin house for days."

Driving north on Central with Benita sitting next to me, I was reminded how beautiful my son's wife was. Older than Jesus in years but younger in maturity, she'd once been Mouse's side-girl, until she started demanding that he leave his wife, EttaMae.

"It feels good to have a breeze," she said, her face leaning into the open window.

I told her about the BNDD agents' movements.

"Yeah," she said, staring up above my head as if there was a TV screen up there showing her memories. "They was drivin' a brown wood-paneled truck, and they stopped at a diner for a long time after they got to Bellflower."

"Then what?"

"Finally, they got back in the truck and went to that warehouse. It looked like it was shut down, but they honked once and the gate to the driveway opened up and they went in."

"What time was all that?"

"It was late. The warehouse was all closed up, like I said."

"What happened after they went into the warehouse?"

"I don't know. I was sittin' across the street in our car and the police drove by. That didn't bother me, but then they passed by two more times. You know, my mama told me that the police was after us and I didn't wanna have to talk to them, so I got outta there and drove back out to Compton."

That was all I needed. But Benita was having such a nice time that I dropped by Basil's Coffee Shop on Central Ave. There she ordered an ice cream sundae, and hamburgers for Essie and Juice. While she ate the ice cream I called Mel.

"What you got, Easy?"

"Sounds like your boys gonna make a deal with the dope at Warehouse Eighty-Six tonight. Sounds like a pass-off but I don't know to who. But from what I hear they do the deal late at night."

"Thanks. I'll get on it."

"There's one other thing."

"What's that?"

"You should probably leave the local cops out the loop."

"Oh. Okay. You wanna be there for the bust?"

"Oh yeah. Motherfuckers wanna mess wit' my boy, I'd love to see them brought down."

He gave me directions.

"Everything okay, Easy?" Benita asked while loving her ice cream and freedom.

"Good. How you doin', girl?"

"Okay."

"Mama Jo's cabin drivin' you crazy?"

"It's all right, I guess. I know we gotta do this because'a what I did."

"What'd you do?"

"I kept tellin' Juice how easy it would be to move all that dope. I didn't even think we could get in trouble. He shoulda taken Essie and left my butt right then."

"That's not my boy," I said.

"No, it ain't."

"But don't worry. After tonight you two can buy a new boat and go anywhere you want."

Across the street from Warehouse 86 sat an office building that was four stories high. The FBI, an organization that had been directed by Richard Milhous Nixon to disgrace and, ultimately, dismiss the BNDD, was running the operation. They had requisitioned the top floor and from there they, along with Melvin and a bald man in a bright yellow suit, were directing more than twenty plainclothes agents and officers, secreted on the street below.

At the entrance of the building, where Melvin had directed

me to go, I was met by two white men wearing similar black suits. The only difference between the two, that I could discern, was that one of them wore sunglasses.

"Not tonight, brother," one of the twins said.

"No? I thought the FBI was advertisin' for new agents out here tonight."

The men glanced at each other and then, in unison, grabbed me by an arm apiece, dragged me down a hall, and then clapped my wrists together in federal irons.

Then one of the FBI men said into his walkie-talkie, "Sanders here. We have a colored man down here talking about the FBI."

"Hold on," someone said on the air.

A minute passed and then the same man asked, "What's his name?"

I spoke up then. "Easy Rawlins."

"He's okay. Bring him up."

After the coordinated operation was over, Melvin told me that the FBI guy running the show was named Clegg, Summerton Clegg. His suit was also black and his eyes a startling cornflower blue. When I was brought before him by Sunglasses, he looked at me and asked, "This him?"

Melvin stepped up then and said, "He's the one."

"Go back to your post," Clegg said to Sunglasses. Then he turned away to watch the street below through a pair of high-powered binoculars.

"Easy," Melvin greeted.

"Hey, Mel. Damn, man, this here is almost like real police work."

He gave me a wry grin and we shook hands.

"Banks and Simmons got here around an hour ago. They're

in there with a few of the warehouse men. No idea what they're doin'."

"So, what do you figure?" I asked. "They gonna use the warehouse to send the dope to other places?"

"No. They bring it and sell it, that's what we think."

"What if you're wrong? What if they come outta there with nuthin'?"

"The dope'll still be somewhere in there."

"So, you got 'em either way."

"Yep," Mel agreed. "Warehouse been closed for an hour now. But the three guys you told us about, the ones that work there, their cars are still parked out back."

It was a long wait. During that time Clegg did not say one word to me, not one. He only spoke to subordinates, and, I supposed, I was lower than that in his estimation, like that male hyena on an African plain. I didn't mind. Most of the time I was out there on some private investigation, my ass on the line. Hanging around there on the fourth floor, drinking coffee and talking now and then to Mel, felt good—like I'd been promoted to the position of private detective operations supervisor and no longer had to get my hands dirty.

At a few minutes past eleven, a black Cadillac sedan drove up to the closed entrance, barked out a short honk, and was allowed in. Over the next quarter hour three more cars, all of them dark of color, drove up and were admitted in similar ways.

"When's your people gonna move?" I asked Mel.

"We figure we let them complete the transactions and then stop 'em a few blocks away."

* * *

At 12:49 a.m., the gate of the warehouse folded upward and one of the dark sedans drove out.

"The first one turned left," Clegg said loudly into his walkie-talkie. "Give him three blocks and then stop him."

Three more minutes and three more automobiles.

Clegg raised his voice higher for each one.

Then a few more minutes passed.

Finally, the brown wood-paneled truck drove out and turned right.

"Get him! Get him!" Clegg screamed. "Get that motherfucker!"

The truck was forced to stop short when police and FBI vehicles came out of nowhere to block its way. At least twenty officers from the various agencies jumped out from the cars and doorways, guns in hand.

The brown truck hit the gas and jumped up on the sidewalk, trying to use that way as its escape route. It might have worked if fifteen officers of the law hadn't opened fire. The wounded truck careered into a furniture store. After maybe half a minute, flames began to lick from under the hood.

The three warehousemen were herded together, their hands over their heads. The furniture store started to burn and so the fire department showed up to add their sirens and bright colors to the already festive tragedy. The bodies of Agents William Banks and Drake Simmons were extracted from the brown truck when the fire was brought under control. Clegg, the FBI bossman, had already descended into the street, situating himself in the middle of the ruckus. That left me, Mel, and the guy in the yellow suit standing at the windows of the fourth-floor vantage point.

"Rawlins?" asked the man I didn't know.

"Yes?"

He held out a hand and I did too. He had a good grip.

"My name is Steinman, Omar Steinman."

"You already know my name. You state police or sumpin'?"

"I'm with an international arm of the government," he said. "Just here to observe."

"Isn't this a national thing?"

"It would be. But the fact is, these guys are bringing contraband in from outside the U.S. My interests are more on the structural side of things. You know, how the money moves and who benefits."

"Wow," I said. "I understand every word and still I don't know what you mean."

The man in the yellow suit moved his shoulder as if he was about to walk away. But then he turned back.

"What do you make out of all this, Rawlins?"

"Pay a man oatmeal wages to cook you a T-bone steak an' you could bet that a little meat will get shaved off the bone before it makes it to your table."

"That's what you think the BNDD men were up to?"

Steinman's eyes were a strong shade of gray. Looking into those eyes, I was suddenly reminded of Carlos Ortega. He had sat me down to see if I was worth saving from the usual beatings men like me got in the county jail.

I was being tested.

"Not only the BNDD men," I said.

"You mean the warehouse workers?"

"The person who told me about this warehouse said that while he was sitting out front, the police cruised by at least three times."

"So?"

"This isn't a high-crime area," I said. "No drugs, prostitutes, or gangs. Police got no cause to be here . . . unless they do."

Omar Steiman smiled and said, "Unless they do," and then he walked away.

When he was gone, Mel came up.

"I'm impressed, Easy."

"With what?"

"A few things. I been wondering how you were gonna get Jesus outta trouble. This sting you put together does it beautifully. But it's not only that. That guy callin' himself Omar is CIA. You're the only one he had words with."

"I don't know if that's good or bad."

"Me neither."

After all that was through, I drove to the WRENS-L office on Robertson and stole a nap on my master bedroom office couch.

32.

When I was a soldier—no, it was longer ago than that. When I was a child of nine and then ten, I slept on the back porch of my maternal grandfather's house in the Fifth Ward. He let me sleep there but I had to scrounge food for myself. I worked when I could and otherwise begged, borrowed, and stole to make the sustenance that a growing boy needs to survive. I didn't waste a goddamned thing. If I lifted a bunch of carrots off a food cart, you had better believe that I didn't peel them. I didn't cut off the green tops. I ate all of what I got, and I would have fought to the death to keep what I had.

That tightfisted habit followed me into World War II. There I'd get myself a half-pound bar of Hershey's chocolate and carry it around in my backpack. Other soldiers would eat everything they ever had right away, but I'd only stop now and then to break a section off from my Hershey bar and eat it peacefully while bombs went off in the night. And even when I bit into a chunk and realized I'd carried it so long that it had turned to chalk, I didn't mind. Because, in some crazy way, that loss proved that I could survive.

That ability to put off satisfaction is part of my nature.

And so, when I awoke the morning after the multi-taskforce bust, I decided that it was time to tear open the letter Anger had received.

There were two sheets folded together into a long, ill-formed rectangle.

The first page was a sheet of white paper, on which had been scrawled a note, written in pencil.

Dear Mama

Hanibal told me to get this here legal documint to you He says that it's real trouble for anybody have it I looked for you but you moved so I'm sendin this to the PO box you got and I am goin to see this negro detective Hanny told me about that might be able to find you I'll be at my cottage if you need me I hope everything is ok

Santangelo

The second sheet of paper was Shelly Dormer's deed to the house in Culver City. I tried to read it, but the print was so small I couldn't make out the words. When I employed my detective's magnifying glass, I could read the words but could not make out what they meant.

That was okay. Somebody somewhere spoke deedish.

Two hours later I was once again seated in the thirty-first floor office of my old friend Jackson Blue.

We talked for a while about the life he thought he missed.

"She was fine?" he asked about the Knockout, Ida Lorris.

"Yeah," I admitted. "Even Raymond had heard about her, somewhere."

"Oh man. All I got is a lawn Jewelle want me to mow. Can

you imagine that? Here I make more money than ninety-nine point nine-nine percent'a people an' she want me to mow a lawn. Horticulture and the PTA, that's where I get my kicks at. I know, Easy, you prob'ly think I'm some kinda fool, I know. I know what you think."

"No, you don't, Blue. I know you not no fool."

"No?" His face was all snarled up, like he knew that whatever I really thought, it was worse.

"No. Tryin' t'straighten you out would be like wantin' Mouse to promise he'd never kill again. Even if he managed not to do it, that shit would eat at him like cancer.

"Shit. The only thing I feel, the only thing I hope, is that you'n Jewelle give up enough for each other that you don't break each other's hearts."

After that candid conversation, I told him what had happened with the drug bust and the various government cops.

"The CIA too?" he exclaimed. "Are you crazy?"

"I'm just tryin' to do what's right."

"Damn, man. Haven't nobody ever told you that a niggah doin' the right thing is worse than suicide?"

"What you got for me, Jackson?"

My friend gave up trying to set me straight, sitting back in his chair and cracking a smile. He put both his small feet up on the desk.

"Me and Mister," he said after his patented pregnant pause, "spent five hours lookin' through every file, computer record, county record, city record, and then had to ask other people to look in their physical file cabinets, just to get one name."

I couldn't rush the man. He'd once told me that his salary, if you worked it out, was more than a hundred dollars an hour. And here, I owed him five hours.

He brought his feet down, sat forward, putting elbows on the desk, and said, "Shelly Dormer's heir, after James Martin, is Constance Brill, née Dormer. You know, I got a call from Von Crudock just yesterday. He made it clear that me givin' him a name like that would be worth a hunnert thousand dollars. Can you imagine that? A hunnert thousand dollars to a niggah like me." His grin would have put the Cheshire cat to shame. "Can you believe that shit? A street niggah like me makin' a hunnert thousand for just a name and some numbers? You know, in the old days when we was boaf hangin' by a string, I woulda sold my own mother down the river for a five-dollar bill."

"Constance Brill," I said.

"Constance Brill," he certified. "She got a address on a canal out in Venice. If you had a telescope, you could probably see her out my windah."

"What you want, Jackson?" I asked. "I mean, if it's not killin' somebody, I'll do whatever."

"You don't owe me nuthin', Easy. Shit. Back in the day you saved my ass more times than I can remember. Yes, you did."

"I appreciate it, Jackson. I do."

"Oh yeah," he said, glossing over my heartfelt gratitude. "I got that other address you wanted too."

Constance Brill née Dormer.

I drove as far as the entrance to the canal. A hundred feet or so down I came to a barge-like boat tethered to a metal pole on the side of the walkway. It was an old wooden craft with most of the paint worn off. If someone were to cut the hemp tether, that useless tub would have floated a few feet before it sank down into the channel.

I climbed up on the deck and located a door, knocked upon it.

"Excuse me," someone said.

I turned toward the land. There was a man, a white man, of course, wearing a tight tan T-shirt on his brawny chest. He also wore sailor pants, but I doubted if he was a seaman.

"Yes?" I allowed.

"Can I help you?"

"Do you live on this scow?"

"What did you say to me?" he asked as his mother probably once asked him when he made some wisecrack.

At that moment the door I had knocked on opened inward. There, three steps down, stood a blowsy woman in a red muumuu dress. Her hair was both the texture and color of hay. Her eyes were pale, but I couldn't discern the exact color.

"Yes?" she said to me.

"Mrs. Brill?"

"Do you need help, Connie?" the man on the shore-street called out.

She glanced at him and then said to me, "Yes, I am."

"My name is Rawlins. I wanted to talk to you about a cousin of yours, Shelly Dormer."

"Oh. Oh yes. Shelly. She passed."

"Connie," the faux seaman said.

"Go away, Frank," she exclaimed exasperatedly. "Mr. Johns told us that you are not a security guard here no more."

The lady looked to be in her fifties, but my calculations, based on Jackson's information, put her at least a decade younger.

Frank didn't like the dismissal, but he accepted it and walked on.

"You ever meet someone that just wants to be mad, Mr. Rawlins?"

"Every day, it seems."

Smiling with me, she asked, "What is it you wanted to know about Shelly?"

"I'm representing a man who's interested in your cousin's will."

"That was a few years ago."

"Yes, but this guy thinks that he can make you some money."

Her eyes widening, she smiled and said, "My place is a mess. Could we go down the street to a little café and talk?"

We sat at an outside table of the Crow's Nest Café. I ordered coffee and said that Connie could have whatever she wanted. She ordered a salami and cheese sandwich on white bread and a glass of red wine.

"Did you know my aunt?" Connie asked while we waited to be served.

"No. I only became aware of her recently."

"She was a very sweet woman. Married four times. She used to always say that she was too kindhearted, and most men took advantage."

"I know people like that."

"Like my aunt or her husbands?"

"Both."

Constance had a nice laugh.

The food and wine came and was placed before the oldest surviving Dormer. There was something formal about this, as if we'd made a nonverbal compact stipulating that she would entertain my questions if I fed her.

"So, Mr. Rawlins, what do you want to know about Shelly?"

"Like I said, I've been talking to people about her will. And as far as I can tell, you're her closest relative."

"Yeah. What she said was that I would receive whatever she had left after other people got what she, um, what she instructed in the first part of the will. But the only thing left was a cultured pearl necklace and a set of rusty old golf clubs that she'd gotten from one of her no-good husbands. I'm sorry. But there's nothing else."

"She owned a house," I suggested.

"Oh yeah. She did. In Culver City. I remember now. Jimmy Martin was left the house."

"But he died, and now, because of the wording of the will, that property goes to you."

"Oh my God. You mean, I own a house?"

"Yes," I said as prelude. "But a very wealthy man wants it. Actually, all he really wants is the deed. He's willing to do anything to get that deed."

"But I don't have it."

"I know that. The trouble is that your claim on the property presents a problem for the rich man."

"Do you work for him?"

"No, I don't. I don't really like the guy."

"So, what should I do?"

She was so trusting.

"You could probably sell it to this guy for maybe twenty-five thousand dollars. But without the deed, I don't know what he'd do."

"What do you mean?"

"Forget that for a minute. What would you say if I could get you a hundred times what that house was worth?"

"That's more than a million," she said doubtfully.

"I can prove it."

"Mr. Rawlins, I'm a cashier at JC Penney's. What the hell do I know about millions?"

"You got a family?"

"A son that took my car one day and then called me a week later to say that he had moved to Reno. A daughter that married my second husband, and a brother who doesn't know what he likes more—little boys or little girls."

"So, what you're saying is that any stranger is better than blood."

Constance Brill laughed, but there were real tears in her eyes.

"I want to retire, sir," she said. "I want to move down around San Diego and buy a house up on a hill that has a view of the ocean. I figgered it would cost me a quarter million dollars to buy a place like that and then to live there till I was seventy, that's how long they say life expectancy is."

"I think that you can do better than that."

Connie couldn't help but cry. She was elated and angry and fearful of the potential heartbreak of hope.

"I don't see how," she said through the tears.

I took ten twenty-dollar bills from my wallet and passed the fold to her, under the table.

"That's two hundred dollars," I said. "Hold on to it for three days and I swear I will make that dream of yours into reality."

33.

From the canals of Venice Beach to North Santa Monica was a short distance to drive, but despite the brevity, I found myself in front of a very different, seemingly commonplace abode. Just a block or two north of San Vicente Boulevard was a small street that had a few restaurants, a pharmacy, and a six-story gray-stone structure that might have been an office building downtown, a small factory in East LA, or a collection of medical offices in Beverly Hills.

On that street the changeable building was the solely owned property of a multimillionaire who had tried twice to kill me, though he probably didn't know my name.

When Melvin Suggs and Charcoal Joe had failed to attain it, Jackson Blue had provided this address.

There were no windows on the ground level and an overabundance of them from floors two to six. The upper casements were the only thing about the rich man's private offices that gave any hint that there was something going on in there. The windows were all different. Some were square, others oval or round. There were star shapes and triangles, crescents, and some formed out of sea urchin–like spines. A few were very long, and here and there were checks and dashes, or a series of horizontal or vertical lines; there was even a window comprised of crosshatched tines of glass. And the differences didn't stop there. Almost every uniquely shaped aperture was filled by a different hue of glass. From clear to foggy white, from red to dusky orange, from shades of green to blue to violet. The upper floors of the otherwise almost nondescript edifice were like a child's toy waiting for a candle to be lit in its hollow core.

It had no signage, not even numbers to indicate the address. There was a door. It was like the portico of a humble house in a neighborhood that was part of a larger county but had no city affiliation. A wood door with a round iron doorknob. There was no buzzer or doorbell, no knocker.

Standing at that pedestrian brown plank, I thought about Amethystine. It was like she went everywhere with me, hanging on my arm, elated by my adventures and decisions. Without her I would have given up on the Santangelo Burris case. She filled me with an excess of life, something I hadn't experienced since I was a boy, surviving vicissitudes that would have defeated most grown men.

So I knocked on that very ordinary door, expecting no answer, hoping that no one came to see what was happening outside. But if wishes were fishes...

I waited for one minute, counting the seconds off in my mind. When time was up, I lifted a clenched hand to knock once more. But before my knuckles could reached their destination, the portal door was jerked inward. It was a violent action. And there I was without even a pistol to defend myself from the big bunker before me.

"Yeah?" he drawled.

I don't know what I expected the person who answered my

knock to look like, but this man was the only one it could have been.

At least six six, he was stooped just a little, as if maybe there was too much trunk for him to stand upright. His forward-tilting chest was massive, and his hairless chin gave the impression that it needed a shave. His forehead was too wide and his cheekbones too close to each other. He probably thought of himself as a white man, though I doubted if many others would. His skin was dark the way some southern Caucasians can be. The whites of his eyes were pinkish with flecks of butter-like fat here and there. The pupils were as dark as gray could get. He wore a sports jacket comprised of square yellow and black patches, the costume of a demon out of Santangelo's and little Gigi's nightmares.

"Waynesmith Von Crudock," was my reply to his one-word question.

"What about him?"

"I'd like to talk with him."

"Who's askin'?"

"Opportunity."

His expression, a big-toothed grimace, probably worked for laughter, pain, and the pleasure of seeing his victims bleed or cry out or die.

"You a smart nigger, huh?" he said.

There was no reason to answer.

"That all you got to say?" he threatened.

"Are you Waynesmith?" I asked.

"I am not," he averred proudly.

"Then I'm not here for you, brother."

"What kinda opportunity?"

"The kind that can be rigged in a land deed."

The giant's unhealthy eyes squinted down to slits; his long-fingered, big-knuckled hands curled into fists.

"Come on in," he commanded.

Before taking a forward step, I had to suppress the desire to run.

The checkerboard ogre led me down one hall, turned left, and walked until getting to an elevator that was made for three normal humans or for me and my guiding troll.

The sixth floor had no halls, no rooms. It was a huge, cavernous space littered with boxes, furniture, and tables that supported everything from caches of jewelry to empty pizza boxes, half-read books to piles of disassembled electronics.

Leaned up into one corner there teetered a large safe that had been yanked out of some wall, broken open, and left to be discarded, like an old beer can on a tenement roof.

In the far corner of the space where all things lost ended up, there was an enormous chair supporting the weight of a man who, at that moment, one could have easily believed was intent on devouring the entire world.

He was tall and fat, with long hair, a grizzled beard, and a face, though mostly hidden behind hair, that blazed with hunger. This prime example of uncrowned royalty wore a black T-shirt and dirty white jeans. His feet were bulbous and bare. The toenails needed clipping. Standing there before him, I could smell that he needed two or three baths.

The first sound from him was a loud, moist fart.

"Who's this?" he growled.

"Says he knows something about a deed," the wolfish doorman replied.

A light beyond the run-of-the-mill, endless appetite dawned in the master's eyes.

Before the sovereign throne, which was made of some kind of metal and cushioned with pillows and carpeting, there sat a small TV tray with a very large hunting knife upon it, reminding me of the man-hating desk clerk from the Orchid SRO, Gina Lima. I wondered what he used that knife for. If I were to answer that question without thinking, I would have said, *For cutting raw meat.*

"You here for Hannibal Lee?" he asked me.

"Why wouldn't I be here for Santangelo Burris, or Lutisha James for that matter?"

"What do you want?" He had no interest in my banter.

"To know the value of a deed," I said like some warrior poet on a lost page of the Bard.

Von Crudock grinned, his teeth the color of aged copper pennies turning green at the bottom of a wishing well.

"Ten thousand dollars," he said.

"Hey," I said, smiling like Jackson Blue used to when he spied a dollar he could steal.

"Do you have it?" the farting monarch asked.

"I know where I can get it."

"Where?" he commanded.

"I can bring it to you."

"Why didn't you bring it now?"

"'Cause Lurch here might'a made me drop it on one'a these tables. Shit. Mothahfuckah look like he could hold me upside down and shake it outta my pocket."

My humor was lost on Crudock.

"This one was at Solomon's Mountain," the ugly servant said then.

"You killed five of my men," Crudock said to me.

"Do you care?"

That was a Kodak Moment. Crudock gazed at me quizzically, not able even to understand the question. Did he care? He struggled with the concept for a moment or two and then said, "Bring me the deed and I won't have you killed."

"You won't have me killed but you will pay me that ten thousand."

"Yes. Of course."

"I'll have it for you by ten a.m. day after tomorrow."

"Why not today?"

"Because I say so," I said, speaking words that I knew Crudock could understand.

He gazed at me from underneath the tangled hair, behind the wiry gate of his beard. His lips pressed against each other as if he were about to spit.

"Day after tomorrow at nine," he said with a nod.

I considered haggling about the time but decided that no benefit could come from it.

Lurch stayed with me on the elevator and then kept me company toward the pedestrian entrance. He pulled the door open. Before stepping out into a world where no one wanted me dead, I stopped.

"Let me ask you a question," I said.

"What's that?" he replied, looking down into my eyes.

"Why'd you kill those people up at the LaCraig house?"

Lurch had a hard face. You imagined that his entire life had been trying to survive a continuous rockslide that broke his body, over and over. He had a hard face, but my question brought a beatific smile to his lips. His eyes went up behind the lids and he moved his head from side to side as if listening to lovely music.

"Sometimes," he said dreamily. "Sometimes you got to squash some bugs."

It was the most beautiful, terrifying confession that I'd ever witnessed. But still I said, "That don't make one bit'a sense."

That sublime smile turned into a boyish grin.

"I was after the Negress," he said. "That's the one that Sasha said was supposed to have the deed. The old rancher knew who I was, he said so."

"The other ones didn't know you."

He hunched his shoulders, ever so slightly.

"Tell me sumpin' else," I asked then.

"What?" the happy killer requested.

"What's your name?"

"Why?"

"I like knowin' the names of people I might have to kill one day."

The fairy-tale ogre laughed out loud. He was tickled all the way down to his fungal core.

"Leon," he said loudly. "Leon."

It took me less than an hour to make it downtown and to Melvin Suggs's disheveled office.

"How'd you even find out where Crudock was at?" he asked me.

"I looked it up in an old phone book."

"Yeah, right," he doubted.

"He as much as admitted he was behind the attack on Solomon's," I said. "They got a big safe on the sixth floor that was pulled out of a wall. I bet it's the one LaCraig had in his house."

"So?"

"What you mean, so? He confessed to me. There's proof of the home invasion. All you got to do is bring him in."

"Look, Easy, that man Crudock got more money than God.

He has residences in four states and in each of them he has at least one senator that owes their seat to him."

"But he attacked Orchestra Solomon," I reasoned.

"And if she attacks him back, I won't be able to do a thing about that either."

"I told him I could get the deed that all this shit is about."

"So either give him what he wants or move to Mongolia."

"You can't do anything?"

"Not within the law."

When I got home, Amethystine was there waiting for me, wearing a classic fifties housedress, black with yellow polka dots on an A-line ensemble that went down to just above her ankles. Her flat black shoes were inhabited by brown feet in white silk socks.

"Are you wearing anything under that?" I asked.

"You'll find out soon enough."

When she pressed her red, red lips up against mine, I tasted strawberries and whiffed the mild scent of fresh-milled soap.

"I hear you been hangin' out with Mary Donovan."

"Yeah," Amethystine admitted. "She's nice."

"If this was three hundred years ago, they would have burned her at the stake."

"You like Mary," she said dismissively. "Me and her being friends is not the problem, now, is it?"

I could feel the breath resonating in my chest.

I said, "One of the richest men in America seems to want me dead."

"Is that all?"

"That's not enough?"

"Is this a flesh-and-blood man?"

"Quite a bit of flesh."

"And does he have anywhere near the acumen of the ways of the world that you do?"

"He has an army."

"Beehive got a queen. But step on her and her army don't mean a thing."

"I love you, Amethystine Stoller."

Jesus, Essie, and Benita made it home that afternoon. By nightfall Hannibal, Violet, and Lutisha James had arrived.

I scoured the standalone freezer kept in a closet on the second floor. From there I brought out gumbo and jambalaya, eggnog mixed with bourbon, and collard greens. While those country delicacies warmed on the stovetop, I made white rice and monkey bread with creole sauce. Benita made a fresh citrus salad to cut the grease and Jesus and Essie threw together a mess of pralines—to end it all on a sweet note.

We had all just sat down to dinner at the long table on the first floor when the front door, which had been locked, was opened.

Feeling for my pistol, I rose from the table.

Then, "Daddy?" she called.

"Baby?"

Feather came in dragging a huge canvas duffel bag.

"Hi-i," she cried.

Most of the room rose to hug her. The dogs leaped in the welcome.

"I didn't know you were comin'," I told her after the third or fourth hug.

"You sounded so sad, Daddy. Bonnie said I should go."

That night was like a furlough in the middle of a world war. I had family, people I loved, and they loved me. There was no tomorrow. There was no war. Everyone had a full stomach and a safe place to sleep.

I was the last one awake, washing dishes and putting away food. It felt so good, so safe and secure doing family chores, that I was surprised to hear the doorbell.

Erculi and Orchestra stood at the threshold, swathed in solemnity. The wise old man bore up under a great weight and the lady stayed close to him, lending him her strength of will.

I ushered my late-night guests out onto the small terrace, where they took seats on two iron stools while I leaned against the latticed-steel balustrade.

"Cosmo is dead," Erculi said.

"I'm so, so sorry, man," I said, feeling his pain in my chest.

"It is not your fault," the proud Sicilian judged. I could tell by his tone that he'd wondered if I was the cause. He thought it over and, I believed, finally decided that he and his sons had failed in their preparedness.

"It's not your fault either," I said.

"Maybe not my fault, but it is my responsibility."

"What do you need from me?"

Erculi wanted to know where he could find the man who was the cause of the death of his son. Orchestra sat next to him, lending her authority to back up the request.

34.

There's a red leather sofa chair in the corner of my third-floor bedroom, diagonally across from the bed. I was sitting naked on that chair while Amethystine slept peacefully, also naked, on top of the jumble of blankets, pillows, and sheets. I was going over and over the unwritten balance sheet of my work, so far, that week.

There was no proof that Jesus had been dealing drugs. There was, on the other hand, a mountain of evidence against the dead BNDD agents. I'd discovered that I had a blood son, Ivy League educated and committed to the struggle. The two most important lovers in my life, Amethystine Stoller and Anger Lee, each one more than I could manage, were coexisting under the same roof. This was a predicament that all Black men, maybe all men everywhere, hungered for even though it was clearly a bad omen.

I wondered if I should offer Niska a limited partnership at the agency but, in the end, decided to shelve that idea for a while.

Somewhere around 5:00 a.m. I realized that I was not going to sleep, so I dressed in a burgundy housecoat that my old girlfriend Bonnie had given me when we still had a future. I made French roast coffee in the kitchen and then went down to the living room to sit near the trickling stream that flowed through the ground floor of our home.

There were plans in motion. These stratagems were not completely mine, but they had something to do with me. I smoked my daily cigarette on the terrace, with the door to the house shut. The dogs had come along with me to look out over the broad plain and sniff the air.

I waited for the sun before turning on a transistor radio. Flipping the dial, looking for music that would soothe me, I happened upon what they called an important news bulletin.

Early this morning Waynesmith Von Crudock was shot and killed along with his bodyguard, Leon Mumford, in front of his office in North Santa Monica. He received multiple gunshot wounds and was pronounced dead on the scene. The SMPD reported that there were no witnesses and no leads.

That week I attended three funerals. The first of these was for the cattle king, his thirty-one-year-old niece-in-law, and her husband. Orchestra came with me because I asked her to. The Ellenbogens were there with Gigi. The minute the orphaned child saw me, she threw herself into my arms. She was crying and laughing, holding on for dear life.

Between her emotional outbursts I said, "Gigi, I want you to meet my good friend Miss Orchestra Solomon."

"Hello," the suddenly shy and definitely suffering child murmured.

Alice Fabricant came up to us around then.

"What are you doing here, Mr. Rawlins?" she asked, without even a hint of friendly concern.

"Came to see my girl."

"She's not yours," the social worker intoned.

"Oh," I said, "of course. Have you met my friend Orchestra Solomon? Sadie," I then said to Orchestra, "this is Mrs. Alice Fabricant, the woman who controls the fate of this child."

"I see," the billionaire said solemnly.

For her part, Alice was dumbfounded. Everyone who had anything to do with fundraising knew about Sadie Solomon.

"It's such a pleasure to meet you," Fabricant sputtered. "Your, your generosity—"

"Mr. Rawlins tells me that this child needs a home," Sadie said.

"Yes, yes, certainly."

"Call my office. Talk to my lawyer."

We left the somber LaCraig funeral with Gigi in tow.

I had to explain to the girl that I was unable to be there for a child and that Sadie, who lived right next door, wanted to adopt a little girl just like her.

"You can come to my house, play with my dogs, and my daughter can teach you all the different things that swimmers know," I explained.

"But—but—but what about that man, that man in the house?"

"You mean the one wearin' the yellow checkerboard?"

"Uh-huh."

"He's dead."

"He really is?"

"They said so on the radio."

With that she finally accepted the new life. And she loved the mountain once we got there.

* * *

Cosmo's burial was the next day, on Orchestra's mountainside. The mourners were all residents of the mountain, people who saw Cosmo nearly every day. Erculi thanked me for telling him where to find his son's killers. He said that it meant that Cosmo could rest in peace.

Two days later we laid Santangelo Burris to rest at Forest Lawn. It was a small affair attended by Anger, Violet, Hannibal, Amethystine, me, and an old guy from the BFNE named Howard Loftus. No one spoke over the grave. We just bowed our heads while he was laid to rest. Amethystine held Anger's hand through the entire ritual, until the backhoe had filled the grave with soil.

Walking down to the parking lot, Loftus fell in step beside me and said, "You know, he was a good man. Not so good with words or ideas that wasn't real. But he believed in his own freedom and the freedom of all Black people. Some'a my brothers at the BFNE didn't agree. They done started to think that bein' more like the white man that made us slaves was the only way to liberation. But Santangelo knew that wasn't true. He knew it in his bones."

Loftus was one of those Black men with great power packed in a small frame. Something about his words, their presentation, reeked of truth.

Down at the parking lot Anger was standing next to the WRENS-L Lincoln Continental. Amethystine and Violet were climbing into the burgundy Buick that Hannibal drove.

"You mind givin' me a ride down to the restaurant, Easy?" my first true love asked.

"No, ma'am."

* * *

We went for quite a while without talking. I turned on the radio but she turned it off.

"I'm sorry, Easy."

"That's okay. I don't need to hear nuthin'."

"Not the radio, fool," she said with a grin. "Back in the day I looked at you like you were a child. Like a little brother, or even my son. I realize now that I done you a disservice. You always been the best man I ever known."

Most times in life I hear words and consider them. But in this case I felt what Anger was saying. Her words pressed down like heavy stones lodged on top of my mind.

"I hope that you and your crooked girlfriend make it," she said into my silence. "And even if you crash and burn, I hope you have a good time on the way down."

Later on that day, back at the house, in the rooftop rose garden, I was sitting with Hannibal. He told me some things about his younger brother.

"He was just mad sometimes," Hannibal told me. "Because he was so rough he thought that people were laughin' at him. But I loved him, you know what I mean?"

What I knew was to let him have his own feelings.

After a decent wait I asked, "What do you plan to do?"

"I don't know. Mama's goin' back down Texas. She said I could come wit' 'er, but them rednecks are too much for me. I got a double degree in literature and economics. I was thinkin' that maybe I could get a job workin' for a financial institution of some kind. Maybe a charity."

"I got an in at P9."

"You do?"

"Yeah."

"What kinda in?"

"If I call the president and say I need to meet, he'll ask when and where."

Surprise showed on the Princeton graduate's face.

"But," I added.

"But what?"

"There might be a way that you could work for yourself."

"Like how?"

"The man who was after Sasha and you, the man that had Santangelo killed, that was Waynesmith Von Crudock."

"Uh-huh," he grunted. "Who did that?"

"The police don't know."

My carefully chosen words had the desired effect. Hannibal nodded sagely.

"What's that got to do with me having my own business?"

"Crudock was the one wanted that deed."

"Yeah?"

"I have it now, and I know the rightful heir. I think we three could work out a contract where you could manage her properties for sumpin' like a five percent fee. You do that and you'll be wearin' vicuna before next year is over."

"Vicuna?"

35.

Funerals wear on me. I've been living through friends' and relatives' last rites for nearly fifty years. First my mother, then my father, and the numbers just rose from there, like levees that are bound to overflow.

I had experienced an entire war zone of dying, and so the marriage between Millicent Roram and John the bartender was a necessary pleasure. Everybody was there. Mouse and Vu Von Lihn; EttaMae and her white servant boy turned lover, Peter Rhone; Jackson Blue; Jewelle Blue; Lynn Hua, the Hong Kong movie star who happened to be in town for a new film; Melvin Suggs, Mary Donovan, and Anatole McCourt; the disbarred lawyer–cum–bail bondsman Milo Sweet; Paris Minton; and Mama Jo in one of her rare public appearances. Fearless Jones was there, of course, along with a hundred and fifty other sundry souls.

Bertrand Hollis and his nine-piece jazz band played the old kind of jazz, not the kind that made you think but the underground rumble that came before, the music that forced you to dance.

Bourbon flowed like water and there was so much food that you couldn't make up your mind. There was fried chicken, barbecued ribs, chitterlings and hog maws, three kinds of greens, corn bread, macaroni and cheese, white rice, turtle soup, and pies of all kinds.

The full range of humanity was there: eighty- and ninety-year-old men and women, at least three dozen squealing kids, beautiful ladies and their decked-out men. Charcoal Joe came accompanied by a small, well-dressed entourage. My sons, Jesus and Hannibal, wore matching blue suits. Violet and Benita and Feather wore silver dresses.

Amethystine was tightly bound in a white silk gown that had been tie-dyed with an entire rainbow of hues. She was the most beautiful person, next to my child's-eye view of my mother, I had ever seen. When she smiled at me, I felt an emotion I would have sworn, before that day, that only women could experience. The feeling caught in my throat, brought my left hand to my chest. All the deaths I had known were with me then, telling me to live harder, better, brighter.

"You're looking very handsome," she said to me.

I guess I could have said something like that to her, but instead I grunted and let my eyes do the talking.

"You look happy too," she continued.

"I'm happy at all of John's weddings."

"You don't think this one will last?"

"Nothing lasts."

She smiled at that dark sentiment, telling me, in a way, that we'd come from similar places.

"So, then," she said, "can I be one of your wives?"

I wanted to say yes but instead I took her hands in mine and squeezed. She rose on the toes of her high-heeled shoes and kissed, then bit my lips.

"Well?"

It was John's day, but still, I felt like the luckiest man in the world.

ABOUT THE AUTHOR

WALTER MOSLEY is one of America's most celebrated writers. He was given the 2020 National Book Award's Medal for Distinguished Contribution to American Letters, named a Grand Master of the Mystery Writers of America, and honored with the Anisfield-Wolf Award, a Grammy, a PEN USA Lifetime Achievement Award, the Robert Kirsch Award, numerous Edgars, and several NAACP Image Awards. His work has been translated into twenty-five languages. He has published fiction and nonfiction in *The New Yorker, Playboy,* and *The Nation.* As an executive producer, he adapted his novel *The Last Days of Ptolemy Grey* for AppleTV+, and he served as a writer and executive producer for FX's *Snowfall.* He divides his time between Brooklyn and Santa Monica.